Familiar Souls

Venessa Knizley

WALK WITH ME SAGA   BOOK III

Selah Press
PUBLISHING

Familiar Souls
By Venessa Knizley

Managing Editor: Loral Robben Pepoon, Cowriterpro
Prepared for Publication by: Kayla Fioravanti, Selah Press
Cover Design: Christine Dupre
Family Tree Illustration: Shweta Mahajan
Proverbs 27:5-6 Art: Alisa Taylor, Etsy.com/shop/AlisaTaylorDesign

Printed in the United States of America, Published by Selah Press, LLC
Copyright © 2019 Venessa Knizley

ISBN 978-0-578-57962-7 Selah Press LLC

Scripture taken from the NEW AMERICAN STANDARD BIBLE®, Copyright© 1960, 1962, 1963, 1968, 1971, 1972, 1973, 1975, 1977, 1995 by The Lockman Foundation. Used by permission.

The definitions listed on the bottom of relevant pages and in the back of the book were compiled by the author from many online sources.

Dedication

To my parents,
I love you beyond words.

Better is
open rebuke
than LOVE
that is concealed
FAITHFUL are the
wounds of a FRIEND
BUT DECEITFUL are
kisses of an ENEMY the

proverbs 27:5-6   © Alisa Taylor 2019

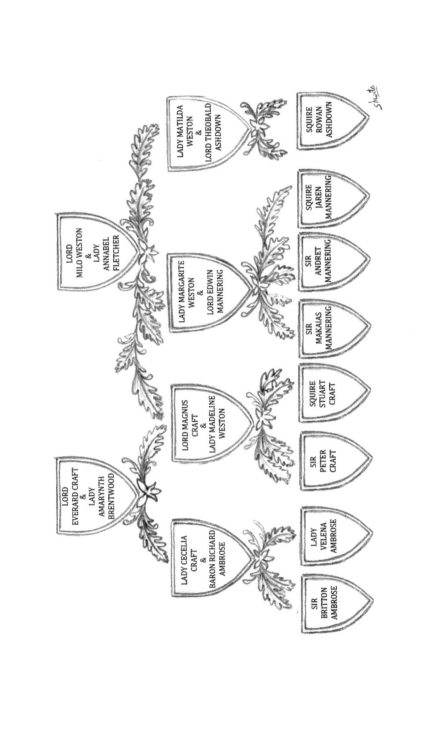

LORD
MILO WESTON
&
LADY
ANNABEL
FLETCHER

LADY MATILDA
WESTON
&
LORD THEOBALD
ASHDOWN

SQUIRE ROWAN
ASHDOWN

LADY MARGARITE
WESTON
&
LORD EDWIN
MANNERING

SQUIRE JAREN
MANNERING

SIR
ANDRET
MANNERING

SIR
MAKAIAS
MANNERING

LORD
EVERARD CRAFT
&
LADY
AMARYNTH
BRENTWOOD

LORD MAGNUS
CRAFT
&
LADY MADELINE
WESTON

SQUIRE
STUART
CRAFT

SIR
PETER
CRAFT

LADY CECELIA
CRAFT
&
BARON RICHARD
AMBROSE

LADY VELENA
AMBROSE

SIR
BRITTON
AMBROSE

prologue

A series of prolonged groans rippled through the knight's blood-encrusted lips as a hazy sort of awareness reintroduced a throbbing pain. There was the smell of dirt in his nostrils and the tightness of dried blood on his face as muffled mewling gave way to louder utterances of consciousness. Opening his eyes, he found himself blinking at solid ground. *Where am I?*

Begrudgingly, Sir Britton rolled from his stomach to his side—his head arching back in sudden agony as a new kind of pain radiated up and down the length of his right leg. He froze, fearing to move again. As the intensity of the moment passed, his breathing slowed, and Britton began to take a mental inventory of his body.

Without doubt, his leg was broken—most likely below his knee. His vision was blurred, and his head felt like it was a watermill churning over a river full of rocks. He pinched his eyes shut, deigning he might wretch then and there. His hands, aching with pins and needles after being constrained beneath his body, seemed to be in working order. His gut, on the other hand, might never accept food again. He moaned—then cried out anew. He'd moved his leg without meaning to.

"God help me…I'm going to kill him!" he shouted. The exertion of exercising his own voice caused his head to reel and tiny bursts of light to flash before his eyes. He fought pain and nausea to push himself up to a sitting position, only to fall back again. Growling out his frustration, he hammered his fists onto the unyielding ground, ridding the road of several clods of earth but not himself of the pain that kept him bound there. Again, he tried sitting up, and by sheer force of will, he succeeded. Again, his head pounded with pain that felt like boulders fighting for space within a skull too small for such monstrosities. He waited for the feeling to pass but had to make do as it only diminished in parts enough for him to pry open an eye to the long, hazy road before him.

A cool wind rustled through the trees to either side of him as he surveyed the landscape for anything that could help his situation, but there was no one else—at least so far as his now imperfect vision could decipher. No horse. No supplies. No sword. No armor. He looked down as another gust of wind chilled his bare chest—no dignity.

"My tunic...my...he took my jerkin[1]." He stared in disbelief at his red and purple splotched ribs. "Was it not enough to take my horse?" He palmed his forehead. "He had to take my clothes..." He massaged his scalp through tufts of hair the color of charred wood and remembered the lice he'd picked up on the journey. A brittle laugh quaked across his shoulders as he hoped more than a few of his pesky passengers would find their new home just as accommodating. "Jokes on you, you b—"

"Ho, there." A man's voice materialized behind him, causing every hair to stand on end.

Clenching his teeth, Britton twisted his torso around for the first time and scowled at his own ineptitude. This was the second time he'd been taken by surprise—the first being the episode that had put him in the situation he was in now. Perhaps, it was the ringing in his ears or that the heavily bearded man had approached from downwind that had kept his presence unknown. Still—an overly laden donkey protesting under the weight of its load should have alerted him.

"You look to be in a bad way," the stranger said, allowing his eyes to rove the tree line, wondering if the men who'd done this to the man on the ground were still lurking about.

"You could say that," Britton answered warily. Against his better judgement, he untwisted himself, unable to keep up with the awkward posture for long. Knowing his time might be limited, Britton searched for something with which to defend himself should the stranger seek to finish him off. Not even his flawed vision could hide the fact that nary a stick lay within reach. Disgusted at his humbled state of being, he swore beneath his breath. *This is not to be my end!*

Wordlessly, the stranger crouched at his side, rubbing his free hand over and through a fully-matured beard as he took in the visible damage colorfully displayed across the wounded man's body.

Britton's forearms flexed. It was possible he could get his hands around the man's neck if he were to act quickly—better to use the element of surprise than to have to try and defend himself against an attack. But judging from *said neck* and the hulk of the man's shoulders, surely the effort would be in vain. Their eyes met—blue to brown—

earth to sky. What were the man's intentions?

The stranger must have comprehended Britton's thoughts, for he nodded his head in understanding even as his mustache twitched at the corners of his mouth, belying a smile that must have been present somewhere beneath the dark mass of whiskers. He began to chortle, the sound echoing from deep in his chest. "You've nothing to fear from me, friend. Why should I finish off someone else's poor job at killing you? Except for your breeches, it looks as if you've nothing left for a man to take. And as you can see," the man stood, dusting himself off, "I've already got myself a pair."

Britton gave a wry smile. "You might as well have them, stranger. They'll not be taking me home today."

"True enough…but you've gone and bled all over them. No, sir, they're no good to me."

"And I'm no good to anyone. I'm unable to move, I'm afraid."

The stranger's brow furrowed, displaying a patchwork of lines and grooves hedged deep across his forehead, revealing his status as one who labored. "Your legs work?"

"One of them."

"The men who did this still about?"

"Long gone…and with them my horse, belongings, armor—"

"You're a knight, then?"

"Sir Britton Ambrose…at your service," he answered. A dull sort of amusement leaked from his eyes, replaced shortly by a look of relief as he applied a goodly amount of pressure to his own ribs, revealing no broken bones—quite remarkable given the look of them.

The stranger lowered his gaze in deference. "Pardon my informality, my lord, it was impossible for me to know."

Britton managed a thin smile. "There's nothing formal about conversing with a naked man."

"Indeed." The stranger chuckled. "I be Edward the Stronger."

"The Stronger, eh…"

"Yes, but you'd be better off if I was Edward the Smarter. I could lift you up on my donkey easily enough, but I don't think it'd be wise. And so, I find myself wishing I knew of a better way of getting you off this road."

"How far are you from home, friend?"

"Five miles." Edward gestured his bearded chin down the road. "I have an inn. Nothing fine, but it'd be a roof over your head where we could get a better look at your damage."

"I'll tell you what, Edward the Stronger. If you can, indeed, get me up on your donkey, I know I can manage the trip. I don't take too fondly to the idea of being fodder for the birds—and in addition, I'd be further in your debt if you could send word back to a man in London for me. How far are we from its gates?"

"A day and no more." Edward took back to stroking his beard. "Who be the man?"

"A friend."

"Shame your friend couldn't have traveled with you in the first place. Might not be in the trouble you're in if he had. Dangerous to travel the roads alone these days—unless, of course, your name be Edward the Stronger." He laughed at himself.

Brittan tried to shift his weight from one hip to the other—cursed and then braced himself as a spasm ran through his leg and side. He gripped his ribs, short of breath. "Yes—well—he was busy wooing a wife."

Edward chuckled deep in his throat. "An ailment of a different sort—but an ailment nonetheless." He returned from his donkey with a piece of leather tethering taken from one of the many worn-out satchels dangling from his donkey's rounded sides. He straddled Britton's legs, gestured for him to put the leather between his teeth, and continued speaking. "Seems we're all damaged in one way or another, Sir Knight."

He reached down to take a firm grip beneath Britton's arms, locking his hands around his torso. "Now—if your leg be broken—this is going to hurt like a kick to the…"

"Just get on with it." Sweat beaded across Britton's forehead as he inhaled deeply through his nose and bit down on the grimy piece of tether, grateful for Edward's forethought. He nodded in readiness as Edward hoisted him up with a throaty grunt. Britton suppressed a cry—thrusting his good leg out for support as quick as he could manage it—but was given no time to catch his breath before Edward had him deposited onto his donkey, rear-facing and with his legs laid out straight before him. The gnawing pain from his leg injury, coupled with the pounding between his ears, was easily one of the more excruciating experiences of his life.

Thankfully the animal's back was flat and wide—and all the wider from the satchels hanging even at its sides. The donkey sidestepped, baulking at the extra weight, and Britton had to fight to keep his balance using only his grip on the bags to steady himself. He grimaced, wanting to fall back onto the beast's neck but sensed the impossibility of such a move, and so was forced to remain upright.

"Are you sure he'll carry me? He's already carrying a substantial load."

Edward's beard lifted at the corners. "He's like me—strong," he said, looking from the donkey to Britton in admiration. "Didn't think I'd get you up there without you bellowing out at least once. I wouldn't have blamed you if you had."

Britton's complexion had turned pallid. "No, no. I could do nothing if not keep my end of the bargain…as you were certainly able to keep yours. You were aptly named, my friend. And I'm grateful to you."

"We'll see how grateful you are at the end of the five miles." Edward grinned as he took up the donkey's lead and began to cluck his tongue in low tones. Careful to steer the donkey away from the ruts and grooves of the uneven road, Edward glanced over his shoulder at the back of Sir Britton's head. He couldn't see his face, but he had a clear view of the knight's white-knuckled grip of the packs. "It might be best if you give me the name of that London friend of yours before we get too far. I have a feeling you won't want to do much talking once I get you to where we're going. I'm still hoping you manage to stay on."

Britton squeezed his lids closed and grunted at his own uncertainty. "Three years, I've survived both France and the Pestilence. If I die now, it won't be from falling off a donkey. I'll hang on—you can be sure of it." As he spoke, another wave a nausea washed over him and he had to grit his teeth against the sway of the animal. *Oh Lord, don't make a liar of me.* "But the name you must remember is Sir Makaias Mannering. He's a guest of the fish monger's daughter on Fish Street."

Edward raised his eyebrows. "Be her name Joanna?"

"You know the woman?"

Edward shrugged and said only, "I know *of* her," choosing to walk the remaining miles in silence for one of the most painful journeys Britton would ever find himself on.

As one who wished to be anywhere but where she was, Joanna

retreated within the recesses of her own head, staring through unrepentant eyes out the window of her father's modest home—too modest for her taste. Her hands were cold as she clutched the sill, the anxious rise and fall of her chest evident as she tried to still the rapid beating of her heart.

She turned around to face the knight behind her. He'd been sitting silent for what seemed an intolerable amount of time—and his silence was deafening. "How could you?" she hissed through clenched teeth. "You might have killed him!"

Sir Makaias sat at the end of an ill-made oak bench—forearms pressed to his knees—trying to gain some semblance of control over his temper. His face sunk into his hands and, with trembling fingers, he began massaging his scalp. Dare he answer? He breathed deep through his nose before speaking slow, deliberate. "Had I come upon the pair of you any later…I would've been very near to killing you *both*. Think more on that." How could he have been so wrong about her?

Joanna turned her head away, her honey-blond hair loose and falling out of its coils. Her shoulders slumped as she clutched her arms at the elbows below her full chest. "I know what you must be thinking of me."

His lids fell closed. "You've no idea what I'm thinking of you."

She glared at him. "Am I not to be given an opportunity to defend my actions?"

"You wish to defend them?" A derisive laugh escaped his throat as he sprang loose from his seat, only to turn aside, not trusting himself to come near her. "There's not been one attempt at an apology—nor one sign of remorse—and now you want to defend your actions? Who are you? Because I don't know! What kind of woman does what you've done? Defend that!"

Indignation snapped in Joanna's eyes—sky blue darkening to stormy gray as her arms unhinged in an animated display of emotion. "I'm the kind of woman who's been alone without her husband-to-be for *four years*…with nary a word from you for all my time. I'm the kind of a woman who's had to live the last three of those years in a city of death and disease! I had no idea if you were alive—or if I'd live till the next day. You judge me too harshly for being alone and afraid."

"That's no excuse."

"Are you going to tell me you were never lonely—or scared? Never visited the bed of another woman in all your time in Calais? That no

French strumpet ever tempted you nor offered herself in trade for your *special* protection?"

Makaias approached her then, his face strained, his voice thick with emotion. "I've never visited the bed of any woman. I promised this to God—and long before you—that I'd have no woman but my wife. I thought that wife would be you. I waited for you. And though I couldn't get word to you...let there be no doubt that I worried for your safety. It was *your* memory that kept me faithfully on my knees— praying for you daily." Makaias' face softened as he recalled such moments. He lifted a warm, calloused hand to caress her cheek. "I only wish it had been the same for you..."

Her body weakened at his touch. "Makaias...please believe me. I didn't know if you were alive or dead," she whispered. "How many years would you have had me wait and mourn before finding another?"

He dropped his hand away. "I'm not so unrealistic as you think. I knew very well I might find that you'd died or married yourself to another."

"Then why—?"

"What I didn't prepare myself for was your deception."

"Decep—"

"When I stepped off that ship with Britton, my only thought was to find you." Makaias turned away and slumped back down onto the bench, the edge of the table biting into the center of his back. "Over and over again, Britton tried to convince me that you'd likely died of Plague—to face reality—to return with him to Totnes."

"Britton never thought much of me."

Makaias' lip twitched. "I should have trusted him."

Joanna blinked. "You agree with him now, do you?"

"How could I not? You're not dead. You're not married...and you had the last three days to tell me that you'd found another! *Three days* to tell me you no longer wanted to be my wife," he said, holding up the last three fingers of his hand, "but instead...you continued on with your indiscretions while my head was turned!"

"I didn't know how to tell you!" she all but shouted.

He rose to his feet, the volume of his voice matching her own. "Well you should have figured it out! I could have left yesterday with Britton—albeit licking my wounds and listening to him gloat—but it would have been better than walking in on you and that...that *deviant.*"

"He's not a deviant!" Joanna shot back. "Roger is—"

Makaias' face twisted in disgust. "By all that's holy, don't tell me his name. Is it not enough I must live with the image of him touching you? It's imprinted in my mind, Joanna! What he wanted from you...by my troth, what he's already had."

"How dare you!" She lifted an indignant hand to strike him, but he caught her by the wrist—tightly at first, his eyes boring into her face. Then taking a breath, he released pressure until he was cradling her hand within his own, gently stroking her palm with his long fingers.

"Oh, Joanna, it's one thing to be unfaithful to me...but another to be unfaithful to God...and to your own virtue. You've given your heart and soul to a godless man, and he'll never give you anything worthwhile in return."

Makaias squeezed her hand. It was cold—like ice brought into contact with the heat of a flame—it couldn't help but slip through his fingers. "I pity you as much as I pity myself."

"Did God make you judge to think such things of me?"

"What I think of you is irrelevant." Baffled again by the hardness of her heart, Makaias brushed past her shoulder to her father's room, where he'd been bedding down since his arrival.

Joanna crossed her arms about her waist and paced the floor, unsure whether she was more angry or hurt. Less than three minutes later, Makaias returned, shouldering a sizable pack containing what belongings he'd entered London with. He paused to face her.

"Where will you go now?" Joanna asked, a lump building in her throat. Reason demanded she beg his forgiveness and ask him to stay—she'd do no better if she let him go—but time had made him a stranger. She remained silent.

"Home." He shifted the weight on his shoulder. "If I'm fortunate, I can still overtake Britton."

"He's got a two-day lead."

"Yes, but he took on a companion, who's traveling on foot." Makaias licked his lips, his brow wrinkling as he calculated the time in his head. "He'll be walking his horse to accommodate. I won't."

Joanna raised her chin. "Well, I guess there's nothing more to say then...is there?"

Makaias held her with his eyes one last time, caressing her image like a water-stained stone pulled fresh from a riverbed. Once, her colors were bright—vivid. Now, they were fading, turning the thing once precious to him to something dull and ordinary. "God save you, Joanna. Tell...this *Roger*...to marry you—else move on. You don't have to be as you are. I know...because once, you were more."

On that word, Makaias turned aside and disappeared into the chill of morning, leaving Joanna alone to consider her life—and the security she'd just allowed to walk out her door.

Having no idea what to do with herself, she stood—she sat, she paced—she sent a full vase of lavender to the floor with one dramatic sweep of her hand...resulting in countless shattered pieces, now resembling the sum of her life.

Roger would come to her again, though marriage would never be his intent. She knew that. And so, it was with tears of self-pity pooling in her eyes that her hired woman found her by the open window, staring blankly into a future she no longer cared for.

"Ma'am?" a meek voice questioned behind her.

Keeping her face averted, Joanna took a deep and labored breath, swiping tears away with the palms of her hands. "What is it Mary?"

"A man outside just delivered this letter for Sir Makaias."

Joanna nodded, having witnessed the stranger come and go from her vantage point at the window. "He's not here," she answered, as if this put the matter to rest.

"I know..." Mary said timidly, "but he left naught but a half hour ago—and he would have needed to buy supplies for his return home. Shall I send Tom to the gate with the letter? He may still have time to overtake him."

Joanna's lips lifted in a mirthless smile. "How did you know he was going home?"

"I..."

Joanna peered back at the girl from over her shoulder, her voice stern and her eyes cold. "I certainly hope your ability to gossip isn't as proficient as your propensity towards eavesdropping. I don't need my misdeeds spread all over London." Joanna's eyes narrowed. "Are we clear, Mary? For I assure you, your employment in this household depends upon it."

"Yes, ma'am, very clear."

Joanna turned one last fleeting glance towards the empty bench where Makaias had cradled his head—her unfaithfulness having bludgeoned his heart—before sweeping past Mary towards her bedroom—her *a dozen times over* tainted bedroom.

"Please excuse me, ma'am, but the letter?"

"Just burn it."

Mary hesitated. "Yes, ma'am, but..."

"But what?" Joanna barked, snapping her head around as a tear slipped from her cheek to the breast of her surcoat[2], marking a dark spot on her otherwise pristine ensemble. "If you'll recall, Mary, what he thinks of my actions… is irrelevant."

[1]**Jerkin:** A close-fitted, sleeveless jacket for men, often made of leather.
[2]**Surcoat:** An outer garment for men or women, made of rich material.

1

engaged

Ignoring the pale strands of hair dancing before his vision, Squire Rowan pulled the bow string back to rest near his fair-skinned cheek and took aim. The wind had died down since their game of quoits[3] in the stables, but it could still aggravate his shot.

Rowan exhaled slowly. Slooowly…he paused, parted his fingers and—ffft! The arrow sliced through the air. Rowan grinned, his pleasure going before him to the bull's eye.

"Well done!" Squire Jaren congratulated him.

"For a squire," Sir Andret added, then proceeded to take an even better shot of his own.

Rowan swore under his breath, to which Sir Andret raised a single brow. "What was that?"

"I said, 'good shot.'"

The knight picked up another arrow, chuckling.

Rowan, too, bent to select another, pausing as he caught site of the stable yard. Was that Stuart entering the stable now? He looked away. He hadn't yet said anything to Sir Andret or Jaren about Velena's engagement becoming official. It'd be common knowledge soon enough.

He thought back to the scene from only a half hour past when it'd been Tristan exiting the stables…alone. Rowan could only assume Velena was still inside. Just short of running, Tristan had been moving fast, his pace easily construed as one of guilt. Rowan should have known something might have happened after he'd left the two of them alone.

Well, what if it did? he questioned himself. What was done was done. Having no misgivings that Stuart was going to make Velena absolutely miserable, he hoped her moment with Tristan had been worth it.

Frowning, he focused his eyes again on his target. Arrow to cheek, he breathed deep…and then let it fly.

Stuart was at the front lines—atop his hill, holding the victory flag over his rival—perceived or otherwise. Yet…the pure preponderance of foolhardy actions he'd exerted before getting here had him wondering if he might still stand to lose.

He'd raised his hand to Velena, and the look on her face as he'd held it aloft…it had shaken him to his core.

He was many things Tristan believed him to be—prideful, self-seeking, calculative—even jealous. But his father? *That*, he could never accept. His father would have struck her—would've brought his palm down upon her cheek without regret or restraint. That's what separated them. Stuart still carried regrets. It kept him human—it kept him from repeating his past mistakes…or so he hoped. Because what he'd done to Daisy…

That…that was a mistake of the worst kind. A black spot he'd never recover from should the truth be discovered. Never was there an action he had regretted more, though it could be argued his remorse was entirely for his own sake. Daisy's personal suffering had yet to reach him. Still—his sin haunted him. For although he knew it couldn't possibly be proved, it could be believed. And that would be just as devastating.

Stuart turned into the wind. Though vastly decreased from only an hour ago, the current of air that fanned his cinnamon colored hair away from his face continued rolling along the surface of the overgrown grasses growing outside his path, bobbing the flower tops up and down like foam upon the water.

He'd already looked in several places before his gaze finally rested on the stables. If his footfalls hadn't announced him, his destrier[4] surely would have, nickering softly from his stall as he entered. Velena was rubbing down Guinevere, her back to him, but he could tell she knew it was him by the stilted manner of her brush stroke. Stuart waited as puffs of dust and horsehair wafted above her, framing her silhouette in the broken light.

"Velena…" Stuart kept his approach slow, "I've been looking for you."

Velena breathed in deep, allowing the odor of horse sweat and hay to linger in her nostrils several moments before setting down the horse comb and leading Guinevere back into her stall. Now, faced with Stuart, she felt herself fall beneath his scrutiny, the emerald color of her eyes remaining curiously glassy as she felt a prick of guilt, recalling the torrent of tears she'd only just shed with Tristan.

Inside, her grief was poignant, but she was resolved to regain the control she'd lost. She regarded her cousin, Stuart, as thoughts, too uncertain to give a name to, flitted through her mind—all of them ugly and full of disappointment. The last time they'd spoken was in anger when he'd raised his hand to strike her. That he'd stayed his hand was a poor consolation. Was this truly the cousin she'd grown up with? The childhood friend she'd once praised as her hero? The resemblance was now merely superficial—and her attraction for him had waned.

"Have you already spoken with your father?" he queried, when she failed to speak.

Velena nodded, letting her gaze fall to the floor.

"Have you nothing to say about it?"

"Not about that."

Stuart's eyes dropped for a moment as well. "You're upset over our quarrel."

"I have a right to be."

Stuart gave the smallest of nods, taking a timid step towards her as if approaching an unbroken filly. She remained still, but by her look, she wanted to bolt.

"Yes, you do…but so have I. You knew I had no tolerance for Tristan," he said, holding out his hand as if to stay her. "And still you baited me with talk of him."

"That was never my intention."

"As you see it, perhaps. But from where I stood, you were once again elevating him—and thrusting me aside." His voice was husky. "I can't understand it." He raised his palms at his sides. "Have I not always loved you? Have I not always been *for* you?"

Velena's shoulders slumped. "You have—and perhaps for this reason more than any other, it was beyond my thinking that you'd ever raise a hand to me. You, who ever received more than your share of the same."

"But I didn't!" Stuart insisted with feeling. He was standing before her now. "And I won't! Not today—not tomorrow. We're not entering into a marriage of convenience, Velena. I love you—and you'll never see me raise my hand to you again. I swear it."

Velena hadn't time to respond before Stuart grasped her by the hand, bending down at the knee before her. His voice was low, sincere—and almost desperate. "I swear it!" he promised again, more adamantly than the first. "You must allow me to make amends. It was a quarrel—a lover's quarrel. Did you never see your parents do so?"

"Of course, but—"

"There. You see," he stood to his feet, "that's all it was. We were both angry—we said things we ought not to have—"

"But I never saw my father raise a hand to my mother…no matter the argument."

Though his patience waned, Stuart nodded in understanding. "It was a mistake."

"But…your father *did* hit your mother…many times." Velena's chin quivered. "It was you who said so."

Stuart planted a fist to his forehead, squeezing his eyes shut against the ugliness of his youth. "I am *not* my father!" he exclaimed through gritted teeth.

Velena's hand stiffened within his grasp, but when he raised his face to her, his look was surprisingly tender.

He inhaled deeply through his nostrils and uncurled his fist to gently stroke the tension away from the hand he'd yet to release. "I'm not my father…" he repeated, more softly this time, his words trailing off like a vapor. "Isn't that what you always used to tell me?"

"Yes," Velena's throat constricted painfully, "but…you *are* his son." Her voice began to break. "And I've come to realize that some things are not so easily cast off…no matter how long we've run from them.

Stuart's eyes drifted back and forth across her face. He saw her pity and it burned a hole through his heart. "I can't change whose son I am. But I can determine the kind of husband I'll be. Forgive me for my thoughtless actions. From the very beginning, I've only ever wanted to be with you."

Velena recognized the truth of it as his eyes sought to drink her in. Suddenly, she needed to breath—to be in the open.

He continued, "This tension between us should have no foot hold, for despite our mistakes, upon hearing this news of our engagement…I couldn't have been more pleased."

Unable to reciprocate the feeling—and not knowing what else to do—Velena quickly pulled her hands away and skirted around him in an attempt to escape the privacy of the stables, lest he attempt to demonstrate more fully his enthusiasm. The Lord knew what kind of effect the enclosed space had on her and Tristan.

Now, aware the winds had changed, the quiet, still sounds of *calm* were a stark contradiction to the tempest still churning within her.

"I know you have hesitations," he said coming up behind her.

She pivoted to face him.

"But you'll see, now, that all will be well."

"I want to believe that," Velena said, closing her eyes. "I want to accept it with all my heart, but—"

"You said you'd accept whoever your father chose. You said you'd accept it as the will of God."

Velena's chest rose and sank, as the exhaling of her breath carried off another small piece of hope. "I did…" her voice held a quiver as she nodded her head in affirmation, "I did—I said that. But now that it's happened—after what's happened—it seems such folly. I'm sorry, Stuart…" She lifted the back of her hand to wipe away the moisture gathering beneath her nose.

"Velena…" Her name dripped from his mouth like the last bit of water from a dried up well.

She sensed his sorrow and found herself groaning inwardly at his pain, for despite her anger, she didn't hate him.

"No, Velena, I'm the one who's sorry…so very sorry," he crooned, wrapping his arms about her body—burying his face into the curve of her neck. He pulled her in, though she remained unresponsive, her arms draped at her sides, the soft texture of her surcoat catching on calloused hands as he stroked her back and shoulders, grasping for what he felt slipping away.

His voice was muffled. "Nothing's happened the way I'd hoped—except for this one thing. Our engagement is the culmination of the only good I've ever had in my life." He pulled back so he could stare her in the eyes. "Please, Velena, don't hate me now." He cupped her face. "Don't you know? You're all I've ever wanted. Tell me you know that…"

Trepidation coiled within her breast, tightening around her heart, but still she nodded, knowing she could do nothing more than accept his love for what it was—for what he claimed it to be. Perhaps it was all he was capable of giving.

Her meager response was less assurance than he wanted, and he gave her a dower smile. What was left for him to do? "You might not see it now, but I'll make you happy. I swear I will!"

Time elapsed quickly for Velena, even as it stood still. Stuart's forehead came down to press against her own, but the moment was nothing like it'd been with Tristan. And despite Tristan's doubts about the genuineness of Stuart's love for her—in this moment, she knew Stuart was sincere…though she could return none of it.

Oh Tristan, what will become of me?

"Your misgivings will pass," Stuart assured her as surely as if he could read her thoughts. He stroked her cheeks with his thumbs. "Neither of us are perfect, Velena. Tell me what to do to set things right, and I'll do it."

Velena took hold of his hands and pulled them off her face, the backs of his fingers unwittingly grazing the front of her surcoat as she pushed him away.

Accident or no, it sent a surge of heat up his arms. *Did she not feel it also?*

Anxious to move beyond heightened emotions that had nearly carried her adrift with Tristan, she set distance between them. "We can do naught but the next thing," she said, remembering the Lord's promise to direct her steps. "We'll toast with our fathers and pray God's grace over our union. Surely, they're expecting us."

With hope in his eyes, he proffered his arm, waiting for her to act of her own volition. "Then let us tarry no longer." When she accommodated with a hand to his sleeve, he convinced himself that all she needed was time—time that was now on his side with their engagement properly secured.

They'd just started back towards the manor when Stuart caught sight of his cousins in the distance practicing their long bows. Stuart detoured.

"What are you doing?" Velena baulked, sensing his motive.

"Before we drink with our fathers, let us first go and tell them the news of our—"

"Oh no," Velena pulled back, "please—not yet." Her eyes swept the landscape to see if Tristan was among the group. She didn't think she could maintain her composure if he was there.

"Why? They've been as family to you since childhood. Wouldn't you like to tell them they'll now be cousins to us both? Have they not always been so in your heart?"

"You know how Rowan will tease. He needs no excuse to—"

"He's a cabbage-eater,[5] and besides, when have you ever minded it? We'll be quick. I want to tell Jaren, myself."

Resistance seemed futile as he dragged her alongside him.

"Jaren!" Stuart called, his voice gaining the group's attention as he approached.

They set down their bows—all except for Rowan, who held his erect by his side like a middle finger.

Stuart clasped his hand securely over hers. "We've an announcement to make. Long in coming—but well worth the wait."

Velena wanted to flee. Despite the years of close familiarity, she still couldn't help but feel awkward and vulnerable before the three men now gawking at her. All the while, she could feel the possessive hand Stuart laid to the small of her back as though he were setting her up for display. Her only solace was in Tristan's absence.

"You are now looking at my future wife," Stuart finished. "Our engagement is official!"

"Long in coming, indeed. Congratulations," Jaren exclaimed, locking wrists with Stuart's free hand, pumping profusely. "And to you...Velena," Jaren bent down to kiss her on the cheek, jerky movements demonstrating the hesitancy of his words. "I know you'll be very...happy together."

Though kindly said, his words were a reproach to Velena's ears. He was telling her to be faithful to Stuart—to abandon Tristan. And though she told herself Jaren should not be faulted for such loyalty to his cousin—his sworn brother—it alienated her from him just the same.

"God bless you both," Sir Andret said in his quiet, matter-of-fact way in stark contrast to the zeal of his younger brother.

As usual, Velena thought the knight's face nearly impossible to read, his smile tipping no more than what polite behavior demanded, giving the impression that he neither approved nor disapproved of the union. Had she ever known his mind? Most likely not.

Velena acknowledged the blessing with what felt like an obligatory grin.

This left Rowan to give his regards—he, who'd remained silently standing by, measuring carefully her every expression. She knew it was a mistake to look at him, but still their eyes met. His were full of pity—and then it happened.

Her dam burst, and unchecked tears streamed down her face, perhaps one for every moment of this absurdly long day. It was dreadful. Appalling. *Dreadfully appalling!* How could she succumb to such a show of emotion while Stuart stood by in the judgment of his peers?

Desperately, she tried to ebb the tide with the sleeve of her tunic, but the well from which her tears sprang seemed an endless supply of grief. It wasn't wailing or sobbing, simply the outpouring of her soul—and there was no stopping it.

Quick to intercede, Rowan took her by the hands. "Nenna, look at you! Crying like it's your wedding day." He raised an eyebrow to Stuart. "You know a woman's really in love when she can't hold back her tears." His fingers pressed into her palms. "At least, it's what my mother used to say when my father wasn't beating her."

Sir Andret chuckled.

Jaren rolled his eyes.

Velena giggled through blurry lashes…until she met Stuart's gaze. He didn't believe Rowan—that much was clear. And why should he? He knew her mind—the raw emotions that had just delivered them over to this moment. She should be the indignant one, having to put up with this charade and yet…she had to acknowledge that her behavior *had* shamed him. Her eyes appealed once more to Rowan for help, and once more, he rose to the occasion.

"Go on, Velena." He gestured at Stuart with his chin, releasing her hands as he did so. "Tell your *sweet dove* how much you love him, and all will be well."

Rowan was handing her an olive branch—a way to make amends. Redemption lay before her, but still it stuck in her throat.

Stuart knew better than anyone that Rowan's speech was hogwash, but still his expression softened to one of expectation as he waited for her to speak. After receiving so little assurances from her, he found himself hungry for any words of love that might condescend from her lips—sincere or otherwise.

He watched as her delicate lips parted—lips that carried with them the taste of salted tears. Stuart was having a difficult time keeping his thoughts in order. Kissing her seemed more inviting now than ever before.

Velena swallowed. What could she say? She'd grown up loving her cousin. It wouldn't be a lie for her to say so now, though sadly, the pool from which she drew that love was now greatly lacking in depth. But she had a choice. When she was still promised to Peter, Tristan had told her that she had a *choice*—that she could choose to love he who would be her future husband. And even though it'd be Stuart destined to walk this life with her now, there was still the same choice looming before her.

God's will be done.

Velena raised her eyes, glistening bright like dew-covered hills. It wouldn't be a lie if she made it the truth. She would choose. "My whole childhood, I loved you, Cousin." She swallowed. "I choose to love you still."

The softness of her voice engaged Stuart's every sensibility, and despite her answer having been prompted—nay, practically forced— his pulse quickened. "And your tears?" he asked, knowing full well why they fell.

"You know as well as I what sorts of *mishaps* have colored our day. Yet, still I'll show myself happy to declare such tidings as we have to give, in the hearing of our friends…our family."

Stuart's insides quivered. "Then let them see that I return your love—love I both *choose* to give…and am compelled to satisfy." He moved in to close the space between them.

Velena only half noticed his response because walking towards them, at the most inopportune moment imaginable…was Tristan.

*Not now…*then suddenly, she was fighting for breath.

Tristan froze mid-stride.

Velena's mind rebelled, as did her body, but Stuart had her firmly about the waist, pulling her against him—locking her into a kiss he'd pressed directly over her narrowly opened mouth.

Under normal circumstances, a public display such as this would have been frowned upon and certainly not tolerated before they were wed. But these weren't normal circumstances, and Stuart's kiss was neither in the public of town, nor in the presence of her father who would certainly object. It was amongst peers—peers who would do little to nothing to dispute his actions. And he was taking full advantage of this now, lingering as long as he dared—undeterred by the hands Velena pressed against his chest in protest of the moment.

For Stuart, it was just as he imaged it would be. He could taste the salt from her tears—the sweetness of her breath. And unyielding, though they were, her lips were soft and warm, and everything he'd longed for. With difficulty, he suppressed a sigh of satisfaction, inwardly cursing the fact they weren't alone.

"Well done, man…" Rowan finally said, his voice dripping with sarcasm, "you've succeeded in embarrassing the hell out of her. Now, stop gushing over your bride and pick up a bow. I think I just might be able to out-shoot you today—now that you've been properly distracted."

Stuart laughed out loud, feeling uncommonly forgiving toward Rowan after such a high. "No amount of distraction could provide you great enough advantage over me, Rowan."

Rowan feigned disappointment. "At least let me try," he said, thinking to give Velena a chance to escape them.

"Soon enough." Stuart turned, noticing Tristan for the first time. A smile crept slowly to his lips. He then added, "For I'll be adequately as distracted for days to come, I should think."

Stuart's expression hid nothing of the pleasure he felt upon realizing he'd just kissed Velena in front of Tristan. He couldn't have planned it better. "Tristan," he said, enjoying the sound of his name for the first time ever. "Your timing is impeccable. Velena and I are to be congratulated."

Tristan looked to Velena only. "Are you alright?"

Velena's mouth parted but if there were words, they couldn't be heard above Jaren's haughty retort.

Jaren stepped forward but was stayed by Sir Andret's palm to his chest. "What do you mean, 'is she alright?'" he asked. "Do you think we'd all be standing here twiddling our thumbs if she weren't? Of all the arrogant—"

"Let the lady answer her own questions, Brother."

Velena nodded her thanks to Sir Andret but had to concede that she barely knew her own mind. Her eyes flitted back and forth about the group with nowhere to land. She saw Jaren glance at her from beneath his bangs, heard Rowan's feet reposition themselves in the grass, felt the flex of Stuart's fingers at her waist and, more than anything else, became painfully aware of the possessive stance he now assumed over her.

Though thoroughly embarrassed over the whole ordeal, Velena forced a mere fraction of a smile and finally managed to say, "I'm alright," actually grateful when Stuart spoke up, giving her an excuse to leave.

"You'll have to excuse us. We're making our way to toast with our fathers." Stuart's look was smug as he attempted to take Velena's unyielding hand through the crook of his arm, but she drew it back without apology.

Blinking back his embarrassment, Stuart nodded a brusque farewell and ushered her away towards the manor house with a hand to her back.

[3]**Quoits:** A medieval game, similar to Horseshoes, involving a ring of iron or rope tossed at an upright peg.
[4]**Destrier:** A knight's warhorse.
[5]**Cabbage-eater:** An insult, as cabbage was a food with an unpleasant aroma, causing equally as unpleasant side-effects; the food of peasants.

2

addled

Knowing he'd have to face them together eventually, Tristan had approached them on purpose—but then, Stuart kissed her. In that moment, Tristan had never wanted to hurt anyone so badly in all his life as he'd wanted to hurt Stuart. He was a thousand times grateful Rowan had stepped in and interrupted their kiss when he had.

This miscreant had ravaged Daisy—and from the pit of his stomach—he was repulsed at the liberties he'd seen him take with Velena. Second only to the satisfaction he would've received from beating Stuart senseless, would've been to heave his disgust all over the swine's shoes. And though the latter might have been no difficulty, no good could have truly come of it. Not for him…and most importantly, not for Velena, so he'd stood, planted, not knowing what to do.

It'd been too late for him to walk away without looking like a coward—and to have given Stuart his usual sarcastic remarks would have only agitated their cause. But what, *exactly*, was their cause?

He'd thought it was for him and Velena not to be parted from one another—or was it simply for their friendship to continue? But did that mean staying together? And if so, what did *together* mean for them? Tristan had been confused ever since he'd left Velena in the stables, crying. He'd tried to run. He'd attempted to pray. But for once in his life, his head had refused to clear.

Now, watching Velena leave with Stuart down the path towards the manor, Tristan flexed his hands and realized he was shaking. It didn't appear they argued, but from the rigid line of Velena's back—and the way the pace of her steps brought her head up and down in a timed bob—he surmised she was in a temper, and rightly so. Nowhere to be seen was the playful sway of her hips that marked her otherwise pleasant demeanor, and all he could think was, *he's stolen her walk.*

Tristan seethed. Stuart had stolen his friend. He'd stolen her kiss.

He'd even stolen her *walk*. Was he to steal until there was nothing left?

Tristan gripped a fist full of hair, welcoming the pain before allowing his arm to drop, followed by his shoulders, truly giving him the appearance of a man vanquished.

Everything works together for good to those who love Him and are called according to His purpose. He knew that, but he refused to believe that marrying Stuart was a part of God's purpose for Velena. *How could any of this work together for good?*

Inadvertently, his mind returned to the stables and the moment they'd been alone. Another moment, and he might have…

He ran his hand over his face, oblivious to the three onlookers still standing by. Tristan tapped his middle finger against his thigh. He didn't want to finish his thought, but it couldn't be helped. *Another moment*…and he might have kissed her.

The impulse had been entirely his own, and he laid none of the blame on Velena—unwilling for a moment to think she'd been seeking any kind of romantic attentions. She'd been distraught! What was his excuse? Was his love for her deeper than he'd realized? He didn't think so, but in this moment, they were acting like something out of Velena's book, *Tristan and Isulte,* and it was driving him to distraction. This was all wrong! The whole thing was wrong. Velena and Stuart. Velena and him.

Wrong! Wrong! Wrong!

"Tristan?"

"What?" He swung his head around as though seeing Rowan for the first time.

"You want to walk?"

Tristan shook his head. "I've done enough walking."

"Anything I can do?"

"No." He glanced at Sir Andret and Jaren, beginning to feel self-conscious. "I'm…I'm just going to go."

Jaren's voice called him back. "It's best if you stay out of this, Tristan."

Tristan huffed. "She's just been thrown to the wolves, and you want me to stay out of it?"

"I'll make sure that nothing…" Jaren stumbled over his words—cleared his throat. "She has all of us to look after her. Don't deceive yourself into thinking you're the only one who cares."

Tristan's eyes narrowed, gripping Jaren with a look—searching. "You know…don't you?"

Jaren made no answer.

Tristan laughed abruptly before shaking his head in disgust. "Of course, you do."

Trusting himself no more to words, he turned on his heel and stalked off along the same path Velena had taken towards the manor.

Rowan and Sir Andret blinked, exchanging glances. "What do you know?" Rowan asked, turning to Jaren.

Avoiding his gaze, Jaren busied himself, gathering up his arrows and longbow as if to leave. "He's just upset."

"We're all upset."

"Well, I'm not!" Jaren asserted.

"Yeees…" Rowan eyed him closely, "and why is that, exactly?"

"Why should I be?"

"Because Stuart is a worm, and you know it. And you know something else too."

"You never let up, Rowan."

"Enough." Sir Andret raised a hand as if addressing small children. He looked to his brother. "Jaren—is there something you want to tell us?"

Jaren hesitated. "Nothing. I misspoke is all. There's no cause for concern."

Sir Andret's mouth pulled into a tight line, his head bobbing up and down as he thought. "Lady Velena's response to her engagement might be considered a cause for concern—to some."

Jaren shrugged. "Perhaps."

"Women don't cry for naught," he continued.

Jaren swung his longbow over his shoulder, "I'll keep that in mind."

Rowan's brow maintained a look of bewilderment as he watched him stalk off towards the barracks. "Why would you say that?" he asked Sir Andret, abruptly.

"Say what?"

"That women don't cry for naught." He tossed up a hand. "They absolutely do."

Sir Andret rolled his eyes. "I was making a point."

Rowan took up his bow again, taking aim at the target. "Well…it wasn't a very good one."

Sir Andret fit an arrow to his own bow. "Do you want to talk or shoot?"

"I'd like to know if we're on the same side."

Sir Andret's arrow flew true to its mark. "Do I need to be on someone's side?"

"Are you ever?" Rowan muttered.

Sir Andret rubbed a hand across his chest as he looked towards the barracks. "I've given an oath to Sir Richard—I'm on his side."

"Very diplomatic of you," Rowan said, cupping his hands over the tip of his bow.

Sir Andret turned to face him, "Not diplomatic. Strategic. I took an oath to a man I respect. You squire to a man you don't. If you want that to change, you'll need to figure a way out from under him."

"And just how am I supposed to do that?"

Sir Andret smirked. "You know better than I how to get out of situations you want no part of." He chuckled. "In fact, I have every confidence you'll figure it out."

3

what's best for her

Tristan stood outside Velena's solar[6], the back of his knuckles poised at the door. For certain, Sir Richard and Lord Magnus would be raising their glasses to the newly-paired couple at this very moment, but he knew in the end Velena would need him. So, he'd come with the intention of hiding away until she returned. All day if need be. How else was he to speak with her—for surely, she'd be under close scrutiny for the remainder of the day.

Assuming her solar was empty, his tap on the distinctly familiar oak barrier was merely a precaution. He was taken aback when Daisy appeared in the doorway, looking wan. Even more so—after making quick check of the hall—she bid him enter without first asking why he'd come.

Tristan found himself stammering out an explanation. "I didn't...didn't think anyone would be here. I—"

"Did you tell Sir Richard?" she interrupted before he could say more.

It made sense she'd want to know. The last time he'd seen Daisy— much to her dismay—he'd told her he'd be going to Sir Richard with the truth of Stuart's treachery. And he *had* tried, but recent events were now clouding his mind, and he suddenly felt exhausted and overwhelmed. His shoulders sagged. "He wouldn't hear me," he confessed.

Daisy's entire demeanor registered relief. Tristan turned away, hating to see the expression she'd make when he told her he wasn't going to give up.

"I need to see Velena."

"Please, Tristan," she pleaded, reaching out to him, "if Lord Richard won't listen, then what possible gain could be had from telling Velena. *Please*, I beg you not to—"

"Ease your mind." Tristan pulled away from her. "That's not why I came."

"You'll be silent on the matter then?"

Tristan ran a hand through his hair, scanning the room for a comfortable place to wait out his vigil. Across the room was another door, leading into Velena and Daisy's bed chamber, which was quite out of the question. To the right, a goodly-sized window fit with tall, rectangular panes of glass was set deep within a window seat. This was more a possibility—as was the longish table and bench set, used for entertaining purposes—but he finally settled on the seating to his left. It was naught but a hard-backed bench, facing a cold fireplace, but it was draped in a sheep skin and in possession of two nicely stuffed pillows.

"No," he said, taking a deep breath. "I've not changed my mind."

Daisy's face blanched. Her blond plait[7] hung lifeless over her shoulder, the curves of her body swaying as if she didn't know which way to go.

Tristan's heart went out to her as he noted the way she gripped the sides of her surcoat. He'd already thought she looked pale, but now he was beginning to worry for her. "I'm so sorry…but what Stuart's done must come to light. It's imperative Sir Richard knows—now more than ever." *Poor thing.* She appeared miserable, indeed.

"Come." He made room for her to sit beside him. "Listen to me. I've given it a goodly deal of thought, and I've decided that if you're shunned—for any reason—because of the confession I give on your behalf…then I'll take you in, myself."

Daisy blinked. "You mean to marr—?"

"No, no…" Tristan's eyes grew large as he made a quick attempt to explain his meaning without stumbling over every other syllable. "I'm offering to…to take you back with me to Oxford. You'd have a place in my household—under my employment that is—for as long as you'd wish to stay."

"You'd do that for me?"

"Without reservation."

"Even after all the grief I've given you?"

Tristan grinned. "Come now, I thought that surely you'd have grown rather fond of me after all this time."

Her smile was shaky at best.

Tristan continued. "You should also know Velena's…engaged."

"It's done then." A forlorn sort of finality echoed in her words.

"For now."

At first Daisy appeared calm, the rise and dip of her chest coming and going in even intervals. Then—suddenly, as if realizing she seated herself on a hot iron—she bolted from the couch. "No!" she protested with all the authority she could muster but didn't possess. "You mustn't let it happen. You can't!"

He looked on in frustration. "Then go to Sir Richard, yourself. Tell him what happened!"

Daisy glared down at him. "I'll do no such thing."

"Then I don't know what else to tell you. For my part, I've tried everything I can think of to keep them apart."

"Not everything," Daisy said, sitting back down.

Tristan puzzled. "What do you mean?"

"You could recommend *yourself* to Sir Richard."

"At the risk of sounding redundant, what do you—"

"*You* could marry her."

Tristan laughed only to realize she was being serious. His smile disappeared. "Did you not hear me? It's already done. It's in writing. And if you don't speak the truth of what Stuart did to you, it's *going* to happen."

"I shouldn't have to martyr myself when there's another way."

"I'm not it," he affirmed.

"You underestimate how much you've meant to this family."

"Sir Richard doesn't want me for a son-in-law."

"But he'd accept you if there was no one else."

"There is someone else." He resisted the urge to shake her by her pretty little shoulders, figuring it was now too late to bring her back to a reality she was bent on escaping.

"But what if you gave him no choice?" she said, suddenly.

"How do you mean?"

"How much would you give of yourself to free Velena from this marriage?"

"Don't play games, Daisy."

"It's not a game. How much do you love her?"

"Enough to be sent away for it, evidently. After our last conversation, I fear Sir Richard won't suffer me to stay much longer."

Daisy ignored him. "Do you love her enough to woo her?"

Tristan did laugh this time.

"I'm in earnest," Daisy insisted, resenting his derisive manner. "If she were…compromised, Stuart would have to abdicate his claim over her for the sake of his reputation, and Sir Richard would be forced to accept you as his alternative."

"If she were…compromi—are you mad?"

"He loves you like a son."

"That is entirely beside the point. I can't even believe you'd suggest…" Tristan couldn't finish. He rose to stand before the hearth, putting his back to Daisy.

She approached, touching his shoulder. "It's the only way."

"I refuse to believe that," he said, shaking her off, "and even if it were, you're forgetting Velena's part in this. How do you think she'd react to my advances?"

Daisy swallowed hard, thinking of her last moments with Bowan, his kind words and gentle passion. "Have faith in yourself. You know she loves you."

"Not like that."

"Only because you've never given her reason to, Tristan." Her eyes lowered. "Perhaps, if you were to…kiss her…or touch her in…in the right way, she may prove more willing than you suppose."

"Good heavens, Daisy—listen to yourself! She'd be no more willing to submit herself to me than you were to Stuart. Have you so soon forgotten the pain of it? Have his actions somehow endeared him to you?"

Daisy's lips pinched together, exposing the dimples that were so lovely when she used to smile. She went to pacing the floor, allowing the truth of his words to coax her back to sanity.

He came to stand by her. "I know you're afraid—but after all you've been through—how could you ask me to betray her in such a way?"

Suddenly embarrassed, Daisy's words tumbled out in defense of her position. "I wasn't suggesting you ravage her. I was simply suggesting I thought it'd be best if—"

"Stop. Enough! I want no more of this. Your grief has blinded you." He looked on her with pity. "You couldn't possibly know what's best for her…not anymore."

Tristan's words shamed her, and she hung her head as hot tears stung the back of her eyes. "That's not true," she whispered, "*You're* what's best for her."

She moved silently towards the door. "Perhaps, I'm not the only one who's blind."

He said nothing as the door closed between them, leaving him alone with the totality of his thoughts…and hers.

---

[6]**Solar:** A bedroom or living space.
[7]**Plait:** Braid (pronounced "plat").

4

truth and a lie

Velena existed somewhere inside herself, numb from having spent so many tears. Silently, she took her place beside Stuart at the table, recalling with regret how she lied to Tristan when he'd asked if she was alright—how she'd wept in the sight of her friends, revealing to all the true depth of her unhappiness. Surely her faith was being tested. Was God calling on her to confirm her belief in His Holy Word—that He *causes all things to work together for good, to those who love God, to those who are called according to His purpose*? If that were the case, every part of her would be crying out for God to help her in her unbelief. For in this moment, it didn't seem true.

She forced a smile as a glass of rich golden liquid was passed into her hands, finally finding a reason for which to be grateful. It wasn't the sweet spiced wine she was used to, but something dry and bitter that puckered her mouth and burned as it slipped down her throat. It seemed fitting.

Encircled about the round oak table within the manor's library, Sir Richard and Lord Magnus sat across from Stuart and herself. They sipped wine and discussed the date for the upcoming nuptials. Any one of them could have observed that she was on her way to downing one too many glasses, but if they had, they made no movement to stop her. For this, she was grateful, taking full advantage of the fog settling over her. Indeed, anytime the conversation came the least bit in her direction, she responded with a placating smile and a raise of her glass—never mind that she had no desire to toast such an occasion.

"I have no desire for a long engagement," Stuart said, fingers drumming out a light-hearted beat upon the wood.

Despite the haze, Velena found his perfectly timed statement comical.

Sir Richard leaned into the back of his chair, rubbing his hands over his thighs. "I understand your enthusiasm, but what would you say to having the wedding follow directly after the tourney[8]?"

"Now, that's a good six weeks away," Magnus stated, matter-of-factly.

Sir Richard shrugged. "It is, but there's still plenty to do before then. We've to plan for food, entertainment—lodging, quite possibly."

Stuart looked disappointed. "That's a whole other fortnight."

Sir Richard's bottom lip protruded. "Events of this magnitude take time. Totnes has seen much suffering these past three years, and—"

"Don't tell us about suffering," Magnus quipped. "We were the ones here for it—don't forget."

Velena noted the familiar edge to her uncle's words—as well as the talent her father had for overlooking them. She glanced towards the door, wishing she had a reason to excuse herself.

"That you were," Sir Richard agreed. "And you suffered your fair share, same as the rest of Totnes—which is why their marriage should be a celebration for all to take part in. And what better way to end the games than to have a wedding—a symbol of new life and renewed vigor." Sir Richard was beginning to show his excitement now.

Magnus rocked his head back and forth, then slapped his hand down on the table. "After the tourney it is."

Sir Richard smiled. "We'll start planning immediately."

Stuart pinched the end of his eyebrow as he glanced over at Velena. He thought perhaps to gain insight into her opinion, but at present, she seemed to be interested in naught but the decorative protuberances encircling her glass.

"For mercy's sake, Stuart, don't act so disappointed," Magnus said, reaching for the pitcher at the center of the table. "The extra time will do us good. I want you knighted before the tourney."

"And what of Rowan and Jaren?" Sir Richard asked, accepting a refill for his own glass.

Magnus pursed his lips. "What about them?"

"Have you any plans for knighting your nephews? They're of age, now, are they not?"

Velena glanced across the table at her uncle.

"This wedding will cost money enough," he scoffed. "Certainly, they don't expect me to pay their way."

"Father, you promised Auntie that—"

Magnus laughed. "Your mother promised," he said, as though a promise made by his late wife to her sister was a ridiculous thing for him to uphold now that she was gone.

"She's a nun."

"Don't be dramatic. She was—was," he said, as if that settled the matter, "a nun. And I need no reminder of that, boy."

"Surely, she has God's ear," Stuart added. "And now that Jaren's father is gone, Auntie could never afford to pay for it."

Velena watched as her uncle maintained an enigmatic expression. Perhaps, he was contemplating whether the indulgence[9] he'd acquired from his pilgrimage to Avignon assured him more than just heavenly entrance, but protection against heavenly retribution over unfulfilled debts, as well.

Sir Richard raised his eyebrows, puckering his lips in disappointment. "A breach of faith could be construed as a promise of future such breeches. To continue with our business discussions would become quite out of the question if that were the case."

Glaring out of the corner of his eye, Magnus quaffed a mouthful of the bitter liquid and swished it around his mouth before swallowing. Gripping the glass by its rim, he clunked it down upon the wood— lastly sucking his breath in through his teeth and grimacing as if catching the taste of something unsavory.

"Very well. I'll pay Jaren's way in exchange for his continued service—but not Rowan's. I'll not have him under my roof forever."

"Has he not also fulfilled his obligations to you?" Sir Richard asked, dryly.

"Begrudgingly so. Taking him in was a favor to yet another of my wife's poor sisters—a sister, along with her husband, who is no more," he emphasized. "And I made no such arrangements with his parents beyond his initial training. I've done that, and I'd just as soon have him gone."

Though outwardly composed, inwardly, Velena hurt for Rowan. It was this hurting for someone else that sparked the first bit of life back into her. She turned to Stuart, but he didn't seem to mind what was being said. He and Rowan had never much gotten along, and there were simply too many other things he was looking forward to—and it showed. He radiated pleasure over nearly every detail of their upcoming nuptials. Velena grew suddenly desirous of even the smallest portion of that happiness and found herself studying him whenever his head was turned.

Dark, wavy hair framed his face, stopping just below his ear lobes.

A scar on his chin, drew her attention to his mouth and the smile she remembered loving as a child. His brown eyes shown bright, and for this one moment, he appeared free of any jealousy or anger.

At one point, he caught her staring, and she lowered her eyes to her drink, giving up her ill-timed perusal. She sat up a little higher in her chair and smoothed out the folds in her surcoat. Stuart might not be her ideal match, but the more she listened to him gush over their future together, the more she thought herself a silly girl for thinking she could keep Tristan as a friend after she were wed. When that happened, neither she nor Tristan would be living in her father's home anymore, which by itself would greatly diminish any contact between them. Furthermore, were it someone else she was marrying, she'd still be faced with the same objections to her maintaining a friend of the opposite sex. And wouldn't she have those same objections if the tables were turned? Suddenly, feeling terribly naïve, she realized it'd been her own willfulness that had kept her believing her friendship with Tristan wouldn't change after she were married. He'd been right all along.

Mortification over her outburst in the stables with Tristan suddenly consumed her. She'd overreacted in the worst way, causing what began as a moment of comfort to quickly evolve into a terrible wedge between them. At first, she'd thought she only imagined it, but the more she brought their interaction to mind—the more certain she was that Tristan had meant to kiss her.

Feeling her face flush, Velena sneaked a peak at Stuart from beneath her lashes, hoping he'd attribute her coloring to too much wine. What would he do if he knew Tristan had almost kissed her? Surely, her forehead didn't count, but could she be any more embarrassed?

This was her fault. Tristan asked her to remember that he was a man…and not just a friend. The nearness of their bodies must have confused him. Velena grew anxious thinking about it. Misunderstandings such as this were just the sort of thing he hated, and she knew he'd have no peace until they were able to set things right again.

So intent on her thoughts was she that it took several moments of staring at Stuart's hand before it registered he was reaching for her empty glass. She relinquished it. They were being dismissed. Velena hoped that none of the decisions made in regard to their wedding required any action on her part—for she didn't recall a thing past their discussion of Rowan.

She attempted a smile as Sir Richard came around the table to kiss her cheek. He looked somewhat concerned but mostly pleased. Surprisingly, her uncle assessed her with uncharacteristic approval. Most likely he interpreted her silence as indicative of a now crushed and moldable spirit.

Stuart was wearing his heart on his sleeve. This time when he proffered his arm, Velena accepted it in an act of submission that she hoped would be preemptive of feelings to come.

She prayed for the future. She prayed that one day she'd be able to find joy in their marriage. Perhaps if Stuart was able to master his jealous nature—or if he rescinded his threat to send Daisy away—it could be possible.

But what of that?

Velena's suspicions lingered. What role did Stuart play in the change that had so removed her dear Daisy from who she used to be? Furthermore, what impetus might he be having on her own life?

As it stood, both questions were of equal concern.

After parting ways with their fathers, Velena and Stuart continued in each other's company, walking the hall and commenting on various pieces of art displayed along the way. She tried to hold her end of an intelligent conversation, but her head was quite fuzzy. The sounds of their leather soles scuffing against the stone—along with the smell of something she thought to be roast pig—managed to catch her attention more than any conversation he sought to contrive.

"What are your thoughts?" Stuart asked, his voice parting through her fog.

Velena stopped. "Of the tapestry?"

Stuart smirked. "Of waiting an extra fortnight to marry." He reached forward, closing the gap to take her hands. "My immediate thought was that I was opposed to the idea. I would just as soon have you as my wife before the tourney. On the other hand, to be knighted and able to fully participate in the games…" He inhaled with a look of satisfaction. "It would make for a grand affair."

He crossed his hand in front of his body and then dragged it above his head like a banner. "Our marriage would be the culmination of the whole event." He dropped it down again and chuckled. "Besides, I don't think your father could really be persuaded to do otherwise. I'd ask you to try your hand at changing his mind, but…" he smiled ruefully, "I know how you don't like to *interfere*."

Velena's brows came together. Her mind wasn't clearing as fast as she would have liked. "How many weeks until the wedding did you say?"

Stuart cocked his head sideways, rolling in his lips. "I might have guessed your thoughts were elsewhere. Were you listening at all?"

Velena looked apologetic. "Not well enough, evidently." She took up walking again. "I know everyone is in a good humor, but if I can be honest, I still don't feel myself. Would you mind terribly if I retired to my room? I think I may have taken too much wine, and I'm afraid I might not last until supper."

"Velena…" He stopped her with a hand to her shoulder and then lowered his chin so his eyes would be level with her own. "It's going to take more than a mere few hours to change your thoughts about us. You need to be patient. We both do." He stepped back to lean his back up against the wall, carefully weighing her reaction. "I know you didn't really mean it before—in front of Jaren and the rest—when you said you loved me."

Velena's face clouded. "Not as you want me to."

Stuart nodded, looking down at the gray stones beneath his soft leather shoes. "Even so…it was a fine thing you did for me—sparing my feelings in front of the others. But it's just you and me now—there's no need for pretense."

"I don't know what you want me to say. It's just—"

"Just…that I'm taking you from Tristan." The muscles in his jaw flexed. "That's the real reason you were crying. Isn't it?"

Velena clutched her hands at her waist. "I'll not deny there's a part of me in mourning for the friendship you intend on denying me—but I'm not pining for him if that's what you're thinking. In truth, I was overwhelmed after our argument. Then you kissed me—in front of everyone," her voice raised before she could think better of it, "and I'm angry with you even now, knowing you did it under the guise of being pleased with my admission of *love*—when its very contents you never believed in the first place." She was now looking him straight in the eyes. "You took advantage of me, Stuart."

28

Stuart tipped his head back to the wall, a casual expression peering down at her from over his nose.

"You don't deny it, then?"

"I don't."

"How could you treat me like that? You know who I am—who we were to each other. I was ever and always your friend! As children, I denied you no shortage of affection and now that I'm a woman, you claim to love me but treat me with contempt."

"Did you expect me never to kiss you?"

"Whether a man is supposed to kiss his bride before or after they're wed, you tell me! I'm obviously naïve to such things, but would it have been too much to ask that my first kiss not be taken from me in public?" She nearly spat the words.

Stuart's forehead wrinkled in quiet confusion. "Your first?"

Velena suddenly found reason to fiddle with the front of her tunic—its modest earthen tones gaining unwarranted attention as she murmured, "I would have thought it quite obvious."

"Tristan *never*...not even once?" He was somewhat incredulous, certain Tristan must have kissed her, if only to spite him after their altercation at Wineford. Or the two nights before leaving the castle when Velena had arrived at the bonfire only minutes before Tristan— surely then. Stuart gave her a hard look, ascertaining the truthfulness of her answer. If she were lying, would he see it in her eyes?

"Of course not." She met his gaze evenly. "He was never a threat to us."

"*Us.*" He repeated the words, liking the way they sounded coming from her.

Velena nodded.

"He *never* kissed you," he repeated, this time more to himself.

A vision of Tristan tenderly cradling her face in his hands flashed abruptly through her mind. She pushed it away. *It was naught but charity.* "Never."

Stuart shook his head in astonishment. "Then he was a fool—but I thank God he was." Using his leg to push himself away from the wall with one smooth motion, he approached her. "*I*, however, am not."

Seeing his intention, Velena stumbled back into the opposite wall, arms poised to resist him.

He stopped, mere inches from her face, dropping his gaze to watch the rise and fall of her chest with unabashed pleasure. He reached for the hands she held to his chest and laced his fingers within hers, grinning boyishly as the heat rose to her cheeks.

Suddenly grateful she'd chosen to wear a modestly cut tunic, Velena pulled her hands free, gently urging him back until he was at arm's length.

"Stuart…" she began, trying to regain her wits.

"I love you," he whispered, testing the resolve of her outstretched arms.

She pushed him back again. "You don't have to do this to convince me of it. There are other ways."

"What would you have me do?"

"Honor me in your behavior just as I seek to honor God in mine. Can you do that?"

He ran a hand over his mouth, shaking his head. "You seek excuses to keep me away."

"No. Can't you understand?" Her voice did nothing to bely her deep frustration. "I *will* choose to love you, but you mustn't keep forcing yourself on me like this."

Forcing? He knew what she meant, but still her comment stung him, and he pulled back. "I'd never force you, Velena."

"You're trying to induce me into something I'm not ready for."

Stuart reached past her hands to her upper arms. Again, her hands splayed open between them. "I seek only to be close to you—not to hurt you." His look was pained as he recognized that the wall between them was not going to be so easy to crumble. He rubbed his thumbs up and down the plaited trim of her surcoat. "You need only bid me stop."

Her voice carryied both the authority of one who knew her own mind and the apology of one who still had no wish to injure the other. "Stop."

He lowered his arms. "For how long?"

Velena blinked in surprise. "Do you really mean for me to answer?"

"I do."

"Until we are wed, then."

The muscles in his jaw worked back and forth as impatience got the better of him. "I'll wait that long to bed you—but sooner than that, I'll kiss you."

Velena's mouth gaped before she began to stammer. "Stuart. How…how can I…how can I know how long? Is it not enough to say that I need more time?"

He stared into the green of her eyes, raising a finger to her temple to push back a small wisp of dark hair that had escaped her circlet. He reached down his thumb and traced the length of her lower lip. "When?" he asked, more gently.

Agitated, Velena pushed his hand aside. "When I have answers," she said, coming to a firm decision.

"Answers before questions? A bit unusual, wouldn't you say?"

"I want the truth about Daisy."

Stuart's heart dropped to the pit of his stomach. *Never.* "Ah. But to this question, you already have an answer?"

"I don't think that I do."

Stuart threw his head back, expressing an audible groan. "I approached Daisy in the orchard for the express purpose of coercing her to spy on you and Tristan. I told you this." His hand sliced through the air. "I didn't trust him then, and I don't trust him now. And as much as you don't like it, a few happy hours have not changed my opinion on the matter."

"This isn't about Tristan," Velena countered, leaving him to stare after her as she stalked down the hall towards the staircase. But Stuart was at her heals, cutting her off so that she was forced into the chapel instead.

"Velena," his voice pleaded, "what do you want from me?"

She turned to face him. "More than your kisses! I want to know why Daisy cries! I want to know why all the joy has gone out of her. Procuring her help as a spy *wouldn't* do this." Her fist thudded against her own chest. "Do you think I'm stupid? You'd truly have me believe she's losing her mind over this, but I know it isn't so." Velena exhaled her frustration and turned aside to sink down onto one of the small wooden pews. Modern and rare, the extravagant furnishing offered no comfort against the hardness with which she seated herself.

Feeling overly anxious, Velena took a moment to gather herself before raising her eyes to meet Stuart's excuses head on—but he made no move to speak nor any attempt to look at her. Instead, he was looking past her—fixedly staring off towards the long, narrow stain-glassed windows that lined the adjacent wall. His gaze was distant, and Velena wondered what world he'd just escaped to.

For her part, she was walking an old dusty road, crossing the path of a certain dark-haired woman who carried a heartful of contempt for her husband. Velena feared what she'd seen in her eyes—feared she might see it in her own. Had she not sworn never to be this woman? She asked the Lord to calm her, and as the memory of the dark-haired woman faded, she again saw Stuart for who she remembered him to be. Standing behind a mask of pride and prowess, he was still that vulnerable little boy living beneath the heavy hand of his father. And who was she, but the one who wiped his worries aside.

Feeling a genuine tenderness towards him for the first time since arriving back at Landerhill, Velena reached out to grab hold of his hand, breaking his reverie as she pulled him down to sit beside her. She spoke softly. "You want my love. *I* want your honesty. Be honest with me so that I can trust you. Whatever intrigue went on between you and Daisy to have affected her so—whatever it is—I want you to tell me."

Stuart swallowed hard, watching as swirls of gray began seeping into the bright green of Velena's eyes as her mood intensified. His voice was a mere wisp of sound. "Only out of my right mind…would I *ever* look twice at Daisy."

"I'm not insinuating you have. I am only asking if you've said—or done—anything to hurt her…or frighten her into such behavior. If you'd only tell me, I could forgive you. Whatever it is…I could forgive you."

Stuart's eyes caressed the smooth contours of the hand she'd draped across his own. "Could you?" he whispered, a sad sort of smile imprinting itself across his mouth.

"Yes, of course. Once this is all sorted out…we can put it behind us."

More than anything, Stuart wanted to be free of his burden—to lay it down before her feet and have her wipe it away. But despite her sincerity, he knew his sin could never be so easily forgiven. This was clear to him, as was the need to end this line of questioning—once and for all. Taking a deep breath, he pulled his hands from her grip and rubbed them back and forth over his thighs. He'd make a confession—but Heaven help him, it'd be a lie.

"The day you accused me of recruiting Daisy as my spy, I let you believe it was so…but in truth, it was the first I'd heard of it."

Velena folded her hands into her lap, waiting for him to go on.

"I never asked anything of Daisy. We spoke in the orchard, but it wasn't about spying. I assume you remember the day of our…*skirmish* on the blanket." He looked sideways at her, giving reference to his inappropriate advances the night of the bonfire—and the ear boxing she gave him as a result.

She nodded.

"I deserved every bit of your disdain, but still, it stung my pride. So, I filled my flask and found myself a spot outside the barracks to drink."

"You'd already been drinking," she murmured, lifting a hand to rub at the tightness behind her ear.

"It takes a king's buttery[10] to drown out one's own self-pity." He chuckled bitterly. "Alas, I had naught but my flask—but that's what I was doing when Daisy approached the opposite end of that same wall, accompanied by a certain young squire. His identity, I'm sure you can guess."

"Bowan."

"Indeed." He nodded, still hardly believing he'd already divulged so much truth about that wretched night. The voice of preservation warned him to be careful as he divulged still more. "We were away from the fire where it was dark. They'd not seen me where I was sitting amongst the shrubbery, so by the time I realized why they'd chosen so secluded a spot, I was bound to remain silent for they were much too...*engaged* in each other's company."

Velena touched a hand to her mouth. "Was she...compromised?"

Stuart's expression became increasingly stoic as he carried on with his version of events. He was shutting down every bit of moral integrity he possessed for this betrayal—telling himself, again, that she would never forgive the truth.

"I don't know," he answered. "Having no desire to watch, I slipped away as soon as I was able—beneath their notice, or so I'd thought. But as fate would have it, I dropped my flask. Daisy found it and concluded I must have observed them in their moment of weakness and came to me, begging that I reveal none of it. I assured her that it was a trivial thing to me what she did with herself—or anyone else for that matter. I agreed to say nothing about it and then dismissed myself immediately from her presence, not wanting to arouse any gossip."

By this time, Velena's eyes were as round as saucers.

He reached over to squeeze her hand. "I'm sorry I kept it from you."

Velena leaned straight back into her pew. "I understand why you did," she finally said.

Blessed Virgin, she believes me.

"Only..."

"Only, what?" Stuart questioned. His explanation of Daisy's *unexplainable* behavior should have been flawless, yet there was still that thread of doubt in her voice.

"It's just that Rowan said he saw you follow after her to the orchard, but you...you just said that she came to you."

Stuart shrugged. "She might have arrived first, but if so, I hadn't taken note of her."

Velena nodded. "I'll not mince words over a matter so small when there are bigger questions to be answered. I can understand any feelings of guilt she may have had upon learning she'd been discovered, but—" Velena bit her bottom lip, retreating deep within her mind to make sense of all the bits and pieces now laying before her. "*Guilt* isn't...it's not what I've been observing from her. I hate to even suggest it—for it seems entirely contradictory to his nature—but do you...do you think it's possible that Bowan might have...forced—"

Stuart's voice sliced through her assumptions. "I don't know—and quite frankly, I don't care to know! When I left them there, she seemed only too eager to accept his attentions, giving no indications of fear or otherwise. Her indiscretion has caused me no small amount of trouble, as it's brought a great deal of friction between us. I must confess to resenting her for it."

Again, Velena nodded. This *would* explain the tension that existed whenever Daisy and Stuart were in the same room together. However, it didn't explain everything. If Bowan was going to force himself upon Daisy, he had three years to do so.

No.

Their affection for one another had always appeared gentle in its substance. So, then why wouldn't Daisy have wanted her to send for Bowan? If she loved him enough to give herself to him willingly— which Velena was now beginning to assume she did—then why wouldn't she want to see him again?

Velena searched Stuart's eyes, but to her dismay, there was nowhere to rest her thoughts. They conveyed neither concern, nor assurance, nor love, nor hate—nor apology. They were disappointingly unreadable—nothing like Tristan's. Despite this, she found herself saying, "Thank you for being honest with me."

His face remained rigid. "If I hadn't given her my word, I'd have been honest from the beginning."

"I understand. I cannot fault you for acting in accordance with your own integrity."

He cleared his throat. "Right." He stood and pulled her up by the hand.

Velena was suddenly exhausted. Before today, she might have rushed off to speak with Daisy about what had, or hadn't, transpired between her and Bowan—but after what'd happened with Tristan, she regretted taking her anxieties to anyone before taking them to the Lord. What she needed to do was pray. Indeed, her spirit was aching to do so. There'd be plenty of time after that to talk with Daisy and—Lord willing—to help Tristan understand, that despite everything, she'd be alright.

Furthermore…she'd be alright without him. She hoped. She began to make her way to the entrance.

Interrupting her thoughts, Stuart pulled her mind back to the present with a touch to her elbow. "And where do you think you're going?" he asked, a telling lilt to his voice, reminding Velena of something she hoped he'd forgotten.

He hadn't.

"You've given me a lot to think about. If you don't mind, I'd still like to take my rest before supper."

He looked down into her face. "But I do mind. I've given you your answers…"

Her breath caught. "Oh."

"I've given you time."

She could see he was serious. "Not very much."

"More than I wanted." The corners of his mouth ticked slightly as he shrugged only one of his shoulders.

"You mustn't kiss me in church."

He leaned forward as if sharing a fine secret. "Though the *church* may deem affection of a physical nature redeemable only through the act of procreation, I'm fairly certain that if that were the case, God wouldn't have created it to be so…*pleasurable.*"

Velena turned away just as he leaned in, her lips feeling the brush of his kiss as she did so. "You speak as one who knows."

Stuart blinked back his surprise as Velena gave him a sidelong glance, her face remaining averted. He straightened to full height and crossed his arms with smile. "It sounds as if you have another question for me."

Now looking him full on, "it's been hinted that you have a certain degree of…experience."

He huffed. "I'd ask you who you heard this from, but Rowan's name drips so readily from my tongue I feel the question to be superfluous."

"But is it true?" Velena asked.

"Should I suppose my answer will hold some bearing as to whether or not you'll kiss me?"

"With no experience of my own, I'm sure I'm not equal to the task."

"And how do you propose to gain some, if not through practice?"

Velena rolled in her lips.

Stuart smiled. "So, this is how you play. First, you push me away, and then you reel me in with promises you never intended to keep."

"I make no apology. You've already stolen your kiss for today. Though to be fair, I should have warned you about my double standards in regard to promises."

Stuart's grin increased. "I've long known of your double standards, Cousin." He brought his lips close to her ear. "But I still want to kiss you," he whispered. "Say, yes."

"On our wedding day I shall."

She attempted to walk away, but his left hand caught her by the waist, a ready smile on his lips until they heard Daisy calling her name from the corridor.

"Before then," he said, releasing her then without argument. It wouldn't do to have Daisy discover Velena in his arms. If she were to ever think he was hurting Velena in any way—no matter that he had no intention of ever doing so—she may be less apt to keep her mouth shut, and more apt to break her silence in order to protect her mistress. With this in mind, he stepped aside with an indulgent sort of grin. "But not today," he conceded and sent her from the chapel alone.

---

[8]**Tourney:** Short for tournament.
[9]**Indulgence:** A grant from church authorities that absolved men of sin and kept them out of purgatory.
[10]**Buttery:** A pantry used for the storage of wine and liquor.

5

charity

Tristan laid his head back upon the pillows he'd adjusted *just so* against the squared arm of the bench seat, his feet propped up at the other end. He couldn't expel Daisy's words from his head.

Blind. Me? Well, perhaps not a completely unreasonable accusation, he considered, *but still it's ridiculous! I can just imagine how wooing Velena would turn out.* He rolled his eyes and began to tap his shoes restlessly on the opposite wooden arm. *She'd laugh in my face!* He pictured the exact face she'd make and then laughed himself.

Tristan steepled his hands at his lips and raised his eyes to the rafters above him. *What's best for Velena is still hidden from my view, Lord—but not from Yours. I'm nothing but a stumbling block. What would You have me do?*

Tristan closed his eyes and thrust his hands deep within his sandy-brown hair, choosing to focus on the pain of having it pulled taught from his scalp rather than on whatever *certain touches* Daisy meant for him to use in coercing Velena into being *friendly.*

Tristan opened his eyes feeling guilty for the unbidden images now flitting through his mind. Yes, he almost kissed her—but it'd been an accident, and there was no malintent in it. Daisy, on the other hand, wanted him to seduce Velena—and that was completely out of the question—unless…

No, it's absurd. Tristan let go of his hair. *But what if we both were to play along? If she only claimed that I mishandled her, and I owned up to it. Her marriage to Stuart would be ruined, and we could marry without my having to actually…*he didn't finish the thought.

Two or three jerky movements later, and he was off his seat. *We could marry?* He shook his head. *Father, what am I thinking?* How could he plan such treachery against the honorable Sir Richard after he'd taken him in—trusted him as a son. And what of Gwenhavare? What were the chances she was still alive—and unmarried? Tristan groaned. *Lord, what do you want of me? Is it your will that I save Velena in this way? Would you have me use intrigue and deception to thwart this marriage? No. I can't accept that.*

His lips began to move as he quoted softly to himself St. Paul's words to the Colossians, "Whatever you do in word or deed, do all in the name of the Lord Jesus..."

You are God of all, he reminded himself. *You know all, You see all, and You accomplish all Your holy will—and all without any interference from me. Help me, Father! And please help Velena.*

There was no *Amen,* for his spirit continued to groan. No longer trusting his thoughts to idleness, he wondered if waiting in her solar was the wisest thing to do after all. Another moment, and he decided to leave. He'd have to wait on God to set up a meeting between Velena and himself. Where was his faith?

Tristan exited Velena's solar with the intention of going below stairs. He thought of continuing his prayers in the chapel, but he could only think of the last time he was there—when he overheard Stuart threatening Daisy—thus it was tainted for him. What he wouldn't give to shed today's burdens and send them tumbling down before him. Wouldn't that be a feat.

Rounding the wall for the steps, he came face to face with Velena. Startled, he couldn't tell if her look was one of relief or regret—or perhaps a mixture of both. Without a word, she grabbed him by the hand and led him past her own solar door to what would have been her brother's, occupied now by Tristan in his absence. Hurriedly, they entered, closing the door behind them. He turned to face her, and she smiled as one who truly knew him. Late night talks, long walks, and horseback rides into the forest—here was his friend.

Thank you, Lord! He took a deep breath and for a moment, his world was sane again. Without knowing whether his elder brother was alive or dead, Velena was the only family he had, and suddenly, his insides ached for all to be back as it had been, while knowing simultaneously that it could never be. Time was relentlessly pushing them towards a future only God could see. And it was good he couldn't, for Tristan had no desire to look into a future where Velena walked along side Stuart.

"Are you alright?" Tristan questioned.

"I take it you didn't believe me the first time you asked."

He shook his head. "Not for a moment, which is why I just came from your solar."

Velena looked surprised.

"I thought you'd need m-" Tristan stumbled over his words, hesitant to say more than he really needed to. "I thought you'd want to talk."

Velena closed her eyes and smiled as one does when all they truly want to do is cry. When she opened them, her lashes were moist. "I thought the same thing."

Tristan grew suddenly uneasy in the presence of her emotion and wondered if he could trust himself around her should she truly take to crying again. He turned from her. "Let's sit."

Velena watched in surprise as he crossed the room to take his seat on a high backed bench, identical to the one in her solar. Her heart sank as she looked from him to the plaited rug at his feet. Though it was clear he expected her to sit beside him, she expected that he would have sat with her on the floor as they always did when they had something important to say to one another. Clearly, her expectations would have to change.

Begrudgingly, she moved forward and settled herself at an angle beside him, giving herself a clear view of his face. He offered only his profile. Surely, if she could get him to look at her, his eyes would tell her all she needed to know.

Tristan leaned back, shoulders slumped forward, all the while clasping his hands in his lap as if continuing in prayer. "I'm sorry I left you in the stables," he finally began.

"As was I."

"Why?" His question was abrupt, giving away the undercurrent of unspoken tension.

Velena bristled at his tone and feigned ignorance of the unspoken in favor of the obvious. "I think you know."

"Velena, listen...I—"

"Because I was *crying*," she interrupted. "Because I was frightened—because I didn't want to be alone—"

"Never mind," he said, holding up his hand. "I was thinking you meant...something else. Never mind. I'm sorry."

"I already said I forgave you."

"No, you didn't. You said, 'as was I,' as if you were sorry that I had to be sorry. Which means you blame me for leaving. And I can't blame you for this because it's the one thing you were afraid I'd do in the first place—and then I did."

Velena frowned. "Why are you being this way?"

"What way?"

"Confusing…and *fidgety*."

Tristan adjusted his pelvis, trying to get comfortable. He repositioned his hand and elbow on the wooden arm. "I'm not fidgety."

"Yes, you are. You're tapping your middle finger. You're uncomfortable."

Tristan popped up from his seat and began pacing the room. "Of course, I'm uncomfortable. You're engaged now. You shouldn't be in here," he pointed out, lowering his voice to a loud whisper in emphasis of the fact. He sighed. "But who am I to lay blame? I shouldn't have gone to your room looking for you. I shouldn't be interfering in your marriage. I shouldn't have gotten so close to you. For crying out loud, I almost—"

"I know." Velena's words plowed through his barricades.

Tristan stopped. "You know?"

"Well…I wasn't entirely sure at first."

"Sure of what…exactly?" He'd play it dumb, just in case there was still a chance they weren't talking about the obvious.

Velena tilted her head in understanding, "First Peter, and I quote: '*Greet one another with a…*'" she paused and waited. "Would you care to finish the sentence?"

"'*With a kiss of love.*'"

Velena dared to smile. "One might also translate it c*harity*. And isn't that all it was, Tristan? Charity."

"You're trying to make me feel better."

"Isn't that all you were doing for me? I don't want you to feel embarrassed."

"It would have been nice if you quoted that before and saved me this long day of embarrassment."

"You don't think I feel the same? It wasn't right for me to lay my burdens on you the way I did. I placed you in an awkward situation. It's entirely my fault. You warned me not forget you were a man…remember?"

He nodded in acknowledgment but didn't raise his eyes to meet her. He came back to his seat looking deflated, trying not to think about what Daisy wanted him to do.

Velena waited for him to speak. Only silence. She dropped to the floor at his feet so he had to look at her. "You're retreating from me—please don't. I couldn't bare it if you did."

"If I stay with you, I'll add nothing but confusion to your life."

Velena fought tears of frustration. "Then leave if you must, but don't hide from me!"

Silence.

"Tristan…" she tried to be gentle.

Silence.

"Tristan!" She snapped.

"What?"

She stood. "A curse on your melancholy! Let it pass right this instant," she demanded, going so far as to stomp her foot.

Tristan rose and walked past her, but Velena followed.

"Look at me."

Tristan spun to face her. "You can't always command me to do as you want," he exclaimed, realizing the absurdity of his statement in conjunction with just having done as he was bid.

"Yes—I can." She shoved him hard.

He stumbled backward. "Stop!"

No, you stop."

Tristan's face twisted, clearly at a loss for what to do next.

Indignant—Velena crossed her arms. "If you can't move past this until you truly know if you wanted to kiss me—then let's put that notion to the test once and for all."

"Pardon?"

"Well…better now…than later," Velena stammered, feeling suddenly and unexplainably winded. "Don't you agree?"

"I'm not sure what I'd be agreeing to, to be honest with you." He lifted a finger to scratch behind his left ear.

Velena bit her bottom lip and then squared her shoulders, determined to snap him back to life. "I think you should kiss me."

Tristan rolled his eyes just before realizing she was serious. He gave an incredulous sort of laugh. "Have you been talking to Daisy?"

"Daisy would never condone such an action, don't be silly."

"You'd be surprised."

"I just think it would put your mind at ease…that's all." She took a step towards him.

He backed away. "Need I remind you that you're now engaged."

"But not married," she reasoned. "The banns[11] haven't even been read." Another step.

Unwilling to take her seriously, Tristan glared at her, this time holding his ground.

She was now a handbreadth away. She twisted her arms in front of her. "Alright...go ahead."

Tristan merely stared.

Now that she'd come so close, she felt silly and almost laughed, though all Tristan could see was that her lips twitched. "Do you want me to close my eyes?" she simpered, her tone all too facetious.

"If you do, you'll be standing in the dark a long while."

Velena laughed through her nose but closed her eyes just the same. "Be serious and get it over with."

The hint of a smile ticked at the corners of Tristan's mouth as his mood lightened despite himself. "I'm not going to kiss you, Velena."

"How rude of you," she chastised, lids lifting as she put hands to her hips.

Shaking his head, he skirted around her, but Velena was quick to follow, tugging at the back of his jerkin like a child begging for attention.

"Kiss me. Kiss me. Kiss meee," she repeated, dogging his every move. "Tristaaaan...stop walking away from me."

Somewhere between amused and annoyed, he finally turned around to hold her back with an extended palm to her shoulder. "Why are you doing this?"

"I'll answer you if you answer me."

"Answer you what?"

Velena gave him an impatient stare. "Why won't you kiss me?"

He rolled his eyes. "I don't know what to tell you, the moment's gone."

"Shall I cry again?"

"For the love—no."

She pushed his hand from her shoulder, cornering him with his back to the fireplace. "Then tell me the real reason?"

He was starting to feel nervous. "Because you're my friend."

"Are lovers not friends as well? Why?"

"Because you're being foolish."

"I'm often foolish. Why?"

"Because you—"

"Why?"

"Because—"

"WHY?"

"Because I don't want to!" he finally blurted,

It was her turn to stare as all jesting fled. Her shoulders sagged. Her voice was a whisper. "Neither do I…"

The implication of those simple words moved him. He'd been trapped in his own head, but she'd not left him to flounder. They were even.

Velena searched his eyes. "Now do you see?"

"How did you know I wouldn't do it?"

She gave his sleeve a quick tug. "Because you're still you—and I'm still me."

The corner of Tristan mouth lifted. "You took a chance."

"No I didn't."

He smiled then, a light coming back into his eyes.

"There you are," she said with a note of satisfaction. "As if one *almost* happenstance could take you away from me."

Tristan let out his breath and with it his awkwardness. "What was I thinking?"

She took a step back. "You *weren't.*"

"You're right." He straightened his posture.

"Of course, I'm right."

Tristan cocked his head to the side and rubbed his fingernails against his jerkin. "And come to think about it, you should be flattered that I even considered kissing you in the first place."

Velena crossed her arms. "Oh, really?"

"Well, you're no lady's maid," he stated, referring back to the only other two women who'd succeeded in stealing one of his kisses, "but you'd do in a pinch."

Velena laughed outright, and Tristan had to shush her, stifling his own laugh in the process.

Velena swooped up a decorated pillow from where they'd been seated and swung it at him, but he was quick and grabbed a hold of the opposing corner. Connected by life's little comforts, they stood upon the plaited rug and gained strength, the one from the other.

Velena lowered herself to sit cross-legged upon the floor, arm raised above her head, still clasping her part of the pillow. She gave it a small tug, bidding him to join her. Inhibitions gone once more, he did.

"I'm glad you're here, Tristan. I really did want to talk with you."

"I was worried," he readily confessed, his focus back to what it should be. "You wouldn't even look at me."

"I was so embarrassed. You saw Stuart…kiss me?"

Tristan grimaced.

Velena forced a brave smile. "Nothing like I'd imagined it."

"You've imagined kissing Stuart?" His tone held immediate disgust.

Velena wrinkled the corner of her eyes at his expression. "There was a time."

"Oh, Lord, help me." Tristan shuddered, lowering his head into his hands. "I'm going to spend a lifetime in purgatory."

"You don't believe in purgatory."

"Well, I'd better start, because after I kill Stuart, your uncle will kill me—and then I'll need you to pray me into Heaven."

Velena frowned. "There shall be no talk of killing. I know it'll never end peaceably between the two of you, but for us—him and I—well…we've known each other our whole lives."

"It makes no difference."

"Yes, it does. And I'll be alright," Velena said, wondering if she said this to herself enough times, she'd really believe it.

"You'll end up a battered woman."

Velena shook her head. "He's apologized for his behavior. He swears he'll never lift a hand to me again—and…and he's made every attempt to be…pleasant and…attentive," Velena said, searching for words to placate him.

"It's not even been a full day, and you've already forgiven him everything? Of course, he's been pleasant. He has what he wants, doesn't he?" Something guttural escaped his throat as he tucked his head down between his knees. "I'm going to vomit."

Rolling her eyes, Velena took a firm grip of his hair and pulled his head up to look him in the eyes. "I will forgive him because it's the Christian thing to do—because it pleases God. And this *is* God's will, Tristan. After all my words to the contrary, I see now that I was wrong to fight it. I was just…afraid."

"This is *not* God's will! God does not give us reprobates as gifts."

"Stop it," Velena demanded. After the way Stuart had kissed her in front of her friends, she needed no one else to tell her how experienced he was, nor how he might have become so. No matter how she detested the behavior, it was common for men to lay with whores. And what could she do about it but hope he'd stop after they were married.

"Not this time, Velena. There are things you still don't know."

Velena blinked. "What things?"

Tristan opened his mouth to speak…but nothing came out. He couldn't do it. Why on earth couldn't he do it? He saw a cloud of anxiety pass over her face in anticipation of what he might share, and he could no more tell her she was about to marry the man who ravished Daisy, then he could follow through on his threats of murder.

"Tristan…what things?"

"Things about Daisy, for instance. Wasn't it you who was ranting only days ago about how Daisy isn't herself and how you're certain Stuart has something to do with it?"

Taking a deep breath, Velena decided not to be particularly honest regarding the subject of her conversation with Stuart in the chapel. For in his current humor, he'd only look for a reason to turn it on its head and find further excuse to disparage him. And she didn't want to resurrect a subject she hoped to lay to rest.

She changed the subject instead. "I know my marriage is less than ideal—less than the dreams and happy endings that we want for ourselves, but I'm…I'm still willing to accept it as my future. Please understand. You've been right all along. Our friendship was always going to change—I just didn't want to believe it. Stuart is my future. Yours is with Isulte."

"You want the happy ending as much as anyone. You can't tell me your content without a Tristan of your own."

"You're my Tristan."

"How can I be your Tristan…if you're not my Isulte?"

Overcome with emotion, Velena looked away. "You're right. I suppose you can't be my Tristan anymore." A single tear trailed down her cheek. She laughed softly. "We are two truly confused people. But you needn't worry for me because you've set me on a good path. I'll continue to learn obedience to Scripture—in action as well as thought. I'll worship our Father in spirit and in truth—and hopefully, one day, I'll learnt to pray before I'm overcome by my anxious thoughts. How much could we have avoided had I done that first? I cannot allow what happened in the stables, though wrought in a moment of weakness, to become indicative of a lifetime of the same."

"You want me to walk away."

"No! Oh, no, Tristan. But I want you to know…that you're able to—and that I'll be alright."

A tear tracked down his own cheek. *You wouldn't be saying this if you knew what Stuart has done. All he had to do was tell her.*

Suddenly, a muffled commotion from below stairs caught their attention. They froze.

"What's that?" Velena asked, startling at what must have been the sound of the front double doors of the manor swinging in upon their hinges, banging into the walls that held them. Next was the urgent voice of a man servant calling out her father's name. He answered. Then silence.

At once, they were on their feet.

"Let me go first," Tristan whispered, cutting in front of her on their way to the door. He could hear Daisy's voice calling out for Velena. "Does she know you're here?" he asked.

Velena shook her head, "I sent her on an errand before I came above stairs."

Hesitant, Tristan peered into the corridor.

"My lady!" Daisy's voice preceded her up the stairwell. She sounded breathless. "Your brother has returned!"

Tristan grabbed Velena by the arm and propelled her out. With no more than a backward glance, she hastened down the hall and into Daisy as she reached the top stair.

"He's back, my lady! Come, quickly."

"Britton," Velena mouthed.

Losing no time, Daisy grabbed Velena by the wrist and dragged her back the way she'd come.

From the top of the stairs, Tristan watched her rush through the open doors of the manor, having no idea what new changes this would bring about.

---

[1]**Banns:** Public Announcement of an intended marriage, announced for three successive weeks (usually in church). Purpose: to provide an opportunity for any objections to the union.

6

homecoming

"He's only just arrived. There—in the wagon." Daisy pointed.

A small crowd had already formed around the dilapidated contraption, less a wagon and more a flat bed of wooden planks stretched out upon wheels. Centered there on his back was a bearded man in rough villein's[12] clothing, struggling to push himself upright. A knight at his side stopped him with a heavy hand to his broad chest.

Sir Richard was already crouched on the wagon carefully examining what remained of his son's visible injuries.

"Father…" Britton's eyes fluttered, then closed as he fell to his back.

Velena came to stand beside the knight, the feel of the splintered wood harsh beneath her palms as she leaned forward to look down into the almost unrecognizable face of her brother.

"What's his damage?" Stuart asked from over her shoulder.

Velena wondered why Stuart addressed the stranger with such familiarity, but concern over her brother's condition took precedence over any curiosity she felt on that account.

"A head injury, a broken leg—just there, below the knee, so take care where you touch him—bruised ribs…" The knight rubbed the sweat from his brow and faced Sir Richard. "It was a difficult journey for him, my lord. He's still in a fair amount of pain and could use a physician—and rest."

A servant rounded his way to the front of the wagon. "I'll see to your horse."

"Thank you," the knight replied.

Sir Richard spoke without emotion, "Totnes is without a physician at present." He put his ear to his son's chest, his head rising and falling to the rhythm of his breathing when a smile broke out across his bearded face—his eyes shining as they hadn't done in years. "It's a strong beat." He searched the ever-growing crowd for a moment, but not finding who he was looking for, addressed his steward. "Sir Tarek, find Geoffrey and see to it that Britton's room is prepared immediately. Tristan can be moved to the guest room."

Hopping down from the wagon, Sir Richard pulled his son to the edge, preparing to cradle him beneath his arms.

"Allow me to help you, my Lord," the knight said. He cut in between Velena and Stuart in an effort to reach Sir Richard and his burden but bumped into Velena's elbow as he passed. He paused long enough to address her. "Excuse me, Lady Velena." Turning back towards Sir Richard, he saw that Sir John of Staybrook had already helped by grabbing hold of Britton's lower half, careful not to disturb the injured part of the leg.

Bewildered, Velena looked up at Stuart. "He knows me?" she asked in a low voice, but not nearly low enough.

The knight turned to address her, his eyes colored by water and mirth. "Yes. I know you, my lady."

Stuart ducked his head, clearly finding some bit of humor in her confusion. "It's Sir Makaias," he answered.

Sir Andret and Jaren's older brother—Britton's companion. Of course!

Sir Richard cast a look in his daughter's direction, and Velena's eyes grew moist, watching the way he clutched his son to himself as if he'd never again let go.

"How can I help, my lord?" Sir Makaias asked.

Sir Richard smiled—his eyes pools of joy. "I have my son again. Do you not also have family you wish to greet?"

"I—" The knight's voice caught in his throat.

Sir Richard's grin spread from ear to ear across his bearded face. "Turn around, Sir Makaias. Unless they be but spirits, your brothers await your attention," he said, gesturing with his elbow, emotion clogging his throat as he tarried no longer but moved to bring his son within the manor.

"Brothers...?" He asked, giving emphasis to the plurality of the word. *Both?* Sir Makaias turned around. True to the Baron's word, there stood Sir Andret and Squire Jaren, laughing at their eldest brother's dumbfounded expression.

"You wait till now to greet me?" he cried, opening his arms wide. "Didn't you know me?"

Without warning, Jaren's face clouded. Able to wait no longer, he drew forward, crashing into the breadth of his brother's chest. Though taller than Makaias, he appeared the younger sibling that he was as he ducked his head the few inches to bury his face into his brother's neck, weeping without shame.

Tears streaming freely, Sir Makaias hooked his arm about Jaren's head, crushing him further as his other hand gripped a fist full of hair as if unwilling to let him go.

Velena thought to follow after her father and brother but found that the emotional reunion between brothers was holding her in place.

Sir Andret approached the duo, putting an arm to Sir Makaias' shoulder. "If you could look in a mirror, Brother, you wouldn't know *yourself.*"

Sir Makaias laughed outright, then pulled him also to himself— kissing his shaved cheek. He looked as one wanting to believe, but who still very nearly couldn't. "Merciful Father," he whispered into the shrinking spaces between them. He released his grip to raise his arms above their heads, biceps bulging beneath his chainmail as he shouted, "Merciful Father! Thank you!" as if no one stood near enough to hear him.

It was a battle cry so joyful Velena almost clapped in praise for what God had done. *He spared them all!* That almost an entire family should be reunited, having been spared from the ravages of the Plague—unheard of.

Stuart stepped towards his cousin, "It's good to see you," he said.

Delighted, Sir Makaias turned, gripping his cousin in a firm embrace. "And you, Stuart! And you…"

A welcome touch of warmth spread through Velena's heart as she watched with what affection Makaias greeted Stuart. How long had it been since she'd seen anyone greet him with such sentiment? She realized she had very little memories of the knight before her—at least eight years her senior, they'd seldom been in each other's company. But his uncommonly sincere and heartfelt acceptance of Stuart did much to endear him to her—as if the burden to remember the good in Stuart had just gotten that much lighter.

The joy before her—the intimate greeting of men—reminded her of the day her uncle had first arrived at Wineford Castle. The day Jaren had first been reunited with Sir Andret, both still anxious for news of Sir Makaias. The day Rowan had taken her up into his arms, cradling her as she wept tears of thanksgiving. The day Stuart told her Peter had died…

So many changes. She'd been a part of the greetings then. It was mostly the same men—save for Sir Makaias, who didn't know her by any means well enough for her participation to be welcomed. She didn't mind. Witnessing their joy was enough. Happily, she'd leave them to themselves. It was time for her to see her brother.

"Where's Peter?" Sir Makaias asked abruptly.

Velena turned back in surprise. Inquiries after his kin were to be expected, but…revisiting anything out of such darkness gave her an uneasy twist in the pit of her stomach.

"Peter's gone," Stuart answered.

Makaias pulled in his bottom lip, his face solemn. "I'm sorry. My condolences…to you both."

Realizing he was including her in his statement, Velena nodded.

Makaias continued, addressing Velena specifically. "This Pestilence has left many a young widow to be sure."

"Wid—?" Understanding dawned. "Oh, no, Sir. You may pity me for the loss of a cousin—but not a husband. He died before we could marry."

"I see," he said, "then I'm sorry for that too."

Stuart locked eyes with Velena, expectantly—as if she should be the one to tell Sir Makaias of their newly acquired engagement.

She knew what he wanted, but an announcement of that sort seemed somehow out of place amidst declarations of Peter's death. "Thank you," was all she said.

"Peter's passing was most grievous," Jaren said, preparing to take it upon himself to dispense what Velena would not, "but there is happy news. Velena is now—"

"Jaren!" she interjected.

He blinked at the interruption.

"It just occurred to me that we should send someone to fetch your mother. Surely, such a reunion won't be complete without her."

Sir Makaias looked so utterly taken aback that Velena wondered what she might have said to offend him before it dawned on her. He still didn't know about his mother.

He looked to his brothers for answers. Sir Andret nodded. "Father didn't make it, but mother is well—not that anyone could have expected otherwise." He smiled broadly. "Death came to her door, and she poked it in the eye. Don't ask me how."

From somewhere deep inside, Sir Makaias began to laugh. One could hardly blame him—he was in complete shock. Silently, it rocked his frame and shook his shoulders. Bending his head low, he held the back of his hand across his lips, still laughing until without warning… it became a sob. Both joy and sorrow racked his body as Sir Andret wrapped his arms around him in understanding.

Velena felt a touch at her elbow and was thankful to find Daisy beckoning her away with a look. Sparing but a parting glance, she knew it was time to go. And though Sir Makaias might never know it, her heart shared in his moment of grief. How could she not, having survived such dark times herself?

The hem of Velena's tunic rustled about her legs and feet as she entered her brother's solar, which until this day had been Tristan's living quarters. She half expected to find him there but one glance around the sitting room, arranged identically to her own, and it was obvious—from the empty table void of books to the abandoned corner by the fireplace where he usually kept his satchel—he'd gathered his belongings and taken himself somewhere out of sight. Britton's arrival had been a surprise, and she wondered if he was feeling displaced— perhaps more so in spirit than in body.

Daisy entered the room only a few steps behind her. "I'll wait here," she said, gesturing to the door that separated the sitting room from the bed chamber.

"I'd rather you come with me," Velena said. "You're as much family as anyone, and your presence is welcome."

Daisy nodded, more than a bit curious to know what had become of Sir Britton since Sir Richard had carried him inside. Was he still unconscious? Preceding Velena to the door, she knocked.

"Come," Sir Richard's voice answered from within.

Daisy pushed the door open. It groaned on its hinges as she stood aside for Velena to pass. The windows had been covered, creating an aura of muted light and shadow so that her eyes had to adjust. Perpendicular to the far wall was the bed where Britton lay…still asleep, Sir Richard hovering by his side.

At the foot of the bed loomed the impenetrable frame of Lord Magnus—legs spread, chest puffed, arms crossed—looking very self-important, along with the most necessary amount of concern as one should hope to find in one's own uncle. He cast her but the briefest of glances over his shoulder, to which Velena showed proper deference as Daisy shut the door behind them.

How arrogant must one man be to desire the honor of being the first person seen upon his nephew's waking for surely, he had no other reason for taking up such a position. And Velena had no trouble believing he'd been standing like this from the moment he'd entered the room. Had he no thought of her father?

Velena pulled Daisy's hand through the crook of her arm as they joined the small vigil, landing a spot by her brother's side opposite her father. "How is he?" she whispered.

"As you see him," Lord Magnus uttered.

Velena glanced from him to her father, whose smile only thinly veiled his irritation as he affirmed the same.

Daisy shifted her weight from one foot to the other. She'd come into service the year Sirs Britton and Makaias had gone to war, and although she had almost no memory of Sir Britton's disposition or character, she thought she remembered him being a handsome man. It was now difficult to tell beneath his dark unkempt hair and tangled whiskers. "His appearance is much altered from what I remember," she said softly.

"I would have known him anywhere," Sir Richard said, smiling down at his son as though his disheveled state affected his looks not at all.

Velena tilted her head as if to take him in from a different angle. "I'm embarrassed to say I may not have," she confessed. "Though that should be of no surprise. I didn't recognize Sir Makaias either. As it was, Stuart had to tell me."

Sir Richard chuckled. "Yes, I heard. Think not too much of it. Neither one was very present during your younger years."

"Still..." Velena continued to study her brother's face. "He knew *me*."

"You haven't been altered by war," Lord Magnus stated bluntly.

"Haven't I?" she asked, softly, daring to question him whilst her father was present. "Has there ever been a time in man's existence that's thrust the entire human race into the clutches of death as we've been? And, I, as much as anyone. I suspect, if my insides matched my outsides, I'd look as haggard as an old woman."

Velena steeled herself against her uncle's reproach for having been contradictory but was surprised when he only nodded, rocking back and forth on his heels. It was the bit of movement needed to propel him from his spot by the foot of the bed to an adjacent wall where a small writing desk and chair stood unoccupied. He slumped into the chair. "Be thankful you weren't in Totnes to see the full force of death's havoc. It was truly something to behold and not ever to be forgotten…though you might spend your entire life wishing it otherwise."

Sir Richard brushed his fingers over his eyebrows. "True. And history may yet reveal that those of us who lived have also died. Died to the world we knew—died to who we were." Sir Richard sat beside his son on the bed, taking his listless hand into his own. "But here is my son—my future. All is not lost and so live, we must.

"How do you live if you no longer recognize yourself?" Daisy asked, her voice a tremulous whisper.

Sir Richard looked upon her with fatherly tenderness. "Should a nursing woman look upon the innocence of her newborn babe and hold it in disdain, longing for the simpler days of being at her own mother's breast? Would it benefit a woman, newly married, to hold her life in contempt because she's no longer able to run about with her companions?"

"'Twould be a silly thing to do," Daisy agreed.

"'Twould be fruitless. As we grow, we trade in our ignorance and childish ways for wisdom and experience. We treasure what we had, but it's an ignorant man who expects it to be duplicated. And life isn't our only means of growth—death, also, has a hand in it—and you've grown beyond your years, Daisy. We all have. And it's up to you whether or not you'll be the better for it. Look to the future, not the past."

Velena slipped an arm around Daisy's waist and squeezed. "The Lord will see us through," she said, briefly laying her head to Daisy's shoulder. Believing it also for herself, she quoted, "*He who has begun a good work in you, is faithful and just to complete it.*"

Daisy turned to her with a grateful smile. "Thank you," she mouthed.

"What a beautiful thought," Sir Richard said, curiosity resting on his brow. "Wherever did you hear it?"

Velena hesitated. "It's Scripture."

Lord Magnus grunted from where he sat behind her. "I've never heard it."

"Tristan learned it…from a Franciscan in Oxford. A Friar Daniel, I believe it was."

"Where is it referenced?" her father asked.

"I'm not sure, exactly." Her words were measured, uncertain if she'd put Tristan under some sort of suspicion of having a Bible. Though not illegal, possessing one without the express permission of the church tended to be frowned upon. Of course, it wasn't owning Scripture, itself, that was the problem, but rather the individual reader's interpretation the Church feared. "I think it was in Ephesians…or Philippians," she continued. "I could ask Tristan if you'd like."

"Do—better yet, search out the Bible in my cabinet and have him find it for me. I'd like to read it for myself. '*Faithful and just to complete it*,'" he murmured. "What a satisfying thought."

Velena's mouth must have been hanging open. "You have a Bible? Here—at the manor?"

"It was a gift from King Edward—a thank you for my service at Sluys." He held up his hand, displaying the two missing fingers he'd lost as a result of it. He clucked his tongue, running the remaining three through his beard. "I don't think I ever opened it, to tell you the truth."

"How have I never seen it?"

"Oh, I keep it put away. It's only meant for display, really—rather gaudy for my taste. Your mother meant to put it out only if the King came through." Looking down at his son, his thoughts drifted to the memory of his wife. "Otherwise, she said it gathered too much dust…"

Velena tried to keep her excitement at bay. "Well, if you have something that lovely, perhaps it's time to display it again. The king may not be here to see it, but Britton is." Velena smiled. "How better to honor his return than to display God's Word in gratitude."

"Don't dust off the cover just yet, Niece," Lord Magnus muttered. "He has to wake up, first."

"Rain belongs out of doors, Magnus! Bring it not into my house. He'll wake up—for certain…he'll wake up."

---

[12]**Villein:** A feudal

7

bruised and broken

Britton would have happily accommodated his father if only he was able to get his worthless body to catch up with his mind. He suspected something wasn't working quite right as he rose and fell through drifts upon drifts of dream world—a world submersed in water. One moment he could hear the warbled tones of conversation above him, and the next, it was as if he was being pushed down into utter darkness. Up and down he drifted through nonsensical thought and bits of noise until finally what was warbled became garbled—and what was garbled became something almost decipherable. If only he could focus on one voice. Was everyone talking at once?

At one point, he thought he heard knocking on a door. He attempted to open his eyes, but they remained stubbornly heavy and unresponsive. Again, he faded into a deep sleep.

Sir Tarek entered with a rather gaunt looking woman.

"Where's the apprentice?" Lord Magnus asked, coming to his feet.

"This is his widow, my lord."

"Your name madam?" Sir Richard asked.

"Agnus Fairweather, my lord. I know I must be a surprise to you, but if it's a healer your looking for, I'm all Totnes has left, at present."

"And what qualifications might you have to call yourself such?"

"I've always had an interest in my husband's work, God rest his soul. He used to take me with him whenever he needed an extra set of hands and whenever I could get my sister to look after our wee ones. I've nursed fevers, administered herbs, and sown back together what shouldn't have come apart. I can set a broken bone as good as any man—and from what I hear, your son has one of those. Have you any objection to me examining him?"

Sir Richard looked hesitant. "I had wanted him to undergo a full physical exam. A woman ought not to perform such things."

"Begging your pardon, but I'm no blushing bride, my lord. I've been a wife and a mother, and there's nothing new he could show me that I haven't looked on before. So, be things as they are—he, needing an exam, and myself being a woman—will you allow it?"

Richard smiled in amusement. "With such a speech as that, how could I say no? And after so long a time at war, I doubt he'd scorn a woman's touch...widow or no."

Velena brought a hand over her mouth to stifle a laugh. Even Daisy managed a smile. "Excuse us, Father, but I'm sure I'm one woman he'd not wish to be present for such proceedings." She giggled.

Once outside the door of the room, Daisy turned to her mistress and said, "You should rest, my lady."

Velena scrunched up the corners of her eyes. "I couldn't hear what goes on through the door if I were taking my rest."

"It's unbecoming a lady to stand with her ear at the door."

"Then you do it," she said, stepping aside for Daisy. "Go on."

Daisy paused in indecision before frowning in the old way. "Alright."

Velena giggled as Daisy held a finger to her smiling lips. It warmed Velena's heart to see bits and pieces of the old Daisy resurfacing. She had, by nature, a tarter disposition—and though often times it'd been directed at one of Velena's many antics, occasionally it allowed her to join in—as long as the intrigue had nothing to do with Tristan.

"What do you hear?" Velena asked.

"From who?"

"Whoever," Velena whispered.

"The healer says the bone in his leg hasn't been displaced—and thinks it'll heal very well, though he mustn't use it for at least six weeks."

Velena nodded. "That's good news."

"But she's concerned for his head injury." Daisy turned away from the door then. "I'm sure it's not nearly as bad as it seems—"

Her voice cut off as Stuart entered the solar, catching them in the act of eavesdropping.

He smirked. "How is he?" he asked, coming up to stand over them.

"He's being examined," Velena said. "The healer is concerned for his head injury."

"Should I wait to go in, do you think?"

Velena shook her head. "You're father's present already. Just knock."

Velena and Daisy moved aside. More accurately, Velena moved aside as Daisy retreated to the far end of the room. Stuart raised his hand to knock…and then turned back to look at Velena. "Why didn't you tell Makaias we were engaged?"

"I could ask you the same question."

Stuart studied her face. "It didn't seem the right time," he admitted.

"I thought the same."

Stuart sighed. "You don't make it easy."

Velena conceded. "Daisy has often told me I'm difficult to get along with," she said, looking to the other woman, only to regret bringing her into the conversation when it was more than obvious she desired to disappear entirely. She redirected the conversation. "Will Sir Makaias be coming up? Perhaps the healer will have some questions concerning Britton's injuries."

"He's below stairs with Auntie," he answered, and then noticed Velena had some sort of nostalgic look to her face. "What?"

"I like that you still call her that."

"What else would I call her?"

"It's the way you said it." Velena's mouth softened. "It reminds me of better times."

"Better times than this?" he asked facetiously.

She smiled, and Stuart reached forward, gently massaging the back of her neck with his hands. They were warm, and she allowed the delicate pressure he exerted to relax her.

"I know how you've worried for Britton—all this time, not knowing. But he'll be alright," he reassured her.

"Thank you."

He nodded and then sensing her calm, he kissed her forehead before letting her go. Forgetting to knock, he disappeared into the room.

Uncomfortable with Stuart's show of affection in front of Daisy, Velena turned away before the door had a chance to close.

"I'm sorry, Daisy."

"What do you mean?"

"I haven't had time to tell you of our engagement. Knowing how you feel about Stuart, I wanted to tell you myself—but we went straight away to our fathers—and then Britton arrived. Since then, everything's turned upside down."

Daisy was quick to embrace her. "No, my lady, worry not. Tristan already told me."

"When?"

"He came looking for you in your solar."

"Then for your sake, I'm glad."

"He worries for you," Daisy said.

"We've already spoken. I was in his solar just before Britton arrived."

Daisy rolled her eyes. "I knew you didn't need any blue thread. Am I to suspect every errand I'm sent on as an excuse to do something you ought not?"

"Not every errand," Velena teased. "Besides, our meeting was by chance this time. The errand was real enough."

Daisy looked doubtful, but her angst was quickly replaced with a small grimace.

"Are you alright?" Velena asked, watching as Daisy pressed a hand to her mid-section just below her breasts.

Daisy blinked her eyes and with it any sign of discomfort. "A momentary feeling, my lady. It's passed now." She let out her breath.

"Tell me if it happens again."

Daisy nodded.

"Alright, then let's be off. I want to speak with Sir Makaias before he…"

Daisy's face twisted.

"Did it happen again?" Velena asked in concern.

"My stomach feels unsettled. Perhaps, I'm hungry."

"Then let's stop in the kitchen. Actually," Velena said, thinking better of it, "let's split our efforts. I'll find Sir Makaias and ask him to come up. You go and eat something and then bring back with you a platter of bread and meats for those holding vigil with Britton. And something easy on the stomach should he awake."

Parting ways at the bottom of the stairs, Daisy's stomach continued to churn in the most uncomfortable way. She asked the cook for some broth, enough for both herself and Britton, along with the bread and meat. While she waited, Daisy wandered out the back door and into the herb garden. Again, she lifted a hand to her stomach and began looking around at the various plants until she found some peppermint. Later, she'd crush it and add it to some hot water to make a drink she hoped would sooth her. In the meantime, she pushed a bit into her mouth, hoping it'd do some good. It had a pleasant taste, anyway.

"You ought to be more careful," a woman said from behind her. It was Agnes—the healer. She was done with her examination and had come down to see if the herb garden had anything more to offer than what she already had at home.

Daisy startled. "I beg your pardon."

Agnes joined her where she stood, close enough so their conversation would remain private. "You hold your hand to your belly. It's a tell-tale sign."

"A what?"

"A motherly gesture."

Daisy blinked. "I'm no mother."

"Nor do you want to be, I'd wager."

"You're mad," Daisy said, bundling the peppermint up into her handkerchief.

The woman raised a shoulder to her ear and moved down the row of herbs. Daisy followed.

"And who are you to care where I put my hands…or for what reason?" she asked.

"I meant no disrespect. I'm but a humble healer who makes her living curing what ails people."

"Just the same, you shouldn't suppose on a person's…gestures, alone, as evidence of their condition. I've been feeling a bit anxious is all."

Agnes ducked her head. "I apologize. But allow me to ask you this. Have you been losing your food, perchance?"

"No."

"But you feel like it now?"

"I already told you—it's nerves."

Agnes nodded. "Have the days seemed endless and sleep never close enough at hand—nor the nights long enough to give you the rest you crave."

"There's always much to do, though…it has seemed that I've been… overly tired. Always tired, as a matter of fact." Daisy seemed close to tears.

"You've missed your flux?"

Had she? Daisy stood still as a statue, her eyes giving the only evidence of life as they darted to and fro across the woman's creased face. "I think you should leave," Daisy said, suddenly.

The healer caught hold of her arm, her grip strong, but her eyes strangely sympathetic.

"I know who you are, my dear. You are maid to Lady Velena Ambrose, and maids ought not to be with child. You have no husband, and you're frightened. I can see it in your face. I can help you..."

"How? Are you a witch?"

"I'm no witch, only a woman who knows her plants. And I have one that can rid you of your burden. No one need know of it. It'll cost you, but nothing you can't pay."

Daisy shook free of her hold. "Let go of my arm, old woman!"

"Old woman, am I?"

"Older than I and not worthy of a tone of respect. What you say is sin straight from the pit of hell, and I don't wish to speak of it any longer."

"Don't wish to speak of it at all...or you don't wish to speak of it here? If you change your mind, I live out yonder. In town, not far from the church. To those who know, I'm called the giver."

"Give?" Daisy snorted. "You don't speak of giving, but of taking. You would take the life of this babe."

"No, dear one, I would give you back your life—the life to which you've been accustomed—comfortable and in the presence of your mistress. Would you be thrown out like a dog?"

"Velena is...Lady Velena is kind. She wouldn't do that."

"The tremble of your hands says otherwise."

Daisy's hand clenched tightly about her bundle of herbs. "Have you considered that your observations might be wrong?"

"I'm seldom wrong when it comes to things of this nature...but I'll leave you to think in peace."

With blood thrumming in her ears, Daisy watched her disappear back into the manor. The healer—the giver—the woman with a heart of stone. Whoever she was, she was glad to be rid of her. Daisy could never do anything so vile as kill her own child—even if it was Stuart's. Could she?

Oh, dear Lord, her heart protested. *Let it not be true...let it not be true.*

8

displaced

Tristan eyed the room he'd now be staying in. It was one of the guestrooms closest to Britton's solar. It was a single room, simple, containing a wardrobe, a table, several chairs and a bed mat—which he currently occupied. Arms propped behind his head, Tristan turned his attention to the ceiling, listening to the footsteps going back and forth outside his door.

Against the door, sitting on his back side—hands dangling over top propped-up knees—was Rowan. Turning his ear to the wood, he could hear the girls as they passed.

"You should be out there with them," Tristan said.

Rowan shrugged. "Britton's a bit indisposed at the moment, and Makaias is probably still with Andret and Jaren."

"I'm sure he'd still be happy to see you. He'd have to be if he was happy to see the likes of Stuart." Tristan smiled coolly and then looked away.

"Now, it's that look right there that brought me to you in the first place. I thought to myself, now I can go and greet my long-lost cousin of four years, or I could go and grab up this bitter shell of a man by his jerkin and stow him away someplace safe before he does something foolish like take off without so much as a *by your leave*. Not that I'd care, myself—but Velena would cry—and we couldn't have that."

"I'd miss you too, Rowan."

"So, how long are you planning to hide?"

Tristan gave a wry smile. "I remember when Velena accused me of hiding the first time she came to my room at Wineford."

"Were you?"

"I suppose in some ways I was. I certainly didn't want to see anyone."

"And now?"

"She has her brother back."

"Oh, come off it! You've got to learn to face your problems, Tristan. And for an added bit of information, Britton isn't one of them. He's never cared much for Stuart, so you've got an ally should you choose to tell him."

"Tell him what?"

"Whatever Jaren *knows* that you haven't told me. Which, by the by, is something I haven't decided whether I'll forgive you for or not. Sharing a secret with Jaren is something of an unpardonable sin—right up there with blaspheming the Holy Spirit and teasing Daisy about her dimples. Especially, as you would see him as the right-hand man to the devil."

"You said it, not I."

"Nooo, I said Stuart was the hind-end of a donkey. I never even hinted at evil. Look, I'm as sorry for Velena as the next person who knows anything about the kind of husband Stuart will be, but…the way you're taking it—"

"The way I'm taking it *what*?"

"Now, I could pretend to be Velena and wheedle it out of you, but fortunately for you, I'm actually no good at batting my eyes."

"That is fortunate," Tristan said dryly.

"Yes, but can you imagine what I'd be able to get away with if I could? I'm thinking the possibilities would be endless—but I digress."

"You certainly have."

Ignoring Tristan's mood, Rowan got right to the point. "Does Jaren know something about Stuart—or about you? You left the stables awfully fast for someone without a guilty conscious."

Tristan sat up, pushing himself perpendicular to the wall. "Nothing happened."

"Did something *almost* happen?"

Tristan raised his eyes to the ceiling. "I almost kissed her. I'm not even sure why—but she was upset and crying, and…"

"Say no more." Rowan chuckled. "Unless the woman is kin, and I suppose by that I mean a sister—because obviously first cousins don't count as close enough in this family—you ought never to be in close proximity to a crying woman. It loosens a man's armor, for lack of a better phrase. I can fight against sword and arrow, but a *pretty woman* crying," he shook his head, "just run."

Tristan smiled for the first time. "Ugly ones are okay, though."

"It depends upon the time of day—and if the light is before or behind you. And if it's dark enough. Even so…you might still find yourself tied to the alter come morning."

Tristan laughed.

"Come on, Tristan. If nothing happened between you, then what does Jaren know?"

Tristan leaned forward over his knees. "I should tell someone."

Rowan smiled. "And I'm the best *someone* I can think of."

"I'll tell you, Rowan, but you'll not like it. You may not even believe it."

"I'm not a child. Just speak."

"I don't know this for sure, but my suspicion is that Jaren has been aware of a certain incident between Stuart…and Daisy."

Rowan looked immediately disgusted. "Is this going to be of an intimate nature?"

"Unfortunately."

"By all that's holy, I thought that woman had better taste." He shook his head. "I never doubted he'd dabble—but Velena's own maid. He's got some—"

"I'm not finished."

But Rowan continued as if he hadn't heard him. "And Daisy— what a waste of a woman. I saw them, you know."

"Daisy and Stuart?"

"At Wineford. The day before we left, I saw them in the orchard together. After that verbal walloping she gave us about being disloyal to Velena, I never would've thought it was something she'd be guilty of herself."

"You don't understand, Rowan."

Rowan huffed through his nose. "You give her much more credit than I," he said, picking at the lint on his hose. It's no secret I've done my fair share of flirting with her, but if I were honest, it was her innocence that attracted me." He laughed dejectedly.

"You mean you actually like her?"

Rowan gave a wry smile. "I know she's not the sort of woman I normally pursue."

"I didn't think you pursued at all. Stripedhoods[13] require very little encouragement, or so I'm told."

"Not everything is as it seems." He laid his head back against the door. "That same night we brought Daisy up to the room after she'd passed out…when I laid her on the bed, I even refused my normal mental indulgences."

"A first, I assume."

"She looked so innocent. I thought that if ever I were to change...she might be worth changing for."

"I had no idea your feelings for her where genuine."

He shook his head. "Fanciful, is a better word. But I was wrong. I suppose she wouldn't be the first woman Stuart's seduced."

"He didn't seduce her, Rowan." Tristan's eyes revealed a deep seeded truth.

Silence hung in the room like an ax about to drop. "What are you saying?"

"He raped her."

"Wha..."

Tristan could see Rowan's mind trying to process what he'd just been told.

"I don't know when it happened," Tristan said. "I mean, it *was* while we were at Wineford, but as to the orchard—I don't know."

Rowan came to his feet, not exactly cognizant of his movements. "You're absolutely positive—positive it was rape, I mean?"

"There's no room for doubt. I overheard Stuart threatening her to silence, myself. I assume you don't like to think Stuart capable of such a thing, but—"

"Stuart be hanged!" He squeezed his eyes shut and clenched his fists, fighting for the self-control it'd take for him to face Stuart again without maiming him. "No matter the miscreant, I'd have it undone for Daisy's sake." He shook his head as if trying to rid himself of the truth. "But that it *was* Stuart..." The muscles in Rowan's jaw worked back and forth. He rubbed a hand over the blond stubble of his chin. He looked back towards the door. *Why her?*

"I haven't told Velena." Tristan said.

"Why not?"

"What good will come of her knowing unless the marriage can be thwarted."

Rowan looked confused. "So, thwart it already. Tell Sir Richard."

"I've already tried telling him, but he was already aware of my objections to Velena's marriage in the first place—and had no desire to hear them again without proof."

"None at all?"

Tristan shook his head. "And now with Britton's return, his thoughts will be elsewhere, and I may be quickly wearing out my welcome."

"Do you think Daisy would accuse him?"

"She swears she'll deny it."

"You've talked to her? What's she thinking? She gains nothing through silence. Surely, she doesn't intend on staying beneath the same roof after he weds Velena."

"I've offered her employment at my mother's home in Oxford. She hasn't agreed yet, but my offer will stand."

"I pray she accepts it. I just can't understand why Stuart would…" He let out a long breath. "Why her? He could have had any woman in the village he wanted—and I know he wants Velena, so why on God's green earth choose the woman closest to her? It doesn't make any sense."

"Perhaps he's done it before?"

"No. I mean, not that I am aware of." Rowan rolled his eyes. "But I didn't know about this, so that isn't saying much. But it doesn't matter. He can't get away with it."

"I don't think it's wise for you to confront him," Tristan said. He stood, thinking he may have to restrain him, but his concerns were for naught.

"I know…I know. As much as it ought to be done, if anyone, it should fall to Squire Bowan to be her champion. I may have let my feelings escape me, but I'm no one to her," he said, grinding the heal of his shoe into the floor. "Indeed, I only add to her discomfort."

"You sound like you're referring to something in particular."

"I was just thinking that yesterday makes much more sense in light of today."

Tristan waited patiently for him to continue.

"I was goading her at the evening meal—trying to get a rise from her…"

"What'd you do?"

"She was doing her best to ignore me, so I gave her a good slap along her backside."

Tristan groaned.

"You said it. She looked at me as though I'd just delivered her a flogging."

Tristan's mouth drew a thin line. "Just keep your hands to yourself from now on."

"That I will. So, what now?"

"Pray."

"We can't do nothing."

"Prayer isn't *nothing*, but if you want for other employment, help me watch over Velena. Make sure that Stuart keeps his hands to *himself.*"

Rowan puckered his mouth to the side. "They're to be married, my friend. Touching is an inevitable happenstance."

"If—God forbid—they marry, there's nothing I can do about it, but before…"

"I wouldn't worry. However little he thinks of Daisy, he wouldn't dare force himself on Velena. And now that they're engaged, he'd have no reason to. She'll be in his bed soon enough."

"Still, I'll need you to promise…because now that you know, I think it's best I leave for a while."

"What? Now?"

"I have something I need to take care of."

"I think you're needed here."

"Wanted, but not needed. If Sir Richard won't hear me, there's nothing more I can do right now. And I'll not watch it happen."

"You'd abandon her? I never took you for a coward, Tristan."

"I'm not afraid. I…" He grabbed a fist full of hair only to leave it to stand on end. "I'm hoping the time away will give me God's perspective on what can be done. I don't know when it happened, but our lives have grown so entangled, I can't see the forest for the trees."

"Where will you go?"

"Back to Oxford. I want to see if my brother is still alive. That, and I need to see that my mother's home is still in order. There may be squatters, and I can't keep my promise to Daisy if I don't have them cleared out."

"But you'll return?"

"Before she marries—for certain."

Rowan paced the floor, agitated. "I don't see how it's possible. The banns will be read five days hence. Add to that the three weeks they're required to wait, and they could be married less than four weeks from *today*," he said with emphasis. "Oxford is at least a nine days journey." He stopped and began counting on his fingers. "You'd have no more than a sennight[14] to find your brother, let alone take care of the other."

"I know," Tristan said, feeling the weight of it.

"Well, don't wait until they're standing before the priest to make your appearance. If you leave it to me to break things up, you know it won't be pretty."

"I'll be back," he assured him.

Rowan let out a deep breath. "Then, back to how I'm supposed to look after Velena. My duties are at Craft Hall. Just how am I supposed to keep watch from there?"

"Surely, you can think of something."

Rowan rolled his eyes. "I thank you for your confidence, but I've no idea how I'm going to do it."

"God will provide a way. And I promise not to leave until He does."

"That cuts into your time," Rowan warned.

"Then add me to your prayers. Hearing the banns is not something I want to stay around for."

[13]**Stripedhoods:** Used to reference a prostitute. In some places, wearing a striped hood was a symbol, denoting their occupation.
[14]**Sennight:** One week.

9

night hours

"Have you had any more stomach pains today?" Velena asked, bending forward so Daisy could help her out of her tunic.

Daisy grabbed the ends of her sleeves first, wriggling the material until the whole of it came over Velena's head. "Not painful. Just…unsettled. But, no. As soon as I ate, I felt fine."

"Good."

Grabbing a brush, Daisy sat with Velena on the bed, first undoing the cord holding the end of Velena's plait together and then working the long tresses of dark hair apart with her fingers. "What did the healer have to say about Britton?" Daisy asked, trying to dismiss her own conversation with her.

"Not much more than you heard for yourself. She did add, however, that if he stays off his leg as he's supposed to, she doesn't think he'll suffer a limp when it's healed."

"Praise God for that," Daisy grinned. Running the brush through Velena's hair one last time, she moved from the bed, gathering up the clothes from the floor and spreading them out over a chair by the door. She'd tend to them tomorrow. "'Twould be difficult for a man's pride, otherwise, I would think."

"Most likely."

"Have you seen him awake?" Daisy asked.

"Not I, though I was told he woke for a short while."

Daisy's lips dipped in sympathy. "I'm sorry you missed it."

"As am I."

"Is it his head injury that keeps him sleeping?"

"She thinks it's merely exhaustion from his injuries as a whole."

"Oh, is that all." Daisy laughed to herself as though exhaustion weren't excuse enough to stay asleep. Her humor faded as she thought of her own fatigue—as if a great heaviness were weighing down upon her entire body. Rising in the morning had never felt more strenuous nor lying down at night more welcome.

But it didn't mean she was with child. The healer could be wrong. Perhaps, some sickness was taking hold of her. That certainly could explain her stomach upset—though it didn't explain why it was usually worse in the mornings. In truth, most mornings, she experienced the urge to seek out the chamber pot—thankfully, not so great that she'd had to do more than think on it. Today was the first time she'd experienced it in the latter part of the day.

"What did Sir Makaias have to say?" Daisy asked next, attempting to focus on the conversation at hand.

"He doesn't agree with the healer's assessment of his head injury. He said when he found Britton, he was complaining of seeing multiples of the same image."

Velena rose to help Daisy undo the cords at her back, laced in such a way as to hold the tunic snug against one's body. "But time will tell," she continued.

"How was he injured in the first place?"

"Sir Makaias said that after their ship landed in London harbor, he'd wanted to stay for a while to visit a friend, but Britton was eager to continue on, so they split ways." Velena motioned for Daisy to face her. "Arms in front," she directed.

Daisy bent low, wriggling out of her own tunic as Velena held on to her cuffs. Daisy smiled as the hem finally passed over her head. "Anxious to be with his family, no doubt."

"I like to think so," Velena continued. "It speaks well of him as a son—that he cared so much to come home.

"And a brother..." Daisy said, retrieving a cloth and bowl of tepid water.

"Yes, he would have had no way of knowing whether we were alive or dead. We know that feeling..."

"'Tis an unspeakable ache," Daisy mused, thinking back to the day Sir Richard had set forth to see about her own family. They'd not survived the Plague. Not one. "Here," she said, wringing out the cloth for Velena to use on her face.

Making thorough circles over her cheeks and forehead, Velena dropped her head back, letting go a sigh as she continued with long strokes across her shoulders and upper chest. There was always something satisfying about cleansing one's self of the grime of the day.

"Did Sir Makaias say for what friend he stayed behind?" Daisy asked.

"Not that I recall—only that he felt awful for it because, had he gone along, Britton wouldn't have pressed on in the company of one who appeared to be a poor traveler in need of an escort.

"And he wasn't?" Daisy asked, eyes growing wide as she began washing herself, her movements much slower, her thoughts completely caught up in the intrigue.

"Poor, perhaps…but not a traveler at all. The man was a part of a much larger gang of bandits—the rest of whom were waiting about a day's distance down the road. There, under the cover of night, they attacked, leaving poor Britton maimed and stripped of everything but his breeches.

"How ever did Sir Makaias find him?"

"It was a passerby who found him. Blessedly, he had a donkey and was able to take him home and care for him. Edward the Stronger, he called him."

"Amazing that he happened along when he did. More bandits could have just as easily set upon him."

"It wasn't chance," Velena said with deep conviction. "The man was an angel in human skin. More amazing was when he sent word back to London of Britton's situation. As it was, Sir Makaias had just started for home. Can you imagine if the letter had missed him?"

"God most certainly had a hand in it," Daisy agreed.

"For certain. It was the kindly maid in the service of his friend's household who received the message—and she who searched him out—finding him just as he was approaching the outer gates. For this, he said, he was eternally grateful, and was hence able to find Britton with little trouble."

"I'm surprised he was leaving so soon." Daisy began to count on her fingers. "You say Britton was only a day out when he was attacked, which means only a day back to send Sir Makaias word. And he was already about to leave? Two days visiting a friend hardly seems worth the delay for Sir Makaias to let your brother set out alone—nor for your brother to be so anxious that he couldn't wait. Surely, they could have compromised and rested for a day only."

Daisy picked up the bowl to deposit it on the fireplace mantel, wrung out the cloth and draped it over a hook to dry. Daisy had a sudden thought. "Was it a man or a woman he stayed behind for?"

"He gave no name."

"You said that, but did he mention a *he* or a *she?*"

"Neither."

"I think that after fighting side by side for so many years, and for as long as they've been friends, that only a woman would have the ability to split them apart the moment they set foot back on English soil. Otherwise, wouldn't Sir Makaias be just as anxious to see to his own family's welfare? You saw how he wept over his brothers. I think only a woman could have kept him away."

Velena drew in a facetious breath, as though taken in by Daisy's conjecture. "And the reason he left so soon," she added, "was because he'd been cockled."

"You're teasing me."

"Only a little," Velena said, giggling.

Daisy slapped at her wrist; Velena flinched playfully.

"You didn't think the same thing when he told you?" Daisy asked.

"He didn't tell me."

"Oh, but he did," she said, holding out her finger.

Velena was enjoying Daisy's animated state, nearly as much as she was enjoying the resurfacing of her friend, in general. This was the Daisy she knew.

"He named Edward the Stronger, did he not? But *not* the name of his friend. *That* says a great deal."

"It says that he is a man of few words," Velena argued. "A family trait he must share with Sir Andret. He says what he needs to and nothing more.

"He lied through omission."

Velena couldn't hold back her smile. "Why must it be a lie and not simply an omission of the unimportant? For if it *was* a woman—and he *was* spurned—what is that to us anyway…but idle gossip?"

Daisy pursed her lips as if this is what it'd take to hold back any additional words she might wish to say. "You're right," she finally conceded, positioning herself beside Velena to draw out her trundle. She waited for Velena to cross over first before laying back upon her mattress. She pulled the woolen blankets up beneath her chin and sighed. "You always think the best of people."

Velena's brows lifted, surprised to hear a rebuke in what should have been a compliment. "You forgot the candle again," she said, settling down onto her pillow.

Rolling her eyes at her own forgetfulness, Daisy threw back the covers to take care of it.

Amused, Velena turned to her side and tucked her elbow flat

beneath her ear, watching as Daisy's curvy silhouette, made visible by the glow of the candle, disappeared as she blew the flame out. Then all to dark. "What people?" Velena asked.

Back in bed, Daisy turned her head to face her. "I didn't mean for it to sound negative."

"What people?" she persisted.

Daisy stared into the nothingness above her. "Rowan, for instance. He's a constant bother to me, yet in your eyes, he can do no wrong."

"Has he overstepped his bounds with you?"

Daisy exhaled, thinking of his slap to her hindquarters. "No," she said, not wanting to cause trouble. "It's no more than I said."

Velena took a moment to really think on it. "I suppose I do give him too much grace, but I'm not unaware of his failings. In fact, I think it's *because* of his failings that I can forgive him so much. He's a lost soul, you know. He doesn't know God—not the way he should. In body, he may be brash—and a bother. But in spirit…he's floundering. And if he never knows the will of God, then one day he'll drown. I think the best of him because I hope the best for him."

"How does one know the will of God?" Daisy asked.

"From St. John, *'For this is the will of My Father, that everyone who beholds the Son and believes in Him will have eternal life, and I Myself will raise him up on the last day.'* For this, he's often in my prayers."

"Do you pray for Stuart, as well?"

"Ah," Velena said, rolling back fully upon her pillow, Stuart's confession again ringing in her ears.

"Do you think the best of *him*?" Daisy persisted.

Velena sighed. "I try not to think the worst."

"After all the grief he's given you over Tristan, how can you be so accepting of him?"

"I have faith that my father's choice for me is God's choice as well."

"Then God chooses poorly."

"Just because God's ways are not our ways doesn't mean He chooses poorly. It just means we can't always understand them at first."

"Or ever."

"Perhaps." She adjusted the blankets at her chest.

"You'll lose Tristan."

"I know."

"And me." It came out before she could stop herself.

Velena blinked into the darkness, wondering how Daisy could have found out about Stuart's threats. "Why should you think so?"

"He senses my dislike for him…and sees me as disloyal."

"I don't care what he senses. I won't let him send you away."

"You may not have a choice."

Velena pressed her lips together.

"Besides, I'm not sure I really want to live under the same roof with a man who doesn't approve of my being there."

Velena shouldn't have rejoiced over this small admission of *falling out of favor* with Stuart, but it seemed to line up with what he told her—and for that her heart was glad. She was so hoping he told her the truth.

"But you've no family," Velena reminded her. "Where would you go?"

"Tristan's offered me work at his mother's home in Oxford."

"What?" Velena sat straight up, blankets bunching at her waist. "Why would he do that?"

Daisy realized her mistake. "I…um…I told him of my concerns with Stuart—that he might not want me around after you were married."

"Oh." Velena's shoulders relaxed. "You should have voiced any concerns you had to me first."

"I'm sorry, my lady."

Remaining upright, Velena sighed. Eyes, having finally adjusted, she was just now able to see Daisy's form on the trundle below her. "It's alright," she assured Daisy. "He's always thinking of others, isn't he?"

"He's always thinking of you," she whispered.

Velena smiled. "If I were marrying for love, I'd want it to be to a man who loved others so well as he loved me."

"Do you think you'll ever come to love Stuart?"

"It's difficult to imagine now, but I hope so."

"Why?"

"Because feeling alone in a marriage seems worse to me than being alone outside of one."

Daisy stayed quiet.

"Daisy?"

"Hmm?"

"Did Bowan ever kiss you?" she asked, knowing Stuart's truth, but hoping to hear it from her.

Daisy fiddled with her sheets. "Yes."

"Did you kiss him back?"

"Yes," she answered honestly. "Did you kiss Stuart back?"

"How did you know about that?"

"I overheard some of the pages talking outside the kitchen. One of them must have seen you."

A frown dipped the corners of Velena's mouth. "That kiss was something of an unwanted surprise. And, no...I didn't." Velena fingered her upper lip. "It was different then I thought it'd be."

If Velena thought Daisy would inquire as to how, she didn't. She remained quiet and Velena wondered if pressing her any more about Bowan was worth the risk of having her shut her out again.

Velena went to her stomach, reaching down to stroke Daisy's hair from her brow. "No matter. This too shall pass. And...if after I'm married, you still want to take Tristan up on his offer, I won't stop you. I won't like it—but I'll understand. Until then...I don't want you to leave. Will you stay with me...please?"

"I'll stay," Daisy whispered, taking Velena's hand and kissing it.

Velena's voice drifted softly over the darkness as she took her arm back beneath her covers. "Thank you."

"Good night, my lady."

"Good night." Velena closed her eyes but found herself tossing and turning long past the time when Daisy's breathing became slow and even. Sleep had claimed her, and Velena wished the same could be said of herself, but she was having a hard time quieting her mind. She was thankful Daisy trusted her enough to speak of Bowan, but she'd not revealed enough to truly support or deny Stuart's confession in the chapel. She'd wanted to ask her about the night of the bonfire and about her conversation with Stuart in the orchard. If she had, would Daisy have admitted to having had an elicit encounter with Bowan? In doing so, would Stuart finally be cleared in her mind of any wrongdoing in the mystery surrounding Daisy's strange behavior? Velena flipped onto her other shoulder, tucking her arm beneath her pillow.

He couldn't be cleared of all wrongdoing because Jaren had admitted that Stuart had made a mistake—that we all make mistakes. So, what was his? And was Jaren indicting Daisy as well? Until this moment, Velena hadn't thought to think of Daisy as anything but an innocent, but what if...

Velena threw the covers from her body, the night air chilling her skin even as the first inkling of a suspicion chilled her heart. She looked down to the trundle—to Daisy—no more than a shadow below her.

No.

Daisy might have thought less of Velena for thinking the best of those who were more than their share of fallible, but she'd be comforted to know Velena still thought the best of her.

Velena crawled out of bed, shrugged into her brocade robe and quietly made her way to the box atop the mantel. Pulling out a fresh candle, she held it down to the hot embers still glowing orange in the hearth. Holding it aloft, she beheld Daisy's sleeping form, the flicker of light dancing across her wheat colored tresses. Without expression, Velena watched her eyes trace a path back and forth beneath her lids. Daisy's was a fitful sleep, and Velena's would be no less. But not yet. Her thoughts were now too active to lay to rest, and she suddenly had a great yearning to be in her brother's presence.

Makaias had barely closed his eyes when the first hint of another's presence crept over him. He felt no immediate danger, so he did little more than slit his eyes and quiet the sound of his breathing should he be wrong. Most likely, it was Sir Richard, come to check on his son. But years of war had heightened his senses so that he was always ready should the unexpected arise.

And so it did, for the slender wisp of a form who entered *was* most certainly unexpected. Makaias watched as Britton's sister—unaware of where he reclined in the shadows—crossed the room to the far side of the bed. A single candle illuminated her way, though light from a dying fire was already casting a warm glow.

He expected her to take watch in the chair her father had left vacant a few hours past, but was surprised when she sunk to the floor, all but her head and shoulders disappearing behind Britton's still form.

So long did she kneel unmoving beside her brother that Makaias was tempted back to sleep. For certainly her prayers were exactly what Britton needed—and no reason for Makaias to make his presence known. At this point it would do naught to startle her. Content to let her think she was alone, and content should he be discovered, he allowed his lids to slide shut until her voice—as low as it was—awoke him again.

10

re-acquainted

Britton's hand was rough. Velena turned it over palm side up…drew it to her cheek. His callouses scratched her flesh, but the breadth of his hand was warm and comforting, reminding her he was still alive. Years of wondering were over, and once again, she marveled at his return.

How different he appeared to her now than when they'd last parted ways four years ago. The war with France had aged him. She curved an arm over the pillow beneath his head and stroked the dark hair laying matted across his forehead. His mouth hung slightly open, drawing attention to his unshaved face. Perhaps, he'd look more himself once he was clean-shaven.

Velena used the end of her sleeve to dab at the moisture pooling in the corner of his mouth. "Sleep well, Brother," she whispered. How odd that even her hushed voice seemed too loud to her own ears, as if Britton's very presence created a certain sacredness to the room. He was her family come home.

"Thank you, Lord." She mouthed it this time, her voice carrying only the hint of sound, and even that, not louder than the breath coming from the rise and fall of his chest. "Do I warrant such a blessing?" she continued. "In his absence, You gave me another. You comforted me with Tristan…and now when it seems our parting may be near—and my heart close to breaking…" her chin quivered, "You returned him to us." Velena smoothed the covers about his arms. "You are truly good to Your daughter, Lord." She wiped a tear from her eye with the palm of her hand, "Please, grant him Your healing. In thy precious Son's name…amen."

It was at the *amen* when Makaias decided remaining silent might not be as prudent as announcing his presence. He'd not been able to discern the murmurings of her prayer, but she appeared in no hurry to leave, and he feared she might continue comforting him with words she obviously thought were private.

Softly, he let down the two front legs of the chair he had tipped back against the wall. He adjusted his position in the seat and allowed the sound of his leather shoes to shift across the floorboards. As thought, she startled but refrained from crying out. He stretched out his arms and yawned, aware her eyes were now focused in his direction.

"Who's there?"

"Forgive me," Makaias said, adding a yawn for effect, "I must have fallen asleep."

"Sir Makaias?"

"Yes, my lady...only me."

Her mouth tipped up at the corners. "See, I recognized you *this* time."

"And in the dark, no less." He smiled, though she may not have seen it, for the majority of light was with her, the single candle casting light across her face, while hiding him in shadow.

Velena pulled her robe more tightly about herself, now conscious of only having her shift beneath. She thought about excusing herself but hadn't worked up the courage to ask him to turn away. If she'd known his mind, she needn't have worried. To him, she was still Britton's little sister—too young and too familiar for that kind of notice. As such, he was unaware of her embarrassment and got up to join her by the bed, carrying his chair with him.

Awkward, Velena gathered her hair around her shoulder. "I'm sorry I didn't recognize you when you first arrived," she continued, "else I would have greeted you properly."

Makaias wondered what properly would have looked like. Women needn't bother with greeting men...except for the purposes of being hospitable. "I wasn't offended."

Silence.

"Nevertheless, I *was* embarrassed, especially since you recognized me."

"You're as I remember—albeit, an older version."

Tristan said this very thing at Wineford—only she'd been fifteen then.

More silence.

"How old are you now?" he asked.

"Eighteen."

He shook his head in wonder. "The years go quickly."

"I thought years of war would have slowed them down. Surely, you yearned for home."

Light reflecting from his eyes, his look was far away. "In many ways." He cleared his throat. "I take it by your presence here tonight that you're worried for your brother."

She overlapped her robe just a bit more and shook her head, freeing some of her hair to fall back from her shoulder. "His very presence is a sign that I needn't worry any longer. I pray only for his speedy recovery."

"As do I."

"Sir Makaias?"

"Hm." His eyes focused, though the color was lost in the darkness.

"I haven't yet thanked you for bringing him home to us."

Makaias cocked his head to the side, an amused expression ticking at his lips as he wondered what else she would have expected him to do. "As opposed to leaving him there?"

Velena smiled coolly in response. "Well," she said, feeling much of the same awkwardness she felt upon her first encounter with Tristan—albeit to a lesser degree. "I should go."

He chuckled, realizing he'd probably annoyed her. "I apologize. I know what you meant."

"Even so. Though we be not alone, my brother makes a poor chaperon in his present condition. And as it is, I'm not quite decent."

Thinking she was in jest, he waved her concern away with a look. Then, casting his gaze beneath the shadow of her chin, he took inventory of her robe, as well as the voluminous amount hair that hung loose about her shoulders. Both worked together to give her a very young appearance, but he had to agree that she was, indeed, improperly dressed. Still, he thought it most unnecessary she should be so self-conscious. Even in so little light, he could discern the lack of curves that Joanna had been in abundance of—at least the ones on top.

He smiled as to reassure her. "Worry not, Lady Velena, I've had no untoward thoughts."

"Still," she said, waiting.

Confused a moment longer, he finally slapped his hands to his knees in realization of what she expected and went through the motions of standing to his feet and turning away.

Affirming the robe was properly overlapped, Velena rose to her feet, using the bedside for support. The frame creaked, and Britton's eyes parted ever so slightly, going unnoticed by anyone for the time being.

Though his vision was still blurred, Britton's mind was the clearest it had been since his arrival. Trying to focus, he discerned it was Makaias' form hovering closest to the bed, but he wasn't alone. There was another shape, and even had she never spoken, he would have recognized it was a woman from the feminine curvature of her hips, along with the flowing mass of shadow billowing about her shoulders. Voice low, she spoke. "If he wakes, please tell him I'll return in the morning to check on him."

Was it his injured eyes or merely the fact that she stood between him and the candle's glow that gave her the incandescent appearance of some sort of dark angel—beauty shrouded in a halo of light? How long had it been since he'd been aroused by a woman?

He wanted to say something to her, but his mouth was so parched. He dared not croak out his first words and ruin the ethereal image before him. So, he remained quiet, content to watch her walk away, knowing she'd return as she said—to check on him. Perhaps, she'd want to do an examination of his leg. He'd succumb to that and more. What had he to be embarrassed of when there was still plenty of him left that should impress?

In silence, he watched her leave but spoke the moment Makaias settled back into his chair. "Don't just sit there," Britton's voice croaked. "My mouth is full of gravel."

Makaias grinned, thinking for a moment to run after Velena, but then realized she'd still be improperly dressed. And anyway, she'd be back in the morning. He leaned over Britton to retrieve a tumbler of ale off the side table. "Parched, are we?"

"And hungry."

"You're in luck," Makaias said, leaving his chair for the desk. "I have here some very cold broth just for such a time as you should wake."

Britton groaned. "It'll do."

Makaias ladled the first spoonful into his mouth.

"You missed."

"Your eye is the same as your mouth in the dark."

"You make a poor nursemaid," Britton grumbled.

"I should get the healer to do it."

"I think I'd like that. How long have I been asleep?"

"Hours."

"Then why do I feel as though I could sleep for hours more?"

"A few more spoonfuls, and I'll leave you to it."

Britton's shoulders sagged. "It's good to be home, Makaias. I've yet to see it in daylight, but I feel it in my bones. We've been away too long."

Sir Makaias delivered another spoonful of cold broth and a sip of ale.

"I'd rather you bring that woman back in here to do this."

"Your—"

"If she wasn't beauty incarnate."

Spoon only halfway to its destination, Makaias dripped broth onto Britton's chest in his confusion. Suddenly, he chuckled, realizing Britton hadn't recognized his sister for who she was, but rather a servant or apprentice to the healer. "Taken with her, were you?"

"If what I saw in the dark was any indication of fine form and beauty, I look forward to morning."

"Just remember…your vision is still blurred."

"But you've seen her?"

"I have."

"Am I mistaken in my judgment?"

"She has a comely appearance—though more girl than woman. But trust me when I say that seen in the light of day, your temptation for her will quickly fade." He laughed to himself, enjoying the game he was allowing to continue.

"I'll see her for myself."

"I think you should see your way back to sleep."

"I know what this is."

"I don't think you do," Makaias said rather smugly.

"You've seen her and you want her for yourself."

"Yes. No. And if I did, I'd have a better chance of winning her than you."

"You underestimate the attractiveness of a man in pain—in need. Women always have a soft spot for that sort of thing—something to do with their need to mend things that aren't broken."

"Except in your case."

"What's that?"

"You *are* broken."

"All the better for me. In fact, I'd wager—"

"You've nothing to wager."

"There's always something to wager. I'll wager a kiss from my sister that I can get…" Britton paused. "Do you know her name?"

Turning his back on Britton, Makaias took the broth back to the desk, concealing his smile. "She didn't say."

"No matter. I'll wager a kiss from my sister that I can get this mystery woman to kiss me before the week is through."

Makaias propped his backside against the desk, hands gripping the wood to either side of him. "I don't think you can reasonably expect to give away your sister's kisses without her consent."

"It's the least she can do for her long-lost brother. That way, if I don't get kissed, at least you will."

"What makes you think I want a kiss from your sister? As far as you know, she's a married woman."

"Is she?"

Makaias rolled his eyes. "No."

"Don't play with me, Kai. You've been spurned and could use the release."

"At your sister's expense?"

"All in good fun—and besides, it's only if I lose—which I won't. So, what will you give me when I win?"

"Listen to you. 'When,'" Makaias mocked.

"I'm in need of a new horse."

"You want my horse?"

"Yes."

"Your father can get you a horse."

"I want yours."

"For the love…you can't even ride a horse."

"If I win the horse that means I'll have gotten the kiss—perhaps the first of many. In which case, I'll have something to keep me occupied until I'm again fit to ride."

"All right," Makaias said, remembering this was a bet he couldn't lose. "If she kisses you—on the mouth—I'll give you my horse. But if not…"

"You'll get a kiss from my sister."

Makaias cocked an eyebrow.

"You don't think she will?"

"I don't think she should."

"Well, it's nothing you'll have to worry over because I'm not going to lose."

"Trust me, Britton, even if you win…you'll lose."

"Don't speak in riddles. You know my head hurts."

"Then enough, my friend. I'll take the wager. Go back to sleep, and I'll leave you in peace. Back to my terribly *comfortable* wooden chair, shall I return. I'll be here if you need anything else."

"Have we not servants for this?"

"I'm not above aiding my friend."

Britton adjusted his shoulders, groaning as the movement trickled down to his leg. He sighed. "Perhaps I'll dream of her."

Makaias took his chair back to a wall where he could sit in a reclined position. "Not if your any sort of fortunate," he said, smiling in delayed satisfaction.

11
familial ties

Britton pushed aside the aging hand that held the foul-smelling concoction. "You're not putting that on me."

Makaias rolled his eyes at his friend. "Do as the woman says."

"Tis the only way to heal your eyes, my lord," the healer explained. "You must apply this mixture atop your eyelids, and this blindfold you must wear as well. Every day, you must apply it, covering your eyes with a fresh cloth after you do so."

"You can't possibly be serious," he said in disgust, noting Makaias was having a difficult time hiding his own distaste for the procedure.

"You must stay in complete darkness for a fortnight. Do this, and I believe we'll see great success in your vision after removing the blindfold. Your eyes need time to heal, and this they cannot do as long as you have use of them."

Again, she attempted to administer that which was now dripping from her fingers in foul clumps upon the floor. And again, he pushed her hand aside.

"This treatment is unsatisfactory. I would just as soon go blind, as heal with that putrid concoction plastered to my face."

"To your lids only, my lord."

"Get her out, Kai."

"But my lord, the herbs and sheep dung are what will bring the healing," she insisted.

"Out!" he ordered, caring not that she startled at the volume of his voice.

Makaias guided her by the shoulders. "I think it best you take your leave, Madam."

"But his treatment—"

"You may leave instructions for the mixture below stairs, and I'll see to the rest."

"For my sake, I pray you do, Sir knight. Sir Richard would be most offended if he thought I'd neglected my work in his son's healing."

"No blame will come to you."

"Just the same—I'll be back in a fortnight to remove the blindfold," she grumbled, handing the cloth to Makaias. She curtsied and left the room.

Makaias turned towards his friend.

"Kai, if you come near me with that—excrement—I'll gouge out your eyes so you'll be the one needing it."

Makaias laughed.

"I'm serious."

"It does seem quite horrid," Makaias agreed, picking up the bowl and taking a whiff. He jerked back. "Sweet mother of—"

"Britton," Velena cried from behind him, trying to keep her voice even, though she wanted to shout. Cradling a rather large and ornate book in her arms, she rushed in. "You're awake!"

"Velena?" His eyes ran up and down his sister in disbelief. Not only was she taller than the little *gnome* he left behind, but she was also a good deal prettier than he remembered.

"In the flesh," she said, twirling in a circle, her cotehardie making a swish of raspberry fabric about her ankles. Her dark hair was looped at the sides of her head into plaited buns, concealed within a netting of beaded pearls. Her smile could have lit up the room, so happy was she to see her brother sitting up and looking well.

"I can hardly accept it! What happened to the girl I left behind? Don't tell me you're she."

"You know I am," she said, barely containing her mirth. "And you're one to talk. You've grown old beneath your whiskers so that I barely recognized you. Nonetheless I'd wrap my arms around your neck and hold on tight if I weren't afraid it'd hurt."

"Come and claim your place, Sister. My neck may be the only thing that doesn't hurt."

Quickly, she drew close to his side, dropping the book to the mattress with a soft thud as she took his head in her arms, drawing him close to her cheek. He smelled of earth and sweat, but still she lingered—taking no mind of Makaias looking on—eyes glistening with unshed tears as they pulled away."

"What's this you have?" he asked, rubbing his nose, trying to overcome his emotion. "Father's Bible?"

"You know of it?"

"Certainly. It used to be on display in the foyer. Though I suppose you were too young to remember. Why do you have it?"

"Father asked me to find a verse for him, and then I thought if you were awake, you might enjoy it if I read to you." She reached out to brush his tangled bangs aside. "You look so much better than last I looked on you. You've been in my prayers."

"I've surely needed them."

"Has the healer been back to see you?"

"She has. But let's not talk of that now."

"She wants him blindfolded for the next fortnight," Makaias interjected.

"Truly, that long? Why ever for?" she asked, taking a whiff of the mixture Sir Makaias held out for her to smell.

"My vision is blurred," Britton answered in irritation.

Makaias chuckled as Velena jerked away, covering her nose. "How foul! What is it?"

Britton shook his head. "You don't want to know."

"But it's supposed to help?"

"So we're told."

"I pity you, then."

"I pity me, too," he confessed. "In fact, I'm in dire need of comforting. Where's that woman who's supposed to check on me?"

Velena looked confused...and then concerned, thinking the damage done to his head was worse than she feared. "The healer already came...remember?"

"Not that old crone. The other woman."

"What other woman?" Velena asked, looking to Makaias, only to see laughter in his eyes.

"Makaias knows of whom I speak," Britton explained.

"Indeed, I do," he said, becoming quite serious, "and it seems she's caught his fancy."

Velena blinked, attention back on her brother. "You've been here all of one day—and were asleep for most of it. How in the world—"

Britton chuckled. "Never mind that. What matters more is that I've struck up a small wager with Kai that I happen to need your help with."

"What could you possibly have to wager? From what I've heard, you were robbed blind."

"You needn't remind me."

"Sorry," Velena said, remembering about his eyes.

Britton excused her misspeak with a wave of his hand. "If I win—when I win—Kai will turn over to me his horse."

"You agreed to this?" she asked of Makaias in surprise, having seen the well-built destrier in question. A beauty to be sure.

"He agreed to that and more," Britton added with a smirk.

Velena turned to Makaias. "What do you get if he loses?"

"Ask your brother. And let it be known it was agreed upon only because I knew I could in nowise lose."

Britton scoffed. "Usually this sort of thing stays private, you understand, but since it does involve you…"

"Me? Your mind's been quite active for one who's only just now come awake."

"I promised him a kiss."

"What?" she nearly sputtered, looking to Makaias, who only shrugged his shoulders and pinched in the corners of his mouth as if to say, he had little to do with it. She crossed her arms, "Well, I hope you're prepared to deliver."

"Come now, Velena, you know I mean you. And as you just said, I've arrived with nothing. Surely, you could take pity on my condition and lend me so meager a gesture to make use of."

"Obviously, you still think me your baby sister with no mind of my own."

"You'll always be such to me." He flashed her a smile meant to appease.

She rolled her eyes.

"But worry not. Look at me!" he exclaimed with a supercilious grin. "I can't lose."

"Yes," Velena said, with a condescending eye, "just look at you."

"Fine. First a bath and then send for the woman who came to me last night. Better yet, fetch the woman and have her come and give *me* the bath," he said, pumping his eyebrows.

Without thinking, Velena's fingers flew to her parted lips as she bubbled up with laughter. "Last night?" She looked to Makaias, who, in all his merriment, could only nod.

"Yes," Britton said, failing to see the humor in her remark.

"Perhaps you don't think of me as your baby sister so much as you think you do."

"What's that to mean?"

"The only woman who came to you last night is standing before you now."

"You jest!"

"Nay, dear brother, whose carnal mind doth need a good cleansing. It was I, and no other, who came to you last night. To pray." Velena watched as the truth of it sunk in.

"You knew!" Britton shouted pointedly at Makaias, who was now doubled over in the corner of the room. "I'm going to be sick…" he moaned.

"Do you need the chamber pot?" Velena asked, flashing him an innocent look. "I would…should I be in your place."

Makaias laughed ever louder. "So, would we all."

"You knew! You knew—you know…and you let me go on about it."

"You went on about it?" Velena asked, curiosity raising her eyebrows. "Pray tell!"

"He called you a dark angel—"

"No more!" Britton interrupted before he could be humiliated any more than he already was. "No more," he said again, his voice breaking as he failed to suppress his own amusement, though it being at his own expense. "Oh, Velena, my eyes have played tricks on me." He ran his hands over his face. "Bring me those nasty things," he said of the dung and wraps. "I'll delay my healing no longer."

By this point, Makaias was wiping tears from his cheeks, his shoulders shaking uncontrollably. "I don't think dung will heal your humiliation."

"You laugh now, but soon it'll be my turn," Britton said, a smirk spreading across his face. "I've lost the wager. Now, collect your kiss, so that I might laugh at your expense."

"Oh," Velena said, pressing her lips together.

Makaias, too, was quick to settle.

"I beg your pardon, brother, but I feel under no obligation to fulfill your wagers.

"Only marriage should stop such an obligation, and Makaias tells me you're under no such enslavement.

Velena's smile faltered, her eyes drifting to her lap, remembering afresh her newly acquired engagement. "Not married at present."

"Then there should be no difficulty. For as long as you're without a husband, might I point out that Kai is also without a wife."

"And *you*…are without tact," Makaias interjected.

Velena waved him off. "Don't scold him, Sir Makaias. He's already had a difficult morning, and I've missed his teasing. I've missed it very much..." She reached for Britton's hand. "In addition, I hope you forgive me, but I must begrudge you your due...for I fear your wager was born of deceit."

Makaias grinned. "That it was."

"Yes, well..." Britton said, releasing a puff of air from his lungs. "I feel a change of subject is due, but...I suddenly find myself in need of a bit more courage to entertain it." He tried to smile but failed. "Can I assume, since mother hasn't yet come to scold me for staying away so long...that she isn't going to."

Makaias reached down to squeeze Britton's good leg where it lay hidden beneath the covers and excused himself from the room.

Velena waited until he'd gone before turning mournful eyes back to her brother. "I'm afraid not."

Britton nodded. He took a ragged breath. "Was it awful?"

"Yes." She swallowed. "It was."

"Will you tell me about it?"

"If you want me to."

He bit into his cheek. "I don't know why, but I want to know."

"Alright."

Britton motioned for her to get comfortable beside him as he did his best to make better room for her on the narrow bed. She wriggled onto her side and tucked her hand beneath her cheek. As well as he could, he turned to listen, but mostly he just stared at the ceiling as she recounted the death of their mother and then of Peter. She told him of their trip to Wineford, her depression... and, lastly, her friendship with Tristan. To this, he listened without judgment.

She would have gone on, but there was a soft rap at the door. Giggling as Britton *helped* roll her from the bed, Velena went to answer it.

"Stuart," she said, surprised he'd come back to the manor so early.

He smiled. "May I come visit the invalid?"

Velena turned to her brother, who gestured him in. She stood back to allow him wide passage.

"How are you feeling, Cousin?"

Britton sighed. "Oh, you know. Ready to take on the French, myself, as usual."

Stuart laughed. "The Scotts, too, no doubt."

"Velena was just telling me about Peter...and your mother. I'm sorry Stuart. I really am."

Stuart produced a tight-lipped grin. "After a little while, you learn not to ask about loved ones, else you'd be offering your condolences to every passerby."

"I'm beginning to see that."

"Besides, I'd rather you offer us your congratulations instead."

"Congratulations...for what?"

Stuart tried to hide his disappointment over Velena not having told her brother, herself. "Velena and I are engaged to be married. Made official only yesterday, as a matter of fact, so you've arrived just in time."

Britton appeared truly surprised. "Then congratulations..." He looked over at Velena, who raised her shoulders slightly as if to apologize for not divulging this bit of news first. "I thought it was only my hallucinations which caused me to smell a fine pig on the spit. And here I thought Father had just run out of fatted calves."

Velena smiled. "It's true, your unexpected return cut our evening celebration short, but now that your home, the occasion is all for you. I happily relinquish any attention Father planned to heap upon us in favor of rejoicing over your return. If there is a fatted calf to be had, then it shall be done."

Stuart's smile confirmed it.

"No. No," Britton protested, "my vision is still far too clouded for me to see properly, and I don't wish to leave my bed at present. But if Velena will stay with me a little while longer, it'll be celebration enough. In fact," he continued apologetically, "if you'll forgive my rudeness, I'd like to spend just a little more time with her before she gets swept away."

"Of course. I'll be downstairs when you're ready for another visit."

"I'll let you know when we're finished," Velena said, as he passed her for the door. He nodded and was gone.

"Shut the door," Britton said softly.

Velena complied before returning to sit by his feet.

"Why didn't you tell me you were engaged to Stuart?"

"I was almost to that part."

Britton studied her.

"You're surprised?"

"Truthfully, I'm disappointed."

"Why should you be?" Velena asked, trying to maintain the countenance of one thoroughly content in her situation.

"Stuart was always…well, he was always…" Britton seemed hard pressed for the right words. "He whined a great deal," he finally answered. "Didn't you think so? At least, that's how I remember it. You were forever dragging him out of his dark moods."

"I don't recall it that way," she answered honestly.

"Well, I don't know how you recall it, but I fear that marriage to him will leave you the constantly doting wife. If he's anything like he was, you'll have little time to do anything else but satiate him."

"Have you always felt this way?"

"I haven't had reason to think on it until now, but I suppose I have. I like Stuart fine—but never the influence he had on you."

"Makaias greeted him warmly enough," she said, easily dropping his title in the presence of her brother. "Was that genuine or does he share your same sentiments?"

"Well, perhaps he has some nonsense feelings of loyalty towards that side of the family that I do not. That would be just like him though."

"To be nonsensical?"

"Loyal."

"I see. Well, I can't change things now, can I?"

"No, I suppose not. Do you know, at one point, though, Father wanted to arrange a marriage between you and Kai?"

"He told me of it."

"And?"

"And what?"

"What did you think of it?" Britton asked.

"I didn't think anything," she said, not wanting to sound offensive.

"He thought your giddy behavior an irritation," Britton said with a grin.

"And I, his stoic countenance," she retorted.

"Now, we're getting somewhere," he laughed.

"You're baiting me."

He pinched his thumb and finger together. "Just a little. But only because I think it's such a shame you're already engaged. I still think he'd be an excellent choice of husband for you.

"It's as I said before; he's too serious."

"Serious? Yes, I suppose, he's a bit on the serious side, but all the more reason he'd benefit from a good deal of laughter in his life."

"I think you provide for that well enough."

Britton hung his head. "I'm never going to live this down."

Velena giggled.

"It's good to hear you laugh, Velena. It is good to see these last few years haven't stolen your voice?"

"They almost did," she confessed. "But God sent me Tristan, and he showed me the love of Christ…and accepted me for all my irritations and loved me just the same."

"How did you explain it before?" he asked.

She brought her lips together, fighting a smile she hoped he'd not misinterpret. "Love—without the marriage part."

Britton shook his head in wonder. "Highly unusual to find a friendship like that between a man and a woman. *I've* certainly never witnessed one."

"We're proof it exists."

"Then I shan't refute it, but let me ask, how does Stuart feel about this very unusual friendship?"

Smiling, Velena bit her lip. "Shall I read the Bible to you now?" she asked with deliberate avoidance of his question.

"'Shall I read the Bible to you now?'" he mocked, playfully pinching her arm. "No, you may not. What you *can* do is tell me how four years has transformed you into such a devious little creature—the likes of which, who goes about staring men in the eyes as if they were her equal, whose closest friends consist of those other than women, and who defies her place as a fallen daughter of Eve by indulging in the reading of Scripture without a proper tutor."

"How do you know I'm without a proper tutor?"

"Have you one?"

"You're awfully demanding for one who just came back from the grave."

"I was never so much *in* the grave as next to it." He chuckled. "Oh, Velena. You've changed. I can see it in your eyes. I'll have to get to know my little sister all over again."

"I disappoint you?"

"Time will tell," he teased again, rubbing the top of her warm hand. "But it's unlikely you will. The world is a changed place, after all, and perhaps the more women we have staring us in the eyes to make something good of what's left of it, the better off we'll be."

She smiled affectionately. "You'd change your opinion of woman just for me?"

"I feel I can make an exception." Again, he pinched her arm, "Now then…" he closed his eyes and adjusted his shoulders below his pillow, "my head is back to hurting. If you'll be so good as to tell Stuart I'll see him after I've had some more rest, I'd like you to read me to sleep.

"As long as you don't ask me to interpret what I read. I'm only a fallen daughter of Eve, after all," she reminded him.

He chuckled. "You wish for me to take it back, but I won't. If I want an interpretation, I'll send for Makaias. He's quite learned in the area of Scripture."

12

changes

The following day, Tristan sat in the great hall as it was quickly emptying of diners. All the large trays and platters of sumptuous foods from the noon meal were being washed and safely tucked away in the kitchen as the trenchers were being collected by half-a-dozen pages to be taken out back for the poor. They'd consume the leftovers and most likely the gravy-sopped trenchers, themselves.

Distasteful to some and common place to others, Tristan paid it no mind as he lifted his elbows up and out of the way, watching as Velena disappeared into the corridor. She was going above stairs to see her brother, leaving him behind to listen, albeit somewhat distractedly, to Sir Richard as he laid bare his concerns over the financial state of the manor.

There were, of course, others seated around him at the dais[15] table. With Tristan seated to Sir Richard's right, Magnus—followed by Stuart—was seated to his left. Across from them, in benches pulled up specifically for this meeting, was Sir Richard's steward, Sir Tarek, and the new bailiff, John the Piper, who had taken the place of Wolfgang Alder after he'd died from the Plague only six months before Sir Richard's return from Wineford Castle. Also present was Sir Makaias, acting as liaison for Sir Britton, who remained confined to his room for the time being.

Tristan glanced from one man to the other. He was exceedingly thankful that Stuart was not in his direct line of vision, though he thought he could still feel his eyes boring a hole into the side of his head. Tristan refused to be intimidated as he rubbed at his nose, trying not to inhale too deeply of the rank odor of too many bodies in need of a good hot soak—his own included. He cleared his throat and tried to keep his middle finger in check as it sought to tap out its usual nervous rhythm upon the table. Magnus was speaking now.

"We have to adjust with the times, Richard. There just isn't the manpower to farm the fiefs."

Sir Richard stroked his caramel colored beard, revealing trenches of gray as he combed his hand through. "Has no one approached the manor for work?" he inquired of John the Piper.

"There's been inquiries, my lord, and we've put them all to work who's asked, but they're wanting more coin for their labor."

"In view of?"

"In view of the fact that they know they're in high demand. Three of the villeins I just recently put to work are here from Berry Pomeroy. They know good and well the consequences for leaving their lord, but they also know you won't send them back to face him. We need them, and that's the truth."

Magnus grunted in obvious disapproval of their ignoble actions. "Disloyal. That's what they are. If they turn tail and run from their last master, who's to say they won't run from you or I once they find someone who'll pay them better. We can't rely on them, I tell you."

Sir Richard barely lifted his eyes in his direction. His brother-in-law irked him—even when he made sense. "Can I afford to pay them what they want?" Sir Richard asked, turning to face Tristan.

Looking a tad flustered, Tristan straightened up and answered truthfully. "Yes, my lord. You can afford it, and for some time to come, but..."

"But what?"

"Taking everything into consideration, it isn't good business to keep doing it. Relying on fief production as your main source of income will eventually deplete your pockets—especially if you have nothing else coming in."

"I see," Sir Richard said, taking a moment too long to stare at him, a sort of regret lingering in his eyes. He swiveled his gaze back across the table. "So, it seems a change is, indeed, in order. What say the rest of you to Magnus' plans for wool production? Do we have the villeins for that?"

"We do, indeed," spoke up Sir Tarek, as John the Piper added in his own nod of approval. "It takes far less men to care for sheep, and we're in the perfect location for it. Close to the ports, we can ship the wool anywhere."

"And should your production go well," Sir Makaias added, "you might even think of investing in a ship of your own."

"And would you command this ship for me?" Sir Richard asked, chuckling.

"Oh, no, not I. I never did obtain my sea legs, my lord."

"Sick, were you?"

"Every day of the trip there and back. I could see the shores of Dover from Calais, and still I couldn't get here fast enough." He laughed good naturedly at himself.

"You see, Richard," Magnus cut in, "the wool business will be good for us. With Stuart and Velena's marriage forthcoming, it's more important now than ever that we leave them with a sustainable income. I have plans for my father's manor to be restored for their use. Starting them with a few hundred sheep of their own will put them right on their feet. If we pool our money, we could purchase more and purchase them now. I've already spoken with a seller."

"Have you now?" Sir Richard asked, turning in his chair to get a better view of Magnus' face.

Tristan watched as Lord Magnus shrugged off Sir Richard's scrutiny of him. "It was necessary to have all in place before coming to you with such a venture. We will be partners after all. Do you not have the best grazing land…and I the business connections to handle both the buying and selling of the wool? Remember, Richard, you've been gone a long time, you'll need me to steer you in the right directions. Furthermore—"

"You need not go on, Lord Magnus," Sir Richard said, rubbing his hands up and down his thighs. "I'm thus convinced. For the sake of procuring a productive livelihood for ourselves and our children—and Lord willing, our children's children…"

Tristan's stomach lurched.

"I'll partner with you," Sir Richard stated. He then rapped his knuckles on the table as though he had another thought, though none were immediately forthcoming other than to ask Tristan to help work out the financial sums needed to draw up the contract for this new venture.

Tristan knew this would be his last act of service before his departure. *Departure*…the finality of word certainly did vex the soul. Tristan watched with an unshakable sort of melancholy as Sir Richard cleared the room of all but himself and Sir Makaias. Having been only vaguely aware of the knight's name prior to his arrival, he was soon to learn how highly esteemed Sir Makaias was to Sir Richard's family—at least to Sir Richard and his son.

To Velena, perhaps not so much. Eight years his junior, any childhood memories she had of him were few, or at the very least, inconsequential. In the entire time Tristan had spent with her family, she'd barely made use of his name—though it had been from her he'd first heard it spoken. Even now, he didn't think she'd pay him much mind, except that he was always with her brother—and, presently, her entire focus was on Sir Britton and his well-being.

Tristan wasn't jealous—exactly. He was happy for her, and quite honestly, having her brother present made his leaving that much easier. She wouldn't be as alone as she'd thought. Still, he felt uprooted, and he wasn't sure how he'd bear the transition, though it was his own idea to leave. He'd informed her of it only this morning. Told her it was time he went looking for his own brother. She listened quietly—though he could tell she'd thought there was more to it. It was near impossible for him to hide anything from her, but she'd let it go.

He wanted it that way—and really should have seen it as a sign of growth and maturity on her part—but her lack of fight had stung his ego. He'd become quite accustomed to—and comfortable with—being her source of strength. It probably wasn't good for either of them, though. This he knew, but what if he still wanted it to be?

Tristan looked towards Sir Makaias, who was listening intently to Sir Richard's praise of him—with a great amount of humility, he had to admit—and wondered what to make of him. Would he be an ally or an adversary for Velena? He was another of Stuart's cousins, after all. But then again, so was Rowan, and there were no doubts where his loyalty fell.

If he were honest, Tristan thought he liked the knight. He was an intriguing sort of man, really. He was better looking—in Tristan's estimation—than Stuart but didn't seem to use his looks to his advantage. No wench coming in from the village to serve at Sir Richard's table had procured more than a passing glance from him, though it was obvious they'd tried. He seemed content to be home from the wars and comfortable in this household, though how he knew this he couldn't say. For when Sir Makaias wasn't speaking, or responding to someone who was, his expressions were nearly impossible to read. Even, now, as Sir Richard gushed his praise of him, Sir Makaias' eyes held little more than the hint of a smile.

Still, his body language and overall countenance suggested that he lacked a pretentious spirit. This alone put Tristan at ease in his presence despite the glances he received from him, which seemed to be more curious than anything else.

"So, what do you say?" Sir Richard was asking. "Will you stay on with me and train my squires? It would be of great help to me."

Makaias locked his hands around the knee he'd slipped between himself and the table and rocked back. While in Calais, his lord—Sir James—had hinted that he might be set up with a demesne[16] of his own upon his return to England, but there had been no written agreement of it. When Sir James died, Makaias' hopes of independence died with him.

Makaias longed to be his own man and run his own land, but his time had not yet come. Sir Richard had always been very good to him, and he decided that if he could be of some use to him, even for a little while, he would do that first above all else. In addition to this, he wanted to stay for the tournament. Entering the games might not win him a fortune, but it was a good place to start. He grinned. "It would be my pleasure to have you as my lord."

Sir Richard clapped his hands together and rubbed them back and forth with satisfaction. "Perfect. I warn you, though, you'll have your work cut out for you. My squires have grown green in their training since the Pestilence has come and gone."

"I can train anyone you put in front of me." He looked to Tristan and grinned for the first time, a question in his eyes. "Even this man, if he has a mind to be taught."

Tristan laughed, suddenly. "Oh, no—not me. Early in my childhood did my father learn I wouldn't be one to take up a sword. So, he allowed me my cock fights and an Oxford education, and I've been all the happier for it."

"His talent with numbers has been invaluable to me, to be sure. It's been a blessing to have a man around I can always trust," Sir Richard said.

Sir Makaias tipped his head respectfully in Tristan's direction. "High praise, indeed. Any man so highly respected in this household shall have my sword. You need never pick one up so long as I'm able to offer you aid."

"A generous offer to a stranger, Sir," Tristan said, surprise showing itself on his face.

"No doubt you wonder at the genuineness of my words, but I assure you, I give no promise lightly. I give it for Sir Richard's sake, as well as for Britton's. He, too, is grateful for the part you've played in his sister's well-being. She's told him of your friendship, and I speak on his behalf, when I say that he approves and thinks kindly of you for it."

"I find that surprising," Tristan answered honestly, looking to Sir Richard. "To many, our friendship is more of an oddity than something to be praised."

"Odd things rise from odd times," Sir Richard said, voicing his approval. "And odd or not, your friendship has been to her a solid foundation, upon which she can now build...for the future." Sir Richard stood. "Come, Sir Makaias, be so good as to make your way to the practice yards, and we'll talk further. I'll tarry only a moment."

"As you like, my lord."

Sir Richard waited till he'd cleared the door and then turned to Tristan with something like grief upon his face. "It's been decided that Velena and Stuart be married following the tourney."

"The tourney? That's a fortnight past the banns, is it not."

He nodded. "It's longer than Stuart or Lord Magnus would like, but it's my wish. That being said...with there being so much time before the wedding...I think it best if—"

Knowing what was about to come, yet unable to wait for it, Tristan spoke first.

"I'm of a mind to find my brother, my lord. I seek your permission to travel home."

Sir Richard's eyes rounded, but he recovered quickly. "You wish to go?"

"Were you not about to ask me to?"

Sir Richard gave a tight smile. "I think it's come to that." He hesitated. "I want to apologize, Tristan."

"No, my lord, it's I—"

"No. Let me speak. I was harsh with you when you came to me last, and I'm sorry for it." He shook his head. "For all my talk of trust, I wouldn't hear you. No doubt, it felt like a betrayal—but I hope you know why."

"You warned me at Wineford not to speak ill of Stuart unless I had proof."

"And you broke your promise," he said, moving around the opposite side of the table as if readying himself to leave.

"I had good reason."

Sir Richard dug his fingers into his beard and sighed. "I'm sure you had—"

"And still do. Will you hear me now, my lord?"

Sir Richard bent over the table, bearing his weight upon his forearms as he shook his head most decidedly. "I've given my word to Lord Magnus. And I keep my word."

"Forgive me, my lord but would he do the same for you?"

Sir Richard rose back to full height. "I suspect you know that he wouldn't...but I can only answer for myself."

"Still, I don't understand."

"I've agreed for Velena to marry Stuart—not her uncle."

"But Stuart is—"

"I know what you're thinking," Sir Richard said, tapping his finger on the table for emphasis, "like father, like son." He crossed his arms. "But though Stuart *is* his son, he has every right to prove that he's *not* his father. You see him now, but I've seen him his entire growing up. He's devoted to Velena. And though you find it vexing, his jealousy towards you is understandable. You have to give him that."

"I give him nothing."

"I see." Sir Richard hung his head, searching for wisdom where there seemed to be none.

"Though discerning in most every consideration, my lord, you're blind in this. You don't know him as well as you think."

"You test me."

Tristan stood to his feet. "He's violated a woman—"

"Tristan—"

"In the worst way a man can do so."

"You speak out of turn!"

"Will you do nothing, my lord?" Tristan's voice rose, his tone pleading. "He must stand trial for his crimes."

"Show me proof!" Sir Richard shouted, pounding his fist down upon the table. "For the love of all that's holy, if it weren't for the heinous nature of your accusation, I'd throw you out this very moment." Sir Richard took a deep breath and brought his voice back to the controlled volume that characterized his steady nature. Though angered that Tristan had continued on with the subject, well past his express wishes that he should remain silent—fair man that he was, Sir

Richard knew he must now be inclined to hear him.

He gestured for Tristan to sit back down and then leaned forward, steepling his hands over the table. "You're telling me that Stuart attacked a woman?"

"Yes, my lord," Tristan answered, his body trembling at the opportunity set before him.

"Under normal circumstances, I would ask if there were any witnesses to this event, but as you've already conceded to having no proof, can I assume there are none?"

"Only the woman, herself."

Sir Richard leaned back in his chair, messaging his forehead. "With no other witnesses, it's just as likely she's lying as telling the truth. But you may bring her before me, and I'll hear her complaint."

Tristan grew silent—his palms sweaty—instantly realizing his confession was for naught. "She...um."

"Well?"

"She...refuses to accuse him...my lord."

Sir Richard let go a deep breath and shrugged his shoulders as if there was nothing further that needed to be said. "So, we're in the same place we were ten minutes ago—only now I doubt my nephew's honor, based on hearsay, and am in an ill-humor. And you wonder why I wouldn't hear you before."

"I understand, my lord. I apologize and yet, how could I keep it to myself? Every hour the knowledge of it plagues me, for this is the man Velena is to marry. A man without morals or scruples—a man who would strike her in a fit of rage."

Sir Richard's countenance was immediately changed. "He's struck her?"

Tristan's spirits rose for no more than a moment before once again, he realized he had nothing to offer. "He only raised his hand to do it. He didn't—but is this not a sign that he isn't in control—?"

"Or a sign that he is," Sir Richard corrected. "As you said, he didn't do it. I'll go out on a limb and assume it was Velena who told you of the incident. Did she say what incited him to anger in the first place?"

Tristan looked down meekly. "She was...defending our friendship. I told her never to do this again."

Sir Richard groaned. "Oh, my boy. It pains me to say it again, but the best you could do for her now is to leave. As soon as Stuart realizes he's not in competition for her hand, they'll find their peace with one another."

Tristan remained silent.

"I'm sorry, Tristan. I wish it were otherwise."

Shoulders slumped, Tristan rose and waited to be dismissed.

Sir Richard's insides ached. Surely all would be put back to rights once he was gone—but now there was doubt—and it nibbled at the back of his mind. "You may stay until the banns have been read," he said, and then after clearing his throat, he added, "If what you say is true, and you can get this woman to come to me before then…I…I give my word that I'll hear her."

"My lord?"

"I consider myself to be a fair man, Tristan—and I can see that you believe what you're saying. If her testimony is convincing, I'll question Stuart." He rubbed at his hip. "I'll question him anyway. For even if I deem it a lie, rumors of this sort would be most damaging. And for this very reason, you must say no more on the subject." It was then a thought dawned on him. "Have you told Velena any of this?"

"No," Tristan insisted, adamantly. "I wouldn't have her feeling trapped, if nothing would be done."

"Then keep it that way," Sir Richard said, leaving no room to doubt the seriousness of his words. "It's in my hands now."

"And God's."

Sir Richard smiled, though it wasn't exactly pleasant. "You have until the banns," he reminded him.

That gave him almost three days. "I understand," Tristan said, hope rising with every breath.

"And…"

"My lord?"

"If nothing comes of this, when you say goodbye to Velena, make sure she understands this may be goodbye…for good. For whether or not you find your brother—and I pray that you do—I'll ask that you stay in Oxford."

Tristan nodded, feeling orphaned in a way he'd not expected. "Then I have one more request before I go."

Sir Richard waited for him to continue.

"When first you asked me to stay, you offered to pay the rest of my way through the studium general[17]. I had no need of your money, but I know someone who does."

"Go on."

"You've been family to me. If I've been anything of the same to you, would you offer Squire Rowan a living in my stead. Velena told me of Lord Magnus' rejection of him, and it pains me, and if you'll take him on as your squire with the intent to knight him, I'll fund both his armor and horse."

"You're a good man to think of him, Tristan."

"Thank you, my lord. He's been a good friend."

"Your request is granted. You weren't the only one Lord Magnus vexed. There may have been no promises made for Rowan's knighthood, but I guarantee there were expectations. If he'll relinquish his use of him, which I don't foresee as a problem, I'll be all too happy to give him his living—as well as armor and a horse. Let it be a sign of what you've meant to us—and still do."

Tristan felt his throat begin to tighten. "You're most gracious, my lord."

"More than I ought, perhaps," he said with a small chuckle. "Half jester, half knight. One never knows what he'll get in a man like Squire Rowan."

---

[15]**Dais:** A raised platform used for a speaker, seats of honor, or a throne.
[16]**Demesne:** Land attached to a manor and retained for the owner's own use.
[17]**Studium generale:** Old name for a medieval university.

13

the banns

Floor length white tippets[18] trailed behind Velena with feminine type grace as she descended the staircase one step at a time, her hand running smoothly down the oil treated banister. She was dressed in a fur-trimmed, burnt-orange, fitted cotehardie with gold buttons and a bronzed plaque belt hanging low about her waist. The boat-shaped neckline flattered her chest and shoulders, and the veiled cylinder caul[19], hiding her rich dark hair, bespoke of the special occasion for which she wore it.

She looks like her mother. This was what Sir Richard thought, as he stood in the foyer watching her approach. His heart swelled with pride, even as he hoped he was doing right by her. If it weren't that this second arrangement of marriage would have been pleasing to his wife, he might have been tempted to break his contract with Magnus over lesser things, let alone an accusation of such proportions as Tristan aimed at his nephew.

Sir Richard had given Tristan the time he'd promised, but his time was up. No woman had come forward, and his accusation was left to linger as nothing more than a whim of Tristan's bitter imaginings. Still, Sir Richard could hardly believe Tristan would lie to him, which left only the possibility that he was right—or misinformed. He hoped for the latter, but for the sake of the former, had sought out to question his nephew.

But in all his years of holding manorial court, he never entertained an accusation with so little information as he'd been given. For the sake of his daughter he would, but when the moment came, he'd not even the name of an accuser with which to question him by.

There were moments Sir Richard regretted not having pressed Tristan for the name of the poor wench involved, but without her cooperation, it would've made little difference. There would be no proof, and without proof, Sir Richard would've appeared a fool to press Stuart for any sort of answer. He felt like a fool as it was—so he didn't pursue the matter. His only recourse was to council his nephew on the wisdom of a monogamous marriage, along with the virtues of fidelity and love.

With little else he could do, Sir Richard had determined to move forward with the banns, compelled to honor his wife's memory by honoring her wishes that Velena be a part of her brother's family—allowing whatever missteps Stuart might have taken to be left to the past—while keeping a close eye on his future.

Sir Richard stood—now with arms outstretched—as Velena descended the last step. "You look like your mother."

"It always makes me happy to hear you say that." She kissed her father's cheek. "I wish she could have been here today."

Sir Richard smiled as one with a great secret. "I think a part of her will be."

Velena's breath caught as he pulled from his pocket the necklace her mother had reserved for only the most special of occasions. It was a blood red ruby set inside a delicate filigree pendant, hanging from a solid gold chain. She could almost hear her mother's voice.

"It's very special", she would whisper. "Your father gave this to me on our wedding day, and someday when you marry…I'll give it to you."

Velena had been eight, but she could still remember watching it dangle from her mother's delicate fingers, feel it slip into the palm of her hands, just as her father did now.

Velena walked up to a front window, smiling at the memory as she let it dangle from the chain so that it might catch the light. It'd be to her, a small glimmer of joy in an otherwise sorrow-filled day.

"Shall I put it on?" Sir Richard asked.

"Please," she answered, still mesmerized by the ruby swinging beneath her fingers, light scattering across her face in tiny flecks of red. Turning around, she stood speechless as her father fumbled with the clasp of the chain, her hand holding the pendent in place. Her eyes drifted to the top of the staircase where Daisy finally appeared. Daisy—but no Tristan.

An hour later she was standing amidst her father, her uncle, and Stuart at the front of the church of St. Mary. It was there that the same motion that had caught her attention with the necklace, again took hold of her as she watched the pockmarked thurifer[20] baby-step his way down the center aisle of the church. Back and forth, back and forth…back and forth. Cupping the incense boat in his left hand, he swung a smoking gilt censer in his right.

Velena fingered the necklace at her throat, as the elaborately designed object flung its sanctimoniously sweet perfume in her direction. In curls and ribbons, the prayer evoking smoke rose from the brazen coals, wafting lazily towards the rafters. It smelled of frankincense and something else she couldn't place. Velena adjusted her stance, inhaled deeply, and then closed her eyes, wishing to catch another glimpse of her mother just behind her eyelids while for the next twenty minutes—kneeling or standing—she bore the extent of the prior's liturgy. Whether it be chanting, consecrating, petitions, or prayer—all were spoken in Latin.

Standing behind them was Sir Makaias with his mother and brothers. One of them cleared his throat, bringing her back to the present, but her attention didn't last long. She looked past the priest to the colored lights filtering in through the stained-glass windows. The light, combined with the voluminous amounts of incense, became a hazy sort of glow that came to rest down upon the small but pious congregation, a building much too large for the few in number the Pestilence had made of them.

When Velena became aware that the priest had begun the benediction, she bowed her head, but his words fell on deaf ears, for her heart's prayers were louder than any words that could escape the mouths of men. Indeed, her prayers were no meager patters of swirling incense lazily wandering the unseen paths towards Heaven, but great billows of silent groans rising from her soul to break open its very doors. Did not the Scriptures say to come boldly before the throne?

She asked Tristan to be here with her today, but he'd refused. How often had he ever refused her something? Less than she could count on one hand, so why now that he was leaving? *He's leaving…*

A pox on his head! She felt like stamping her foot. Hadn't she been brave enough to merit one last favor? Hadn't she kept her protests to herself—thinking of his well-being above her own—recognizing his need to go despite the part of her that felt like it was dying? But it was decided, and there was nothing for Velena to do but accept it. Tears pricked the back of her eyes, but she held them at bay, reminding herself that he promised to say goodbye. She'd cry then. She'd let her sorrow be known then—in front of her father, in front of her uncle— in front of Stuart. It'd be her last protest.

Opening her eyes, Velena turned around to catch a glimpse of Daisy standing in the back. She looked peaked. Velena caught her gaze and gave her an encouraging smile. Daisy returned it with one of her own, as well as a small spin of her slim finger, gesturing for Velena to turn back around to the front. Velena put on her most serious face her, grateful to have this small piece of Daisy returned.

Ever since their candid discussion of five nights past, Daisy had begun to come back to herself. And though she wasn't all she'd been before returning to Landerhill, Velena could see that she was putting forth an effort to re-engage with those around her, and this seemed more important than the undigested patchwork of information she'd come to accept as the truth of what had happened between Daisy and Stuart.

Once mass was over, Velena exited the church along with everyone else and stood quietly to the left of Stuart, mirroring a woman's place beside the rib of the man from whence she'd come. The priest raised his voice as he read the banns, publicly engaging them before all. Her insides flinched with every syllable.

When it was done, she rallied herself for Stuart's sake and smiled politely as they received the blessings of those surrounding them. She bowed her head and curtsied when necessary but was always scanning in the distance for Tristan. It was another who caught her eye. A fair-skinned woman, standing a head taller than any of her female peers, and with hair as dark as her own, weaved her way through the small crowd, raising her arm in greeting.

"Nenna!" the woman called out, not at all caring who should hear her speak so informal.

"Rainydayas," Velena cried, leaving Stuart's side at once. Daisy remained beside Sir Richard.

The women embraced. "I heard rumors you were still alive," Rainydayas said, looking down at her friend. "But as I'm not one for gossip, I thought I'd better come and see for myself."

"I'm overjoyed that you did. It seems that when the Lord removes a thing, He's faithful to provide a thing in its stead."

"I'm not sure what that means, but if I'm the thing provided than I'm happy to be."

"One of many. My brother's home!"

"I'm so happy for you," she said, grabbing her into another tight hug.

"Oh, Rainydayas, it's so good to see you. It seems a lifetime ago, does it not?"

"Indeed, it does."

"I've thought of you often."

"Then why haven't you come calling?" she said, placing her hands upon her hips, a wide grin stretched across her face."

"I couldn't even begin to tell you in one sitting about all of the distractions that have held me captive."

"I can see one of them, now," Rainydayas said, gesturing back in Stuart's direction.

Velena had only to cast a slight backward glance over her shoulder to see the perpetual look of pleasure still plastered all over Stuart's face as he accepted the congratulations of one after another. She turned back, not meaning to give the tight-lipped sort of grin that belies the truth of what someone is really thinking when they're trying to indicate something else entirely—but she did.

"Oh. I see," Rainydayas said, choosing to lower her voice, so as not to embarrass Velena in front of anyone who might hear. "You're not happy with the arrangement, I take it."

"I'm less inclined towards its eventuality...than I should be...perhaps. But I have been, and ever will be, in the will our Lord. And in that, I can still take joy."

"But for the marriage, itself?"

Velena lowered her head so that not even her lips could be read should someone be looking. "I'm resigned to it."

"Resigned? Was he not your childhood companion? I would have guessed that you'd make a good match."

Velena shrugged away what she couldn't presently explain and instead reached forward to grip her friend's hands. "Never mind any of that. We're both well—body and soul—and that's enough reason to celebrate. Furthermore, I'm desperate for a woman's company to divert my thoughts away from myself! I so need someone to..." Velena's voice trailed off as her eyes focused past Rainydayas' shoulder.

"What is it?" she said, turning around.

"I'm so sorry," Velena said, feeling an army of butterflies take flight within her belly. This was it. "You'll probably think me horribly rude, but I have to talk to that man."

Rainydayas lifted an eyebrow. "Is he one of your many *complications?*"

A brief shadow passed over Velena's face. "No," she answered honestly. "He's my friend."

"Go and talk with him then," she encouraged. "It looks as if he's waiting for you."

Velena hesitated. She looked back at Daisy, who had such a look of discomfort upon her face—as if the mere act of standing were a chore—that Velena's chest tightened. And if she wasn't already able to read Daisy's thoughts, her barely discernible shake of the head would have been enough to know that she disapproved of what she knew to be forthcoming.

Daisy could be as inconstant as the wind. One moment she hated Velena's friendship with Tristan, the next she expected him to be her savior—now back to disapproval. Perhaps, she was merely against her making a scene. Either way, Daisy would have to bear with her one more time, for this was quite possibly the last time—and she was determined.

Rainydayas' voice brought her back to present. "Go on. I'll wait."

"You really don't mind?"

"Only a little," she teased, "but not if I can steal you away from your father for the rest of the day. I wish to take you up on your invitation of invite without delay. Come and spend the day with me at my home, and we'll have all the time in the world to catch up."

Still holding hands, Velena and Rainydayas exchanged places, pulling away as they spoke until their fingertips at last parted.

"I'm afraid that tonight's banquet will cut 'all the time in the world' a bit short but speak with my father while I'm delayed. I'm sure you can arrange it."

With that said, their dark heads parted, and Rainydayas approached Sir Richard—and Velena, an awaiting Tristan.

---

[18]**Tippets:** A long, narrow strip of attached material hanging from a sleeve or hood.
[19]**Caul:** Close-fitting headdress.
[20]**Thurifer:** In Catholic ceremony, it's one who carries the censer.

14

letting go

Tristan straightened his legs in Augustine's stirrups and adjusted himself in his saddle for what felt like the hundredth time. He looked to the church several streets down, watching as the parishioners exited and gathered around Sir Richard and his daughter. The banns were handed to the priest, who in great pomp and circumstance, began reading aloud the intent of Squire Stuart and Lady Velena to be married, thus providing ample time for anyone to dispute the marriage should they so desire. This was why he stayed away. Even now, his stomach lurched as the crowd of onlookers clapped and cheered the upcoming union of the Baron's daughter to Lord Magnus' son. If only Daisy had come forward.

For the last three days, Tristan had shadowed her every step, pleading with her to see reason. But a more stubborn woman he never met, and she adamantly refused. She even went so far as to threaten him with a pair of cutting shears should he ask her again. It was then Tristan realized that if anything was to be done to stop Velena's marriage, it would have to be done without her. He knew his accusation of Stuart had brought strife to Lord Richard's home, but even so, he'd not repent of it. And if Sir Richard wouldn't allow him to return to Landerhill, he'd have to do all he could before leaving.

Tristan smiled as Velena embraced someone she seemed to be well acquainted with and became hopeful that she may have reunited with someone to whom she could confide. He watched her without hurry, trying to memorize her face and form, which was, at present, too far away to observe well—but no matter. He knew her movements and the way she carried herself. Other woman might parade themselves about with more poise and grace, but Velena had energy and spirit—and a beguiling sashay that could outdo them all. Tristan chuckled. He was surely going to miss her.

As soon as it appeared that she'd seen him, his heart beat faster for knowing what he had to do. Though she was still afar off, he raised his arm in greeting. He could see her pulling away from the dark-haired woman at her side. Now, she was walking towards him. He inhaled and held it several seconds before releasing his breath. *How am I going to do it, Lord?* He pressed his fingers against the spot where the letter rested beneath his jerkin. *How do I give this to Sir Richard and leave her to bear the burden of it alone? Will he even tell her?* He dismounted as she approached his horse. *How do I say goodbye?*

"Hello," Velena said, after Tristan declined to offer any first words.

Tristan smiled at her simple greeting. "How was the service?"

"I don't remember anything about it, actually."

"Was it dull—or did you just forget your Latin?"

"It could have been in Greek for as little as I paid attention," she confessed. "I kept seeing this image of us saying goodbye. I even had a whole torrent of tears saved up just for the occasion."

"I'd be flattered except your eyes seem quite dry at present."

"It does seem odd."

"Perhaps, you're still angry with me for not accompanying you to church?" he suggested, the corner of his mouth lifting slightly in jest.

Velena drew her hands up to her hips. "Yes," then down again "...and no." Her eyes swept back to High Street, to the road that would lead him away from Totnes. "I know why you didn't."

"Still, some tears would be nice," he said, a far-off look passing over his face as he followed her gaze. His insides twisted as his newly formed resentment began to surface. "You should ask Daisy for some. I dare say, she's had them in abundance."

Velena blinked at his unfeeling remark. "Tristan."

"I'm sorry," he said, taking in a deep breath. He knew it was wrong of him to feel the way he did, but he also knew that if she were only willing to come forward, this day could have been avoided. The Lord, himself, would have to remove his bitterness. He looked past Velena towards the church. "I think she'll finally be happy now that I'm gone, though."

"Don't say that. You know she cares for you...in her own way."

He nodded.

"Regardless," Velena continued, "remember to keep her in your prayers. I think she's ill."

"How so?"

"She's been in some sort of discomfort, and this morning, she barely made it to the chamber pot before retching. I should have made her stay in bed, but she assured me it was only spoiled meat. Yet, I ate of the same. I'm growing concerned."

"Well, for her sake, I hope it's as she claims."

"And if she grows worse?"

"Your care of her will be enough," he said, wondering if his persistence over the last few days had been the cause of it. "I think she's probably more weary of mind than anything else."

"I hope you're right." A moment went by as Velena's eyes drifted over his face, arms twisting behind her back.

He waited.

"I wish I could ask you to stay."

"You know I can't."

"When did we run out of time?"

He smiled, sardonically. "Time was always something we had a limited amount of."

He wanted her to know he was still praying for a way to come back, but as with all things, his intentions could fail. He could fail—and what were the plans of men in the hands of a wise God? Truly, last night had found him on his knees, struggling to submit to this and more.

Velena's spirit felt wilted, and her emotions unearthed. "I know you want to find your brother, but part of me can't help thinking that you're actually relieved to turn your care of me over to mine."

"That's not even close to being true."

She continued. "And though it'd hardly be wrong for you to do so—being that it was only by my request that you've stayed so long as you have and gained nothing but ill treatment for your troubles," her chin began to quiver, "it still hurts that you're leaving."

Tristan looked past her shoulder, surprised Stuart wasn't bounding up behind her, ready to pull her away. "You don't think it pains me to go? How can I reassure you when our time is nearly spent?"

"Tell me I haven't been a burden to you."

"We're all tangled up, Velena. Surely, you see that. Your burdens have always been my burdens…but never you." He pushed some pebbles aside with his foot. "Never *you*."

An ill awaited silence followed, each of them knowing what came next.

Tristan spoke first. "Velena, make me a promise before I go?"

"I'll make you a hundred."

"Just the one." He smiled, but it didn't last. "Don't let Stuart kiss you again—not until your…" he swallowed, "your wedding day." The words stuck in his throat, his heart crying, *may it never be.*

"Tri—"

"Please," he said, closing his eyes, lest her next words be in protest. "Please…just do this for me. You know he's had other women. Don't let him treat you like one of those. Make him wait."

Velena nodded her head as a wave of emotion washed over her. With blurred vision, she stared into his eyes, allowing Tristan time to see the tears that would follow.

"DON'T!" he exclaimed with more force than he intended. He'd startled them both and with wide eyes, she gaped at him. "Don't," he said again, laughing softly. "You know what happens when you cry." He lowered his voice to whisper. "Almost kissing you in private is one thing, but in public…?"

Recovering, Velena's hands came over her nose and mouth, and he could tell by her eyes that she was laughing. Swiping her fingers across her cheeks, she held them out for him to see. "Just a few."

He reached out to take hold of her hands, then remembered himself and pulled back. "I don't want you to get into any more trouble with Stuart," he said, rubbing his hands up and down his hips as if they needed a good wiping. "In fact, I'm not sure why he's allowed me to speak with you at all. Doesn't he still think I'm in love with you?" he questioned, clearly disgruntled that he might not.

She giggled. "Oh, he does…but he's finally come around to the idea that I don't love you. At least, he believes that I believe that I don't." Velena paused, appearing slightly confused by her sentence. She sniffed and used her tippet to wipe the moisture gathering at the end of her nose. "Though, he may still think I'm merely blind to it, which I can't really help."

Tristan rolled his eyes. "Well, if it makes you feel any better, you won't be the only one to be accused of blindness."

"Who accuses you?"

"Daisy. Says I'm the best thing for you, only I'm too blind to see it. Says if I marry you, it'll solve all your problems. What do *you* think of that?"

"I think your Isulte is alive and waiting for you…and would be very sad if you did. Find her. Make a home with her. It's your dream, and I wouldn't take that away for all the world."

Tristan shook his head, a sentimental smile sliding easily into place. "It's *your* dream for me."

"Then thank me when it proves true."

"Lovely thoughts, but I can't free you if I don't come back."

"Is that what you're planning to do? No, Tristan, please don't. As much as I don't want this to be the last time I see you, I want you to live your life. Untangle yourself and be free of my burdens. If you're to marry anyone, it must be your Isulte. And when it happens, send word, and I'll write to you so that you can see what the Lord has done in your absence. If God wishes someone else for me other than Stuart...then He'll do it."

"Then, I leave you in God's hands."

"It's where I've always been."

He nodded, acknowledging she spoke the truth. "Goodbye, Velena." He pressed his lips into a thin smile and made a half turn to leave, his movement broken as if he wanted to say more.

"Tristan, wait..."

Her voice pulled him back around, and it pained him to see just how lost she appeared in that moment.

"I just... I just wanted to say..." she paused to breathe, "your friendship has given me more happiness than I could ever have asked for. You were a light for me in a very dark time—and I'll always remember that."

Tristan ran his hands through his hair in a way Velena had seen a million times before, and it made her insides ache, believing she'd never see it again.

"You've been the same for me," he said with feeling. "I know it's sinful to say so, but in moments like these, I truly find myself wishing God was merely concerned with such things as our happiness. Alas, he's also about our holiness. And especially mine, for He'll have to do a great work in me if I'm ever to forgive Stuart should he hurt you."

"God has forgiven our sins, Tristan. Forgive because you've been forgiven."

Tristan smiled in disbelief, her courage and faith, once again, humbling him. She'd come so far from the frightened girl she used to be. "Do you forgive me for leaving?" he asked.

She took a ragged breath. "Only if you forgive me for letting you."

Tristan's smile faded, as the tears he'd been strong enough to hold back finally stung the back of his eyes. He nodded absently as the reality that he was, indeed, letting go of all control came crashing down upon his shoulders like a giant wave, and he felt as if he was losing his mother and sisters all over again. Velena had become his family, and not even the thought that Gwenhavare might be out there somewhere, still living, could assuage the grief he felt in this moment.

Suddenly remembering, he withdrew the letter he'd tucked away in his tunic. "Here," he said, placing it into her hands, "I almost forgot."

"Shall I read it now?"

"Oh, no...uh, it's for your father...actually. Just a few final words."

"Did you write one for me?" she asked, disappointment coating her words.

Tristan looked apologetic. "I tell you the truth when I say, I've written you a great many letters, though none that satisfied me enough to deliver into your keeping. I hadn't the words for it...not for this."

Velena gave a small nod.

"I...I did, however, copy down a piece of Scripture for you in your room. I was going to leave it for you to find later, but it's probably best you know it's there. It's short...but it sums up what I need you to remember."

It was then Tristan noticed Rowan approaching from behind Velena, Rainydayas by his side. A panic welled up inside him that he hadn't yet said enough—hadn't truly told her how much she meant to him. Suddenly, he began stumbling over his words in an attempt to hang on to their last bit of privacy. "If I could add to it now, I'd say that I want you to know that it's been my privilege to know you. And that...that through you, I have learned more about myself—and females in general," he chuckled, "than I ever would have on my own. Thank you for allowing us the opportunity to have such an honest friendship, for I have always been—and always will be—honest with you...even if it takes me a little while to get around to it. Remember that."

Velena knit her brow together at his last statement but was too overcome by his declaration to think more than a passing thought to any secondary meanings. "No more words," she managed to say just before Rowan overcame them, "or it'll be you who breaks my heart."

"Well, you're quite the spectacle," Rowan stated, coming alongside them. "Trying to stir up a bit of gossip before you leave, are we?"

Tristan looked towards his feet and smiled, but Velena bit her lip, steeling a glance over her left shoulder. "Is he upset?" she asked.

"Who—Stuart?" Rowan exclaimed, with much facetiousness, "Why should he be angry just because the woman he's supposed to marry is off talking alone with some other man that he just so happens to hate?"

"He hates him?" Rainydayas asked, her curiosity peeked.

"With the strength of a thousand suns," Rowan added for emphasis.

Rainydayas laughed in a way that belied the fact that she *did* laugh, and *would* laugh, at most anything spilling forth from Rowan's mouth, instantly reminding Velena of Rowan's confession that she was in love with him.

Rowan broadened his grin, obviously happy with the attention he received, despite his not returning her feelings. "But how rude of me. Lady Rainydayas, allow me to introduce to you Esquire Tristan Challener, son to The Challenger."

"Sir Tobias Challener," she said, her already large eyes growing rounder, "Well, that's quite the legacy."

Tristan looked surprised. "I'm surprised you know him by his name."

"My brother was a herald," she said, as though this explained everything.

"So," Rowan said, turning his attention back towards Velena. "This lady tells me she's received permission to steal you away. Are you going to keep her waiting? Give Tristan a kiss, Nenna, and let's be off with you.

"Don't tease me, Rowan. If there was ever a serious bone in your body, please bear the weight of your jests upon it now."

An honest look flitted across his face before he tossed it aside like the stone he now kicked with his shoe. "I wasn't in jest when I said you were stirring up gossip for yourself. I've come to save you—*again*."

"I don't mean for you to have to—"

"Cease," he said, shedding his sarcasm. "What would you have me do?"

Velena turned back towards Tristan, who had been all the while looking at her. "Tell me how to say goodbye."

Rowan smiled with an heir of superiority. "If closure is what you need, I can indeed supply it." With his back towards the church, he stretched his arms in both directions and pulled Velena and Tristan into his chest for a giant bear hug, hiding them behind his taller-than-average frame. There within Rowan's arms, Tristan rested his cheek upon Velena's head and she upon his shoulder. It was a small gesture—brief but poignant.

"Now push me away as if you're angry about it," Rowan said with a smile.

Though inwardly protesting, Velena was quick to comply, shoving herself away and taking several steps back. She even put her hands upon her hips to appear angry at the inappropriateness of his touch.

Rowan dropped his arms and laughed louder than he needed to. He had no qualms about accepting all the blame. He cared very little for what others thought, and only for what pleased him—and in this circle of friends, he found great pleasure. "You're getting good at this, Nenna. We should start a stage routine, you and I."

Rainydayas laughed despite the small pang of jealousy pricking at her heart, noting the open affection Rowan felt for her friend. That he would tease Velena was not a bother to her, only that he didn't share with her the same unguarded expressions.

Rowan slapped Tristan on the back before pulling him in tight to his side by the shoulders. "Time to go."

With a tight-lipped smile, and an apologetic look, Tristan gathered Augustine's reigns back into his hand and turned to follow Rowan.

"Where are you going, Rowan?" Velena asked.

Tristan answered for him. "Just to the edge of town...to see me off."

"Oh," was all Velena said, unashamedly jealous of whatever extra moments Rowan would have with him.

"Nenna," Rainydayas whispered at her side, softly pulling her attention away, "Come with me."

Allowing herself to be led, Velena fell into pace beside her friend, her eyes deep pools of green liquid as she stole several backward glances over her shoulder. Slowly, they made their way back towards the church and Velena's horse. "I suppose you must think I'm a terrible person for crying over a man who isn't to be my husband." She sniffed back her tears, no longer desirous that Stuart should see them.

"No," Rainydayas answered simply.

"I thought maybe you might have thought I was in love with him."

Rainydayas laughed. "No, I didn't think that either."

"Then you would be with the first not to."

"He is a man of character, is he not?"

"Yes, but how would you—"

"Rowan said so."

"Oh. But what has that to do with it?"

Rainydayas' mouth lifted into half a smile. "Women don't fall in love with men of character. If we did, the world would be a much better place, would it not?"

Velena gnawed lightly at her bottom lip in thought. Rainy had always adhered to a very individual perspective on life, which she kept safely tucked within neat and tidy little boxes of her own making, leaving her with a very definitive answer for any question she might be asked.

"Then whom do women fall in love with?" Velena inquired.

Rainydayas looked at Velena as though the answer was most obvious. "We aren't allowed to fall in love. We don't love our husbands and our husbands don't love us. We enter the state of holy matrimony as bitter people. Bitter people, begetting bitter children, which begets a bitter life for the next generation."

Velena scrunched up her forehead, "That's dreadfully cynical."

"What's cynical about it?" she asked with a straight face.

"You're assuming the worst about people. I have very little experience in the matters of love, myself—but I've known others who do it very well."

Rainydayas raised an eyebrow and gave a one-sided smile. "You think the best of everyone because you generally like people. I, on the other hand, hate people."

Velena cocked her head to the side, "You do not."

"I do," she said, matter of factly, "which is probably why I think the worst."

"I can think of plenty of people whom you've liked."

"Perhaps, but I hated them first," she said with a wry smile.

"Did you hate me?"

"Yeeeesss," she answered, long and slow as if addressing a child. "But not for as long as some." She laughed.

Velena rolled her eyes at the other woman's forthrightness.

"All, except for my current house guest," Rainy continued. "I liked her right away, which was a great surprise to me."

"You have someone staying with you?"

"Yes. I was in Oxfordshire the month before last with my Aunt Sabine and ran into the most interesting person."

"Oh, really. In what way?"

"You'll know when you meet her. We got along so well, in fact, that I asked her to stay with me indefinitely."

"She has no family?" Velena inquired.

"No one except her mother. Her husband died on the night of

their wedding, along with…well, I'm sure she'll tell you all about it someday but brace yourself, for it was quite morbid, really. I will say, however, that the baron she married was a horridly unpleasant man, so you needn't worry about being sensitive to her loss. She doesn't stand on pretense."

"None of us should," Velena said, stealing a final glance over her shoulder as they arrived back at the church. "There's no time for it."

Tristan and Rowan reached the edge of Totnes where they came to a halt. Sidestepping a pile of horse dung, Tristan turned to face him. "I suppose you'll be missing me," he said with a forced smile.

Rowan chuckled. "Things have definitely been more interesting with you around."

Tristan pushed out his lower lip, shaking his head. "Velena will keep things plenty interesting." He laughed, just thinking about her and her list of double standards. "You'll have to be sure to pay her plenty of attention while I'm gone."

"You know I'll be there whenever I need a good laugh."

"Knowing you, it'll probably be at her expense."

"She handles it well," Rowan retorted pleasantly.

"That she does…" Tristan's voice trailed off as he peered pensively down the familiar road he'd just come. "In all seriousness, Rowan, remember to look after her for me."

"I told you I would."

"And in case something happens, and I can't come back—"

"You'll be back," Rowan reassured him. "You told Sir Richard and—"

"And it came to nothing."

"Not so. It'll be like a fly buzzing about his ears. Believe me. He'll not be able to rest until he learns the truth."

"I'm hoping so, but just in case, I've left him a letter, letting him know it was Daisy who was violated. I'm hoping it'll make a difference."

"You should have told him that to begin with."

Tristan shook his head. "I wanted to give her the chance to come forward on her own before risking her reputation. This morning, I tried to persuade her one last time, and she pulled her dinner knife on me."

"She certainly has a bite."

"Yes, and, she's given me little choice now."

"Did you already give it to him?" Rowan asked, referring back to the letter.

"I asked Velena to."

He raised an eyebrow. "And, you trust her not to open it?"

Tristan smirked. "I'm hoping if it comes from her and not me, Sir Richard will feel the importance of knowing what I have to tell him."

"If only you could wield a sword as good as you do the art of manipulation."

"It's called logic."

"Well, I hope it works," he said, pulling at his earlobe. "In any case, I'll remain vigilant until then…and for some time after. When the time comes, I plan on taking my oath to Velena."

"Not to Sir Richard?"

"Him, as well. But this way, I'm certain of serving a good lady, who will most likely forgive all my misbehaviors…and hopefully grant me some land based on my looks and not my achievements, of which I have none."

"I just thank the Lord you'll be at Landerhill while I'm gone."

"Thanks to you as well, or so I've heard."

Tristan smiled. "When do you leave Craft Hall?"

"One more trip to gather my things, and I'll not look back. A pox on my uncle. If I'd known he'd never intended to knight me, I'd have found a way out from under him long ago."

"Well, it's done now."

"Yes, and now I can move on to bigger and better things," he said, rubbing his hands together.

Tristan watched in amusement as Rowan's mouth suddenly stretched into a wide, toothy grin. "Do I want to know what you're thinking?"

Rowan threw his head back and laughed. "What I've planned for Stuart is far better than a beating. Not only am I going to protect our dear, sweet and innocent little dove—I'm going to drive Stuart mad whilst doing it."

"You have my full attention."

Rowan rubbed his hands together enthusiastically, clearly aroused by his own idea. "I believe a little courtly love is in order."

It was now Tristan's turn to laugh. "Only you could think of something so absurd!"

"Only I could think of something so brilliant!"

Still chuckling, Tristan mounted his horse. "Indeed. That's what I meant. I just hope Velena is able to survive your version of vigilance."

"She'll *love* it," Rowan said, putting some space in between himself and the horse. "She used to love me, you know?"

"We all have our failings."

"Be gone," Rowan exclaimed, swatting Tristan's horse on the rump. "And God be with you," he called after him.

"And with you!" Tristan yelled back, turning around for one last look, but Rowan was already walking in the opposite direction. Shoulders squared and head set, his long-legged strides carried him back towards the church. Tristan turned forward and his spirit groaned. He knew Rowan hadn't spoken to Stuart since learning about Daisy, but he also knew he'd break silence sometime. Tristan only hoped he'd keep his head about him when he did.

15

thwarted

By the time Velena and Rainydayas reached the church, the crowd of people had dwindled considerably so that there was now no one in Velena's line of vision to block the look of displeasure overshadowing Stuart's face as they approached.

Velena remembered Tristan's letter and pressed it to her side, sliding it down her cotehardie until her fingers felt the hem of its pocket. She slipped it in, not wanting to chance any misunderstandings as to who it was intended for.

Rainydayas addressed Stuart first. "Good day, Squire Stuart," she said, clearly unruffled by his expression.

"Lady Rainydayas," he returned with a nod of his head, "it's good to see you well."

"In body and in spirit," she said, producing a small curtsy. "And fortunate enough to make a new acquaintance this day."

The muscles on the sides of Stuart's jaw twitched as he acknowledged her reference to having been introduced to Tristan. "A family friend," he said, forcing a smile.

"Then he's a person to hold dear, for in my experience friends have always proved to be of infinite more value than family."

"Squire Jaren has always been such to me," Stuart affirmed.

Rainydayas smiled. "Then I don't have to tell you what a loss it is to see a good friend go. And this Tristan fellow seems just the sort of person to whom one would want to stay. I'm sorry for you both."

To say that the air between husband and wife-to-be had grown suddenly awkward would've been a gross understatement. And it seemed to Rainydayas that she'd suddenly faded into the scenery as Stuart took a deep breath, obviously frustrated that Velena's goodbye to Tristan had even happened.

"Your sympathies must remain entirely with Velena, for to me, he was naught but a great interference."

Velena raised her chin. "As he is no longer with us, I would say that his *interference* is over."

Stuart feigned humor. "Much to your dismay, I assume. And I can only pray that his absence will now end any future aptitudes towards impropriety."

Velena's mouth hung slightly ajar, as Stuart had never dared humiliate her in public before, but it didn't take her long to recover, admitting to herself that she had, indeed, put him to the test this day. She cast aside his insult with an over-exaggerated sigh. "I remain by your side, do I not?"

"In body."

"Dear Cousin," Velena said, setting hands upon her hips. "As I cannot please you, have you anything else to say ere I depart?"

Finding a strange sort of enjoyment in their banter, Stuart crossed his arms and grinned, owning it was better to argue than to exist in a suspended place of quiet angst. He shook his head. "I yield...and apologize for my lack of decorum in front of our guest."

Lady Rainydayas ducked her head in acknowledgement.

Stuart continued. "Lady, ours is not going to be a marriage without its imperfections...as you can see."

Rainydayas smiled coolly. "I have a great tolerance for such things, my lord. If it pleases you to remember, I grew up with ten brothers. It could very well be said we were without anything akin to perfection at all."

Stuart rubbed at his nose and chuckled. "I remember them well. You must have grown quite a thick skin as a child."

"Truly. And as a consequence, I'm not easily offended nor put off by others. Not even you," she said with a wry smile.

"I'm happy to hear it. Sir Richard has conveyed to me Velena's desire to visit with you this day. Afterwards, if you find you still have stomach for more, we look forward to your presence at tonight's banquet."

"I have stomach for both your food and your company. You will find me most pleased to banquet with you this evening."

"Very good," Stuart said, feeling the mood lighten as he turned his attention back to Velena. "Until then, we best not waste the day,"

Velena nodded as she looked around. "Where's my father?"

Stuart nodded towards the church doors. "Back inside with a few others to discuss this business of raising sheep."

"Not the most stimulating of conversations," Rainydayas said wryly.

Stuart shrugged. "Perhaps not, but it's to be our livelihood, so you'll have to excuse me as I intend to join them. I only waited to see Velena off." *And to make sure she didn't get it into her head to sidle up behind Tristan on his horse and make a break for it,* he thought ruefully.

"I shan't disturb him then," Velena said. "I thought to say goodbye before I left, but if you'd please do it for me, it'll be well enough."

Stuart nodded. "Your father will send for you when it's time. I'll come, myself, if I can." He then took up one of Velena's hands and laid a kiss to the backs of her fingers, smiling his own goodbye as he let his gaze travel down the length of her body, admiring the lovely figure standing before him. He'd won, and he warmed with the knowledge that Tristan was finally gone. Who was left for him to contend with now?

Just then, Daisy rounded the corner from somewhere around back of the church. He dipped his head towards Rainydayas and turned away, ignoring her as he entered the priory, the doors making a definitive thud as he disappeared within.

"My lady," Daisy said, a look of concern alighting upon her face. "I didn't know you'd returned. My apologies if you had to wait."

"Not at all, but where have you been off to?"

"I…was talking with the healer. I told her of my stomach upset, and she took me back to her house and gifted me with…some herbs. She lives only that way," Daisy said, pointing behind her.

"That was kind of her," Rainydayas said, in surprise. "I heard last week that she'd drowned a new litter of kittens, and I thought to hate her for it. But—I suppose kindness to people trumps injustice to animals," she finished with a sigh. "I suppose I'll have to warm up to her, now."

Velena exchanged a look with Daisy, which almost set her to laughing, but she maintained her composure, instead saying, "Daisy, I'm going to visit with Lady Rainydayas, but I'd really rather *you* go back to the manor and rest. It'll give you an opportunity to take those herbs."

Daisy looked apprehensive. "You don't mind?"

"I insist," she said, coming forward to peck Daisy on the cheek. "Oh, but I'll need you to do something for me later," she said, reaching into her pocket. "When my father gets home, give him this."

"Who shall I say it's from?"

"It's from Tristan."

Daisy's countenance stiffened, though her smile remained doggedly in place. "From Tristan?"

"Yes."

"Did he say if it was important?"

"If she asked you to do it then it's important," Rainydayas said, as if addressing an unlearned child, clearly irked by Daisy's failure to obey without question.

Velena intervened, as Daisy looked about ready to slap her. "She's merely asking if it's better to take it in to him now. And, no, there's no hurry," she said addressing Daisy again. "It's naught but some last words. You may even leave it on his desk if you'd like."

Daisy continued to stare at Rainydayas as if she wanted to box her ears.

"You may leave and take your rest," Velena encouraged, drawing Daisy's eyes back to herself. "I'll need you to help me change for tonight." She touched Daisy's arm, giving her a look of apology as she left her there by the church to make her way home. She'd speak with Rainydayas about her treatment of Daisy once they were out of earshot.

A short distance away, Velena collected Guinevere by the reigns as they headed for Rainydayas' home on foot.

Daisy brushed her hand along the wall of the church as she rounded the corner. The stones were rough, and in some places sharp, scratching her fingertips as she moved along. Assured she was alone, she leaned her back against the aged building and held Tristan's letter out before her.

She stared at it. She turned it over repeatedly. She rubbed her thumbs over its surface. She toyed with the edges of its seal. The wax was smooth. It wouldn't take much to…

Daisy's breath caught as a small section broke free of the parchment. She exhaled slowly, popping it back the rest of the way. Hands frozen, Daisy envisioned the mournful gaze of the Virgin Mary looking down on her with disapproval. "Forgive me," she whispered.

Velena would have told her that the Lord's mother had no power to do so, but she hadn't the courage to ask it of the Christ child. Too late to go back now, she opened the letter, scanning its contents for what she hoped wouldn't be there—but it was as she suspected. For days, Tristan had been hounding her to confess Stuart's misdeed to Sir Richard. Every day, he'd come asking her this, and every day, she'd refused. And now this. Tristan might have left, but the moment Velena had told her this was his letter, she'd known in her heart he hadn't given up.

Refolding it quickly, she shoved it deep within her pocket. But no sooner had she done so, then a voice caused her to jump.

"From anyone I know?" Rowan asked, meandering towards her, a long piece of grass hanging out the corner of his mouth.

Startled, Daisy wanted to run, lest the letter somehow fly out from her pocket and give her away, but she knew better and stood her ground.

"Squire Rowan, you…you startled me."

"Unintentional, I assure you. I was merely passing by. I didn't mean to interrupt you from reading your—"

Daisy wiped her palms down the sides of her surcoat. "Oh, no, it's nothing. It's…from family."

"Are they well?"

"As well as can be expected."

"Good…" He hesitated. "Actually, Dimples, I'm glad I ran into you because—"

"I don't like it when you call me that," she interrupted.

Rowan smirked. "I have a feeling you wouldn't like anything I called you—including your name. But…" he cleared his face of all humor, "I apologize."

"You apologize?" her eyes narrowed. "What ails you, Squire? Has your quick wit grown tired of running its mouth?"

"Today it has," he rocked his head from side to side, "if only in this moment. Minutes from now who can tell," he said, glancing absently towards the horses.

"I have no desire to banter with you. Is there something you need?"

"Just a moment of your time, if you'll allow it."

"I'm actually feeling rather unwell at the moment." She began to turn away from him. "I was about to go back to the manor to take my rest, so if it could wait until—"

"I'll be quick," he assured her. "I'd like to speak with you *before* the banquet."

She sighed, feeling she'd be rid of him no other way. "Very well. If it's quick."

"I'll do my best," he said, maintaining his serious demeanor. He ushered her towards a pair of headstones nearby—just two of the many that side of the church.

He stood opposite her as she sat on a particularly low one, forcing herself to relax. He had no way of knowing what she'd done. Again, her stomach churned. The dried grass beneath her tunic pricked at the ankles of her stockings, and she curled her toes within her shoes, fighting for an unexpected bout of nausea to pass. "You had something to say?" she asked, noting the way he stared.

"You look pale, Daisy. Are you well?"

"I told you I wasn't."

"So you did," he apologized, "and I promised to be brief. I wanted to be the first to tell you that Sir Richard has seen fit to bring me under his care for the remainder of my squire training."

Daisy looked surprised. "At the manor?"

"In the barracks."

"But with us—with us at Landerhill."

He nodded. "Clearly, this bothers you, which is why I wanted to tell you, myself."

"I didn't say I was bothered. But why would your uncle let you go?"

"He had no intention of knighting me, and Sir Richard has been most generous in his offer to do so. Besides, my uncle was all too happy to be rid of me, I think."

Daisy looked smug. "I wonder why."

Rowan gave her a sardonic smile. "This brings me to my other topic. I wanted you to know that while I'm there, I have every intention of leaving you alone."

"I don't know what you mean," she said, looking down.

"I think you do," he said, taking his seat on the headstone across from her, his long legs just shy of brushing the ends of her knees. "I've made sport of you on more than one occasion. I thought myself playful, but I'm not too proud to admit I've been offensive."

Daisy looked doubtful. "And what brought you to this change of mind?"

Leaning forward to rest his arms upon his thighs, he looked her steady in the eye, deciding at that moment to be honest. "Tristan told me what was done to you."

He might as well have punched her in the face. Daisy felt light-headed. She closed her eyes, as a wave of embarrassment threatened to topple her over. Bowing her head down to her knees, she held tightly to her skirt, feeling the letter stiff at her thigh.

"How could he?" she mumbled.

"How could he not?" Rowan asked, taking a step towards her, crouching down upon his haunches. He ducked his head to look into her face. "Do you think me so unfeeling?"

She sat back up. "Yes—I think it. You, who keep me always in your line of vision—who winks and touches what he should not. Because I've been taken by one man doesn't mean I make myself available to another."

"I'll never touch you again."

She laughed with derision.

"My flirtations will cease, I swear it. I offer you my friendship…and my protection."

"Why should you bother? You've never thought of anyone but yourself."

"Let's just say, my concern happens to be a little further reaching at the moment."

Daisy rolled her eyes. "If you tell anyone about Stuart, I'll deny it."

"You didn't deny it to *me*," he said, a small tick bringing up one corner of his mouth.

"I should have." She glared at him. "What are you smiling at?"

"I'm just glad you don't hate me as much as I thought you did." Standing to his feet, he held out his hand to help her up.

She looked around. Navarre and another page were just then walking past. Was that a wink she saw pass between them?

She stood, unaided. "You said you'd not touch me," she reminded him.

"So I did," he said pulling back his hand. "See how easily I acquiesce?"

Daisy's lips pressed together.

"You give me that look, but you'll soon learn you can trust me." He lowered his voice. "I mean to protect you, Daisy. Should you need me—for anything at all—you need only to ask."

Daisy's eyes flitted from his face to his feet to his face again. His eyes were sincere, the set to his jaw unwavering. Would she be a fool to trust him? "I need you to save Velena's life without ending mine."

He blinked, realizing the true extend of the burden Tristan had left him with.

She looked him in the eye, a cool breeze pulling a wisp of golden hair loose from beneath her veil. "It was the same with Tristan. He was never so concerned for me as for Velena," she finally said.

"Not true," he pointed his finger at her. "It was concern for you that kept him from naming you to Sir Richard in the first place."

Daisy felt the weight of Tristan's *concern* like a stone in her pocket— once a threat, now fodder for her fire. "A nice sentiment...but it comes up short."

Rowan's eyes grew soft. "Then allow me to go the distance. If God will grant me the means...I'll save you both." Hands at his sides, he bowed his head and walked away.

16

baroness ladawn

Rainydayas hooked an arm around Velena's shoulders and pulled her close as soon as they gained some distance from St. Mary's. "I'm sorry if I made things worse for you with Stuart. I tend to speak out of turn."

Velena smiled sadly, briefly leaning her head into her friend's shoulder. "If anything, I made things worse for myself...though I admit he was more tolerant than I expected."

"Still."

"No, sincerely, it'll be alright. If you must regret anything, let it be your words to Daisy. She may be my maid—but she's as close as a sister. You mustn't speak to her the way you did."

Rainy dropped her arm, silent for a moment. She sighed aloud. "Alright. I accept your reproval. I may be quick to judge, but I'm also quick to change."

"Thank you," Velena said, truly relieved. They continued walking. "I don't suppose you knew what sort of a mess you were walking into this morning."

Rainydayas raised her eyebrows. "Not upon arrival, but putting what pieces I have of the puzzle together, I'm sure I know more than you think."

"What do you know?"

"I know you were engaged to Peter when you left Totnes and that he died of the Pestilence while you were away. I assume your friendship with this Tristan person began at your father's castle and that when Stuart went with Lord Magnus to fetch you...he found the competition most unpleasant."

"How did you know Stuart came to Wineford?"

"Everybody knew. My dear friend, Totnes is only half what it used to be. Not much goes on that another hasn't heard about by midday—

and everyone knew that Squire Stuart wanted to take his brother's place."

Velena's eyes rounded. "I suppose what I should be asking is if there's anything you don't know."

"How long were you at Wineford before you learned of Peter's death?"

"Three years. I knew nothing of it until Stuart's arrival."

"Then assuming you thought Peter was alive all that while—or might be—had you any checks on your friendship with Tristan due to your betrothal to another?"

"There wasn't a need. My father treated him as a son, and he was to me as a brother."

"But to Stuart, a threat?"

"Yes, though there was no need for such jealousy." Rainydayas gave no argument, though from her expression, Velena felt she disagreed.

"I know *you* don't love Tristan—but does he love you?"

"No. I mean, yes. But it's not...it's not the sort of love one marries for."

"And what kind of love does one need for that when most are bound to marry for no love at all?"

Rainydayas didn't wait for an answer, but continued speaking along the same vein of thought, allowing Velena time to contemplate her meaning until they reached South Street and the steps of Rainydayas' narrow two-story home sandwiched in between two others just like it.

"I'm sorry I gave your maid grief over the letter," Rainydayas suddenly said.

Velena looked surprised she should bring it up again.

Rainydayas shrugged. "I've had time to think on it, and I didn't mean it before as much as I do now."

Velena shook her head in amusement. "Well, I forgive you twice then. It means a lot to me that you should like her.

"I'll do my best," came Rainydayas' genuine reply as they took their first steps towards the front door.

Velena entered Rainydayas' home, blinking her eyes until they adjusted to the dim lighting within. It didn't take her long to realize how bare the entry room was. There were no tapestries, no portraits, no decorations or ornamentation of any kind except for a few empty tables and a stained rug.

"What's happened here?"

Resting her hand upon her hip, Rainydayas pursed her lips as she surveyed her own home as if seeing it for the first time. "Pitiful isn't it? It was ransacked during our absence. My family stayed in Totness for the first year of Plague before convincing father it'd be in our best interest to take refuge in Oxford with Auntie Sabine."

"I wouldn't have thought Oxford would have proved any safer."

"Yes, well, my aunt's house isn't exactly in Oxford proper, but in Oxfordshire county, half-a-day's ride from the nearest church. Anyway, it was only six of my good-for-nothing brothers that accompanied us. Two stayed behind with their families and two were left behind to protect that which would stand to be lost otherwise—namely, our home. Unfortunately, while we were away, they allowed it to be overrun with their friends, opening it up for parties, orgies—and only God knows what else, as if there could be anything worse," she raised an eyebrow, "but with them, one should never underestimate. They ate everything, drank everything, broke everything—and urinated on everything else…" Rainydayas' voice trailed off, more annoyed than angry.

Velena took a fresh look at the stain on the rug and grimaced. "My uncle said people were living as such, but I didn't want to believe it."

"Accept our home as proof."

"Where is your family now?"

"Liam and Jonathan, who'd stayed with the house, are dead—and as far as I'm concerned, good riddance. While at my aunt's, my father died of an infection, and my mother…well, she committed suicide after receiving word that Bently died of the Plague in the bed of some stripe-hooded harlot—which was actually quite fitting, as Bently was born of a tryst[21] that we all pretended not to know about."

Velena could only stare. "You've grown callous."

"But not you," Rainydayas said, looking down at her friend.

Velena shook her head. "By God's grace."

Rainydayas exhaled slowly, "I suppose, with ten brothers, I was used to being practically invisible. I used to resent it…but now I just wish for it to remain so. Five of my younger brothers have chosen to remain in Oxfordshire, leaving me in Totness with only my elder brothers, Robert and Leon. They allow me to do as I please so long as I don't interfere in their business. So, for once in my life, I answer to no one."

"What's their business?"

"Drinking too much—and thievery. If you ever happen to see them…turn and go the other way."

"Do they care so little for you?"

Rainydayas laughed. "Possibly even less than that. If they cared at all, they might have at least brought over a few new furnishings from all their spoils."

Velena giggled. "Yes, but then you'd have to explain to Tilda Borrows why you had her best tumblers the next time you had her over."

"I hadn't thought of that," Rainydayas said. She narrowed her eyes, then smiled. "Oh, don't worry for me, Nenna. I'm unmarried and my own woman. Who ever heard of such a thing?"

"Will you remain unmarried?"

"No," she said with a crooked smile, "I intend on marrying Squire Rowan as soon as he attains knighthood…and as soon as I can convince him to ask me."

Velena laughed before she could think better of it.

"You don't think I'm serious?"

"On the contrary," Velena said, grinning, "I believe you mean every word—though you'll have your work cut out for you."

"I'm a patient woman."

"Still, there will be hurdles to overcome."

"If you're talking about the expense of his knighthood, I'm quite prepared. If his uncle has no plans to do it, then I shall pay his way."

"You have money?"

"Enough."

"Enough to replace your furnishings?" Velena asked, sweeping her hand to indicate the bare room.

"Unfortunately, it's one or the other—but all in good time."

Velena gave a tight-lipped grin, recalling her conversation with Rowan while they were still at Wineford Castle and wondered if Rainydayas knew that Rowan didn't return the strength of her affections. "And what of love?" she asked.

"The love of an honest friendship may not be enough for some, but it is for me."

Velena didn't have long to contemplate Rainydayas' answer before she was ushered down the hall and above stairs to the second level of her home.

They stopped in front of a closed doorway, and with her hand still upon the handle, Rainydayas turned to Velena, a great deal of satisfaction in her eyes. "The truth is even if I could've redecorated by now, it'd matter very little for I never spend any time in the front room. I do, on the other hand, spend nearly every waking moment in here, so I think you'll find it much more to your liking."

The anticipation of a smile played across her face as Lady Rainydayas opened the door and stepped aside for Velena to enter. The room was of medium size. It had wooden floors sprinkled with rushes and sweet-smelling thyme. Velena enjoyed the pleasant aroma as she eyed the plastered walls—decorated in a vivid colored floral fresco—and the large framed window adorned with bright green shutters.

Secured open, it let in the full light of day, resplendent in long trails of swirling particles, which streamed across a smooth rectangular wooden table standing center of the room. There, the light came to rest upon a very feminine and manicured hand working various stokes of charcoal across a large piece of parchment paper.

The hand paused, and the woman glanced up. She had a heart shaped face framed in a wine-colored wimple[22], which wrapped beneath her chin and up over her head, fully concealing her hair. Velena noticed that, like herself, the woman had green eyes, as well as an open expression that immediately disarmed Velena of any reservations she might have had upon meeting someone so lovely.

"Baroness LaDawn, I'd like to present to you Lady Velena Ambrose. Lady Velena—Baroness LaDawn."

Velena immediately lowered her eyes, giving a slight curtsy as the woman rose to her feet. "It's a pleasure to meet you, Baroness."

"Oh, no," she protested, waving her hand in dismissal. "Please, I'm Gwenhavare—or Lady Gwenhavare if you cannot bring yourself to be so informal."

"You care not for your title?" Velena asked, as Rainydayas turned to give some instructions to a boy appearing just outside the door.

Gwenhavare's mouth curved into a smile. "Only because it's a title I barely own. It's in dispute, as we speak," she said, gesturing to the chair across from her.

Velena sat down. "Who disputes it?" she asked boldly.

"The son of my deceased husband. You see, my marriage had no time to be consummated before his death, and so his son is now seeking his rights over his father's fortune."

"I'm sorry," Velena said, stealing a peek at the sketch in front of Lady Gwenhavare.

"I'm not overly concerned," she replied. "He was only a stepson from a previous marriage, himself, so I don't believe his case is any stronger than my own."

"I'm glad of it. Though, I meant…that I was sorry for the loss of your husband," Velena said, now looking her directly in the face.

Gwenhavare cocked her head to the side, a thoughtful expression flickering behind her eyes. By the time she smiled, it was sincere. "I thank you."

Rainydayas rejoined them at the table. "Timothy will bring us some refreshments. What have I missed?"

"Nothing you don't already know, I'm sure—but if I may change the subject to this sketch…" Velena said pointing to the upside-down portrait across from her. "How intriguing…"

Gwenhavare smiled broadly. "It's nothing, really. I draw only for my own pleasure."

"You're too humble," Rainydayas chided. "Your sketches are brilliant! She did one of me just the other day. Here, I'll show you," she said rising from her seat to fetch it off a much smaller table in the corner of the room. She laid it before Velena.

Once again, the medium used was charcoal. The lines and smudges ranged from very dark black to the lightest of smoky grays, blending together in the most harmonious movement across the paper to create an almost perfect likeness of Rainydayas.

"Amazing," Velena said, hovering her fingers just above the lines. "You truly have a gift. How did you learn such an art?"

Gwenhavare looked down lovingly, clearly admiring it as one gazing down upon her own child. "Much practice," she whispered.

"She's self-taught," Rainydayas boasted of her friend.

Velena shook her head in wonder. "Who's this you're drawing now?" So far, it was fairly indistinguishable, mostly just shapes and shadows—the beginnings of a man's face, she thought. The eyes looked familiar.

"Oh, this," Gwenhavare said, growing slightly self-conscious. "It's someone I used to know…but it's difficult to draw someone's portrait when they're not in front of you."

"I thought perhaps it was your husband," Velena said, unsure why she wanted to know.

"No…a friend. Well, not even a friend—more of an acquaintance, really. Something about his eyes continually draws me back to paper—but I can never get them right."

Velena let her thoughts turn to Tristan for the first time since entering the room. He had wonderful eyes. Her chest felt tight. She told herself she shouldn't continue to probe—but she asked, "Was it someone you loved?"

Not bothering to look up, Gwenhavare continued to smile down at the half-done portrait. "No," she said honestly. "Though I fancy I could have...given different circumstances. He seemed an interesting sort of man, though not your average sort, by any means. At first, I thought him rather awkward, but he was also kind, witty, well-thought—and honest. But I was at least three years his senior, so I felt a little silly giving him any serious consideration."

"Age has nothing to do with love," Rainydayas remarked as the boy she called Timothy entered the room with food and drink.

He set the platter down upon the table, obliging Gwenhavare to gather her drawings up and out of the way. "Will there be anything else, my lady?" he asked.

"Yes," Rainydayas said. "Timothy, how old are you?"

"Me...my lady? I...I don't rightly know. My mum died when I was real little, and I don't think my sire remembers too good. I figure I'm about fifteen."

Rainydayas rolled her eyes. "Next time someone asks, just say *fifteen,* and skip the story about your parents. Not many people desire so long an explanation. Now then, Timothy...if a woman loved you who was...age eighteen, let's say, could you be persuaded to love her in return?"

"Love her, probably...but marry her—not likely."

"How cheeky. And why is that?" Rainydayas, demanded to know.

"Well—if I were to marry a woman that much older, as I see it, she'd be inclined to think she was my mother. And I don't see as how I could discipline her then—if ever there was a time that called for it. She'd not likely take a beating from me without giving one in return."

Velena inhaled sharply, covering her hand over her mouth to hide her smile. Rainydayas and Gwenhavare, however, burst into fits of laughter that continued on until Timothy grinned stupidly, as though he'd said something awfully clever.

Catching her breath, Rainydayas dismissed him, calling out to the lad as he left that she would now be calling on him whenever she felt the slightest bit melancholy, which seemed to suit him just fine.

"Another person I've decided to like," Rainydayas declared, happily. "What an honest lad. I shall keep him around for always, I think."

Velena smiled—and then without warning gushed out an unexpected sob. She covered her mouth as tears made tracks down her cheeks. "I'm so sorry," she said, wiping them away before anymore could fall. Looking up, she took a deep breath through her nose before letting it out through her mouth. She did this more than once and managed to hold the rest of her emotion in check, though her eyes remained glassy.

Gwenhavare looked on with both confusion and compassion. "Whatever have you to be sorry for?"

"She had to say goodbye to a dear friend, today," Rainydayas answered for her, reaching over to touch her hand. "And she's bound this day to a man she doesn't want to marry. It's a bit too soon for true gaiety, perhaps."

Velena choked out a laugh at her friend's direct manner, not at all upset she'd just offered up her most personal information to a stranger.

"Still, she's in desperate need of cheering up," she added.

"You poor thing," Gwenhavare said, sincerely. "What can be done for you?"

"Nothing," Velena said slumping back in her chair. "I thought I was alright but have found that I'm capable of tears whenever I least expect it." Frustrated with herself, she wiped again at her eyes.

Gwenhavare nodded in understanding. "Well, I can tell you from experience…tears are never obedient. They neither come when we want them, nor stay away when we don't, but you'll always be able to use them to your advantage…for they have the loveliest effect on your eyes."

Velena giggled, at Gwenhavare's attempt to lighten the mood. "We share the same color," Velena said.

Gwenhavare wrinkled her nose. "Don't be absurd," she said, raising her voice a pitch higher. "Mine are more grey than green. No— yours are like a grassy field or…or an emerald. Furthermore, set against the dark color of your hair—they're quite stunning. I can't help but be jealous. My hair is a very drab shade of brown."

Velena smiled. "I'm sure it's not."

"No, really, it is," Rainydayas agreed.

Gwenhavare rolled her eyes, though without offense.

"What color would you wish it to be?" Velena asked, feeling herself drawn back into a good humor.

"Red," she said without hesitation.

Velena and Rainydayas both laughed.

"I do *not* jest. I'm positively in love with rich and vibrant colors. Once when I was little, my mother made a dress for one of my dolls, dyed red with beet juice. Even then, I remember thinking that someday I wanted hair of such a color. I even tried sneaking into the kitchen to find some beets to boil but was caught before I had the chance to try it. Just as well," she laughed, "I probably would've scalded myself trying."

"I have beets!" Rainydayas announced loudly. "We should do it. We should color your hair, Gwenny. What say you to that?"

Gwenhavare pursed her lips in thought, looking slyly in Velena's direction. "Would it cheer you up to see my hair as red as my dolly's dress?"

Thinking back to the time Tristan had chased her around the house trying to cut her hair, Velena couldn't believe she would be so brave as to dye it, herself. Again, she felt the prick of tears behind her eyes but willed them away. She breathed deeply through her nose and lifted her chin. "I think it actually would—though don't do it on my account. I wouldn't want you to regret it the next time you saw your hair down."

Rising to stand, Gwenhavare laughed, as though at her own joke. "Oh, I shouldn't worry about that," she said, unpinning her wimple. The scarf fell away to reveal, perhaps, a finger's length of hair growth in all directions. "I haven't got anything to let down, you see."

Velena failed to hide her shock. "What happened?"

"Her mother," Rainydayas said plainly.

Velena looked incredulous. "She cut your hair?" she asked, watching Gwenhavare retreat somewhere inside herself for the briefest of moments.

"No. She tried marrying me off again, despite my being opposed to it. So, I made myself unpresentable by cutting it, myself," she said, squaring her shoulders in a way Velena was sure she'd done for her mother the day she'd been so brazen as to defy her.

Velena had a hundred questions but could think to ask only one. "Had she chosen a cruel man?"

Gwenhavare shook her head. "There was just so much...so much death." She closed her eyes. "Whether you loved someone or whether you didn't...it didn't matter. To me—marrying a man was the equivalent of marrying a corpse. Death was inevitable, and...I...I wanted nothing to do with husbands...or children. Who could know if the Plague was truly gone?" She cringed at a memory. "I knew many a mother, who left their children behind in their effort to live whilst those around them were dying. How could anyone live with themselves, knowing they'd done such a thing. I thought it better to be alone, lest I discover I was the same breed of coward."

Rainydayas left her seat to wrap an arm about her shoulders, her silence bespeaking her sympathies.

Gwenhavare gave her a warm smile and then turned to Velena who'd been watching her intently. "I know it sounds absurd. You're probably thinking I've taken leave of my senses," she said, her eyes burdened in a way Velena could fully understand.

Could it really be that I've never known this woman before today? Velena mused, feeling close to her in a way she didn't expect. Maneuvering around the table to stand before her, Velena took her hand. "Not even the smallest part of me thinks so," she whispered. "For there isn't a person left alive, who can say they've not been burned by the touch of death. *That* is the absurdity—is it not?"

Gwenhavare's face relaxed into a grateful smile, and she squeezed Velena's hand in return. "Rainydayas has very good taste in friends, I think," she said, warmly. "Now...let's make my dolly's dress jealous, shall we?"

Rainydayas smiled her approval, as they all turned in pursuit of the door. "Ahh!" she squealed, running back to the table. "We almost forgot the wine," she said, gathering up the flask and glasses into her arms. "We'll need this, if we're to follow through on such a plan."

Velena and Gwenhavare giggled, helping to displace the goblets from her arms lest she drop them. *Could this be You, Lord...*Velena thought as she trailed after them into the hallway, *staying me in this time of grief?*

Gwenhavare paused to link arms with her, bringing Velena a deeper sense of His peace. *I see Your hand in it,* her heart whispered, *and I thank You. I couldn't have borne it for long.*

---

[21]**Tryst:** A romantic meeting between lovers.
[22]**Wimple:** A head covering made of cloth, worn around the neck and chin.

17

another tristan

Bending over a basin positioned in a corner of Britton's bed chamber, Makaias pushed his sleeves up to his elbows and splashed water over his newly-shaven face and head. Coming to full height, he vigorously rubbed his hand back and forth over what hair was left, flinging excess beads of water across the floor.

"I don't want to go," Britton said, sitting at the end of his bed with his legs spread and hands dangling between his knees.

Makaias smirked as he pushed down his sleeves. He brushed them smooth with the backs of his hands and then reached for his jerkin; the brushed leather fit comfortably snug over his well-muscled chest. "Because you have to wear a blindfold or because you've no more hair than a wee babe at its mother's breast?"

Britton ran a self-conscious hand over his head and frowned at the half inch of fuzz still left him. "Both."

Makaias scooped up Britton's jerkin and tossed it in his lap. "Come on—for your sister. You can't stay hidden away forever. It's only hair."

Britton muttered a curse and then set to dressing himself blindfolded.

"Look on the bright side," Makaias teased, "you could be blind, bald…and smell like dung."

"And I would, too, if that healer had anything to do with it. Good heavens," he said, fumbling with his buttons.

"You've got them lined up wrong," Makaias said, helping Britton correct his error. He chuckled. "She'll be angry when she finds out you forewent using her *recipe*."

Britton scowled. "If men were meant to have dung on their faces, we'd be using the garderobe[23], standing on our heads."

Makaias didn't argue, waiting patiently for Britton to finish his ablutions[24] before leading him from his solar. By the time he strolled into the great hall with Britton by his side, the room was already hot and muggy from too many bodies. To gain some ventilation, the windows had been secured open, allowing the evening air to mingle with the aroma of fresh meat and sweet-smelling rushes newly added to the floor. Esteemed manor folk and guests, all dressed in their finest, filled the two long tables set perpendicular to the dais. Each table was draped in elegant linens and decorated with garden flora and high-stick candles. Small wooden soup bowls were set out alongside trenchers and tumblers full of the buttery's best ale.

The room buzzed with the hum of conversation as Makaias attempted to guide Britton between the row of tables to join his father on the dais, but he could feel Britton grow stiff at his side.

"I don't need you to lead me about like a woman," he grumbled.

"Then do it yourself," Makaias said, removing his hand from Britton's elbow. "Lead on."

"And fall flat on my face?"

"You can be led like a woman or complain like one," Makaias said from the side of his mouth, "the choice is yours...*my lady*."

Britton scowled. "Fine friend you are. Where's Velena? I'd sooner have *her* at my arm."

Makaias scanned the room, but she seemed to be nowhere in sight. "I don't see her."

"Isn't she with Stuart?"

"No, but come on, let me take you the rest of the way." Meeting with no resistance this time, Makaias deposited Britton beside his father before making his way back to one of the lower tables. He straddled the bench beside his brother Squire Jaren and gave him a firm pat on the shoulder. "How fair you, Brother?"

"Hm?" he grinned, distracted by the noise of the room.

"Are you well?" Makaias inquired again.

"Oh." Jaren nodded with a smile. "I am. Well, enough and better for having you with us."

"I feel the same," he said, still in awe to be home among his brothers. "Where's Andret?"

"I'm not sure."

Makaias puzzled, "Wasn't he sent to fetch Lady Velena?"

"'Tis done," a voice sounded at his back.

Makais brought his other leg over the bench so he could turn and face Sir Andret. Their mother was at his arm, her face beaming. Makaias attempted to stand, but she stopped him with both hands to the sides of his face. She kissed his cheek in greeting.

"Keep your seat, my son," she said, running a hand over top of what was left of his hair. "Soft. Reminds me of when you were but a wee babe," she said, a mirthful look upon her face. "Did it offend you that you should cut it off?"

He grinned. "Not the hair, but the lice, who called it home."

She nodded without the slightest hint of disgust. "After, did you wash your head in sea water?"

"I did."

"Good boy," she said, taking her seat beside him, "but if you find they're still there, I'll make you some lye."

"Thank you, Mother." Then looking past her to Sir Andret, who was now seated, himself, he inquired, "Where's Lady Velena?"

"Still getting ready, I imagine," he said, with some nonchalance.

"What's happening?" Jaren asked, looking past Makaias to hear what was being said.

"Eat your food," Sir Andret called back, not wanting to carry on a conversation across two people.

Makaias chuckled before unsheathing the dinner knife at his waist. He reached for a trencher of meat and took a stab at a rather juicy looking chunk of pork. His mother, Lady Margarite, did the same.

"Why do you look for her?" she asked.

"Britton was asking," Makaias explained, his mouth already half full.

Lady Margarite raised her eyebrows following a brief sip of ale. "But not you?"

Makaias looked confused. "Why would I be looking for her?"

"Has it crossed your mind that if Lady Cecilia hadn't wanted Lady Velena for Sir Peter all those years ago, this banquet might have been for you."

Before he could react, the room broke into applause. All present stood to their feet, and Makaias shook his head dismissively as he popped an especially moist morsel of wastel[25] into his mouth, freeing his hands to clap with the rest.

Stuart had already risen from his place at the dais and crossed behind Makaias towards the doors, essentially blocking his view of the women entering. As Stuart moved aside to take Velena's arm—giving

Makaias a clear view—chewing suddenly seemed a little less important. He swallowed, but the bread caught, and he found himself reaching for the ale.

Lady Margarite twisted back to look at him. "How about now?" she asked, a humorous glint to her eyes.

He offered naught but an indulgent smile, "Beauty is only skin deep, Mother."

"'Tis true," she conceded and turned back as Stuart presented a rather resplendent Velena to the room of cheering onlookers—more than a few of whom cast upon her a critical eye, knowing nothing except that she'd left her intended standing at the church for a private moment with another man.

Entering just behind Velena were her companions, Lady Rainydayas and a woman Makaias didn't recognize, as well as Velena's lady's maid, Daisy. All were lovely, dressed in their finest, yet it wasn't difficult to tell Velena's ensemble was put together to outshine them all.

She wore a boat-necked, calf-length surcoat of cranberry brocade, inlaid with gold threading and pearls. The richer, truer red of the fitted cotehardie beneath was displayed at her neckline, sleeves, and below the hem, embroidered with an intricate flower and leaf pattern. The front half of her dark hair, thus complimented by the separate shades of red, was plaited over her ears and concealed within ruby-encrusted reticulated templars[26]. The back half was interwoven with a cream-colored ribbon and plaited with horsehair to provide length and thickness, bringing her plait down well past her knees. The finishing touches to her ensemble were a sheer scarf pinned into place, wrapped loosely about her face from her chin to the crown of her head, and her mother's ruby necklace.

Pivoting his head, Makaias followed her progress as Stuart led her from one end of the room to the other, watching as she boldly met the eyes of her guests, maintaining a brave smile as she went along. It faltered only a moment when her gaze passed over Makaias as if he were a stranger, settling instead on the person of his mother and brothers. An unfamiliar man standing among those familiar to her must have given her reason to pause because her eyes returned to him, recognizing him at last.

Makaias dipped his head in acknowledgment, noting with amusement how his lack of hair had again hidden his identity just as surely as a full set of whiskers had when first he arrived at Landerhill.

He noticed also that Britton received a similar look of surprise as Velena took in his shaven head and smooth cheeks. As a young man, Makaias could remember Britton teasing his sister mercilessly, but there'd never been a doubt that he adored her, and so it was no surprise to him to see that Britton had removed his blindfold to watch Velena's ascent to the dais, grinning from ear to ear with as tender a look as ever his father could give.

Enjoying the scene before him, Makaias only looked away when Britton raised an eyebrow in his direction. Makaias knew what his friend was thinking—the same as his mother. If either of them had their way, it'd be Makaias on the dais with Velena instead of Stuart. As soon as was appropriate, Makaias lowered himself back to his seat and indulged in a minced pie, thinking back to the night Velena had entered Britton's room to pray, hair strewn about her shoulders and dressed in naught but a shift and robe. The woman before him was a sight more put together—beautiful, in fact—but so too had been his Joanna. Beautiful—and unfaithful. He chewed without tasting before reaching for his drink.

He wouldn't apply unfaithfulness to Velena without cause, but her tasteless display with Tristan after church that morning had certainly been nothing to admire. Indeed, he deemed it folly, for even if her greatest sin had been naivety, which he didn't believe—it was a sign of latent maturity not to be endured in one as old as she, who ought to know better.

No. If wedding Velena meant enduring treatment such as that, she'd have to offer her husband-to-be more than the obligatory smile she wore now—a smile that barely touched her eyes. Another shame, for they, too, were worthy of attention.

As the head table was again seated, Velena now in their midst, Sir Tarek came around to the front of the dais to call the room to order. "Those swearing fealty[27] to our lord, Sir Richard, the Baron of Landerhill—you will now come forward."

Coming to his feet, Makaias gave Lady Margarite's hand a quick squeeze in response to her look of motherly pride and received a firm slap on the back from Jaren. He approached the dais with a quick and even stride, unsheathing his sword before planting it before him. Genuflecting on one knee, Makaias swore fealty to Sir Richard as his lord, promising both his sword and life's blood for the extent of his service.

Once done, Velena came to her feet, extending to him a rose from across the table. "We welcome you to our household, Sir Makaias."

Their fingers touched, and Makaias felt pleased his body held no reaction. "I thank you," he said, bowing his head low.

Sir Britton's voice cut in. "Promise not to cry, but I do *not* have a rose for you," he said, earning himself a smattering of laughs from the tables below.

"Then don't expect my protection," Sir Makaias warned, pointing a finger at him as he walked away.

Having already re-blindfolded himself before the ceremony, Britton raised a tumbler in salute. "I have my own sword."

"Much to our dismay," Makaias retorted.

The whole room broke into bouts of laughter, ribbing Sir Britton for his poor sight and what he might or might not cut off should he attempt a swing.

"Alright! Alright!" he shouted above the din. "No sword. No sword!" By now he was laughing along with the rest of them.

Still smiling, Sir Tarek motioned for Squire Rowan to approach the dais. Yet to be knighted, he'd still be swearing his fealty as a new member of Sir Richard's household.

Rising from one of the lower tables, Rowan shed every trace of his cocky demeanor. Face set like flint, he bowed his knee, sparing his Uncle Magnus not even an acknowledging glance as he swore his oath of service to Sir Richard.

Again, Velena proffered a rose. "We welcome you to our household, Squire Rowan," she said, bestowing on him the kind of smile reserved for a friend.

"Good riddance," Lord Magnus muttered under his breath.

Rowan bowed. "I thank you, Lady Velena." Upon rising, his eyes settled on Stuart seated beside her. Rowan looked him full in the face for the first time since hearing of Daisy's misfortune…and smiled, all traces of seriousness erased. "Sir Richard," Rowan exclaimed, addressing his new lord so all could hear.

"Squire."

"Since, there are no more present to bow the knee, might I obtain your permission to address the fair maiden by your side."

Sir Richard smiled warily. "If she wishes it."

"I thank you. My lady?" Rowan questioned, "If you would indulge me, I'd like to share with you a story."

By now, Velena's curiosity was growing. "By all means," she said, leaning forward.

He bowed low. "Again, I thank you," he said and turned to face the lower tables. "Though there be not many here ignorant of the story of Tristan and Isulte, for the sake of what I have to say, I would refresh your memories."

Smiles beamed back at him, and a hush filled the room, for there wasn't a man nor woman present who didn't covet the telling of a good story.

He began, "It's a love story of the best and worst kind. It's the story of a man, named Tristan, who loved his king. So much did he love him, and have reason to be beholden to him, that he sought to bring his lonely sire great joy by winning him a bride. The king agreed to the benevolent act, and so Tristan set off to do as promised. By contest, he won the fair maiden, Isulte, and brought her the great journey home. But Isulte was not so assured she would love the king, so her mother mixed an elixir into a bottle of wine for her to take with her on her journey. Upon drinking said potion, she could expect to be thrust into the throngs of love for the first man she sees.

"On the journey back, thus keeping the bottle a secret, Isulte's dimwitted maid mistakes one bottle of wine for another and gives her mistress the enchanted wine by mistake. In walks Tristan," Rowan said with a sly smile, "and I'm sure you can all guess the rest."

"Tell us!" someone shouted from below.

Then another, "You've gained not only a squire, but a bard[28] as well."

A cheer rose up from the room, and Sir Richard and Velena exchanged looks of amusement as Rowan held up his hands for silence.

"Hush. Hush, friends. You've convinced me to go on." He rubbed his hands together and pumped his eyebrows. "So, in walks Tristan, only to partake of the same wine. There can be no doubt but that they fall madly in love, one with the other—but still—Tristan loves his king and delivers the maiden as promised. In ignorance of their love, the king weds her," Rowan began to laugh, "and Tristan and Isulte spend the better part of their time in an attempt to exercise self-denial—when all they want is to be together. But fortunately, their will to do right is strong—and in this self-denial, they succeed."

"Liar," the crowd cried in unison.

Rowan smiled, doubling over at his own attempt to deceive. "They failed!" he shouted, pumping his hand into the air. "They failed miserably," he continued, laughing, along with those around him. "The Tristan of this story is not to be emulated, my friends. So, what moral can we gain from such a tale?" he questioned of the crowd.

"Never trust another man to bring you back a wife," a portly man in front called out.

"And never let your mother mix your wine." This from his wife beside him.

The guests cheered.

"So true…so true, my friends. But, alas, I call upon you to pity me—for I—am that Tristan." Rowan waited for the room to quiet. "Now, some of you may have heard of a more recent Tristan—a man who lived here as brother to this fine woman up until this very day," he said, gesturing back towards Velena, who was now looking at him with some trepidation. He gave her a reassuring smile and continued.

"True, he was born to that name—but for purposes of our story— he is, in actuality, the poor dimwitted maid who mixed up my wine."

A smattering of uncomfortable laughter.

"You see, he loved this woman as a sister, and in loving her, he asked me to care for her in his absence. I vowed that I would, but with that vow I was struck with an arrow. An arrow of love…" He placed a hand to his chest.

He let the silence linger. "How long have I known this woman, but that I now find myself, not only bound to protect her, but also to love her for all eternity."

Velena choked up her drink, laying the back of her hand to her mouth.

"So I ask you to pray for me. For unlike the Tristan of old—not to be confused with the Tristan who left today in search of his brother," he said in a rush of words.

"You mean the dimwitted maid?"

"That's the one," he said with a laugh, "who will pray for his success on this journey?"

"I will!" a knight from the back row, called forward happily.

"Good man." Rowan pointed in his direction. "Now, unlike the Tristan of old, who failed in every respect, I will prevail in my self-denial. Chivalry demands it. God demands it. Her father would forbid otherwise," he spoke from the side of his mouth. "And I demand it of myself—for I am Rowan—and I do not fail!

The people cheered.

"Thus, satisfied in my own conscious, I declare courtly love for this woman—in all of its glorious absurdities!" he yelled above the noise. "Lady Velena," he dropped to his knees, "my love for you is not born of this earth, lusting after that, which it cannot have—but of God, holy and faithful, desiring only your good."

"Squire Rowan...honestly," she said, fidgeting in her seat.

"Fear not, lest you be overwhelmed with my declaration. My love for you is innocent in its every intent. It need not be requited in order to flourish. It need not be a source of contention between you and your husband-to-be—though if it is, all the merrier," he said, provoking a glowering Stuart with a pump of his eyebrows, causing a round of ribbing at Stuart's expense.

Rowan twisted around, holding a finger to his lips, speaking in a whisper. The effect, dramatic, as he cupped his hands in front of his chest. "To me, she is as the Virgin Mary, perfect and unattainable. Forever will I commit myself to holding her up on that pedestal of the mind, running for her favor, and..." he glanced over his shoulder at Stuart with a smile, "dodging the king."

Velena bit her lip at the hoots and hollers that followed.

Rowan stood to his feet. "My lady," he said, reaching over the table to take her hand to his lips. "Will you accept my love and all that comes with it."

"If she will not, I will," a woman giggled, from one of the tables below. Her mother cackled her approval.

Velena's smile was brilliant though her eyes remained uncertain. "I hesitate to ask what that might be, but to the former...yes—so long as it comes with a repeat performance—for I dare say you've gained yourself quite a following this day." Standing, she called out to her guests, "Were you not entertained?" and then clapped along with her guests in jovial acceptance.

Sir Richard wriggled his finger for Rowan to lean forward. "Tristan put you up to this, did he?"

"No, my lord," Rowan answered, with something akin to a twinkle in his eye, "it was entirely of my own invention."

Lord Magnus snorted at his side. "He's your problem now, Richard."

Sir Richard ran a hand up through the underside of his beard before dismissing Rowan with a wave of his fingers. "You may be seated, Squire," he said, pondering the truthfulness of Rowan's statement.

"What do you make of that nephew of mine?" Lady Margarite asked of Makaias, befuddled as to what could have brought on such eccentric behavior.

"He's ever the same as he was," Makaias said looking past his mother to Sir Andret who was supporting his chin in his palm. Makaias laughed more at his brother's exasperated expression than he did at Rowan's shenanigans. But should Makaias have looked around, he would have seen two very keen looks of displeasure. Jaren's being one. Stuart's, the other.

As for Daisy, she sat ever watchful, fingering Rowan's note in her pocket and growing more and more curious about this would-be protector.

Returning to their food, it was no more than fifteen minutes later before the sound of flutes and lutes[29], coming from the minstrel's gallery filled the room with a light and airy sound. In perfect timing, the cittern[30] and the psaltery[31] joined in, delighting the senses as the stronger wine was passed around—coursing through their veins to the beat of the drum.

Arms crossed, Makaias left his seat to lean up against the oversized stone fireplace. It's inner hearth, tall enough for a man to stand in, was still radiating heat from the coals burning bright beneath the spitted pig half gone.

Velena approached, tumbler in hand. "Will you not join in the festivities, Sir Makaias? Or is it you prefer to remain stoically aloof?"

He chuckled.

She continued. "Surely you can let down your walls for only the briefest of moments to join in the festivities."

"What makes you think they're up?"

"You don't drink with us."

Makaias smirked. "That is for the benefit of all, Lady. You may desire that my walls should crumble, but if I lift that to my lips, you'll soon have a change of mind—risking callouses and broken nails to rebuild them as fast as your hands can manage it."

"You don't handle your drink, Sir?"

"Not in the slightest," he answered, noting that though she looked at him, her thoughts appeared to be drifting elsewhere as he watched her slide her finger round the lip of her tumbler.

"Tristan doesn't indulge in anything of any strength either." Appearing wistful a mere moment longer, she shook her head as if to clear her mind. "Though not because he can't tolerate it—well, actually, he can't tolerate it…but because—"

"He doesn't care for it?"

"Yes. But he also thinks it's wrong to drink to excess." She smiled meekly. "He's chided me often for indulging."

"Indulging to excess?"

"Never purposefully," she answered, immediately recalling the self-induced fog of just that morning as she toasted her engagement with Stuart. *That might have been on purpose*, she confessed to herself.

"Accidentally?"

Drink still in hand, she folded her arms and ignored the inner prick to her conscience. "You don't believe me?" she questioned.

He smirked. "I think it's not that my walls are too high, but that I have them at all that leaves you astonished. I'm neither stoic nor aloof, my lady. I simply have command over my own body. And once you learn the same…*accidents* will be fewer and farther in between."

Employing an overly polite smile, Velena squinted her eyes.

Makaias' rounded in question to her look.

She did the same.

"Have I offended you?" he finally asked.

Velena turned her head so as to glare at him from the corner of her eye. "Weeere…you trying to?"

Unruffled by her agitation, he chuckled.

Velena stared at him from over her tumbler, taking a sip.

Conceding, he dipped his head. "Forgive me. I often sound more critical than I intend to."

Setting her drink upon the mantle, she gave a self-satisfied smile. "Not due to a lack of discipline, I hope."

Makaias raised his eyebrow, amused at his own words used against him. "I only meant to impart a little brotherly advice," he said with a crooked smile lifting one side of his mouth.

"A strong position to take with one who already has a brother."

"You forget; I've known you a very long time."

"You've known me?" She choked back a laugh. "You know *Britton* is what you mean—for surely, you've said no more than two sentences to me in my entire growing up. No, Sir. You've only known *of* me."

Finally standing erect from the fireplace, Makaias widened his stance and crossed his arms as if battling wits with Britton's sister was enough to topple him over. "It's true I never made a habit of conversing much with the opposite sex, but I took note of you. I take note of you still."

"And what do you see, pray tell?"

A child in a woman's body, he said only to himself. And honestly, that was his feeling on it. She was uninhibited and unrestrained—impetuous, even. In the short time he'd been back to observe her, he thought her a person who ought to be capable of making better decisions than he'd seen thus far. He held nothing against Tristan, but for her to encourage a friendship with a man in that way—pure folly. And now she was paying for it, both with her reputation, and in her relationship with his cousin, Stuart.

And then there was the way she stared…looking every man in the eye as if she thought herself his equal. A woman's expression ought to convey more modesty.

"Well?" Velena prompted.

"I'm thinking," he said only.

Shaking her head, Velena reached for her drink—but a fraction of a moment too late. Suddenly upon her, Lady Rainydayas was pulling her away from Makaias and back towards the center of the room. The scrape of wood clearly heard above the music as tables and benches were immediately pushed back so men and woman could help form a circle.

Removing himself still further from the throng, Makaias watched from the outskirts as men and women linked hands, moving to the rhythm of the drums. First left and then again to the right, their hips pivoted to the music in a way that reminded Makaias of a Jewish dance he'd seen once. Then palm to palm they began weaving their way through the circle in opposite directions, the rich hue of Lady Velena's attire pulling at the eye, making her easy to follow.

Her movements were fluid, and her smile now genuinely in place. Makaias had never been one to dance, but the energy with which Velena suddenly lit up the room was enough to propel him forward—or at least enough for him to think about letting it do so. Instead, he walked past the dancers and on to the dais to join Sir Britton.

Makaias bent down to his ear, "How fare you?" he asked.

"If one can enjoy the feeling of spinning in circles, then I do well, but as it is the commotion is too much for me, I think. Would you escort this old woman back to her room?"

Makaias gave a wry grin. "Certainly, but I'll not be kissing your hand at the door."

"I'll try to hold back my disappointment," Britton said, before begging leave of his father. And then, unlike before, he allowed Makaias to direct him by his elbow and through the crowd without complaint.

"I'd like to say good night to Velena," Britton said, raising his voice above the music.

Without hesitation, Makaias changed directions and caught Velena's attention with a nod of his head. Seeing her brother by his side, she broke free from the circle and approached them, her smile still in place.

"I can't get used to your hair," she exclaimed to Britton, reaching up to rub the soft fuzz hovering above his scalp.

"I look a disgrace, I know."

"Not at all! You look handsome."

It wasn't lost on Makaias how she failed to meet his eyes this time, nor how she kept her compliments for her brother only.

"It was a sin to hide such pleasant features beneath your whiskers. If I thought better of it, I'd have shaved you, myself."

Britton moved a self-conscious hand to his head. "I thank you, but it has me feeling like an old friar."

She giggled. "You'd have to shave your crown for that. But tell me…if you hate it so, why not have left the length at your ears?"

"'Twas necessary for getting rid of the lice."

Palms held out, Velena stepped back. "They're gone now, I hope. My hair is far too thick to think about such things without cringing."

"We'd be forced to cut yours as well," Britton drolled.

"Oh no, Brother. It's been tried before—fortunately, without success."

"Tristan?" Makaias queried, realizing too late how his question must have sounded more like an accusation.

"Fear not," Britton exclaimed, "you now have Rowan to keep you safe."

"Oh my," Velena said, placing a hand to her cheek with a laugh. "I think he must have over-imbibed on the wine."

Makaias almost cracked a smile as her eyes dared him to make a comment.

"Then, if you need a protector to *protect* you from your protector, you may call on Makaias," Britton added.

Makaias did chuckle, then, at his friend's generosity on his behalf.

"Is that not a brother's role?" she queried.

He shrugged. "I'm an invalid, as you can see—incapable of wielding even my own sword," he acknowledged with a wry grin.

Velena slapped at his arm. "I don't believe that for a moment—and I didn't laugh with those who said so."

A corner of Britton's mouth lifted in disbelief. "It's my eyes that are injured, not my ears. I heard you well-enough."

"All in good fun," she said, crinkling her eyes in delight, finally turning them back towards Makaias. "Well, then. It seems you've been given no say in the matter, but fear not, I've no intention of holding you to it."

"Same as the kiss," Britton teased.

Velena shrugged her shoulders, despite her brother's inability to see through his blindfold, her expression a shade dismissive of certain obligations he felt she owed.

"I just swore an oath to your household, my lady," Makaias reminded her. "Your well-being will always be of the utmost importance." Again, he was taken aback by the frankness of her stare. Did the woman ever look away?

"And now, by all accounts, you're the most well protected woman in Totnes," Britton chimed in. "This should make your friend happy."

Velena opened her mouth to speak but closed it again as a wave of emotion sought to undo her. Forgoing speech, she opted for a quick nod.

"You miss him?" Britton asked in earnest when she didn't answer.

Nodding again, Velena compressed her lips and closed her eyes. When they opened, they'd taken on a glassy sheen. She raised a hand to the constriction in her throat and remembered her brother needed to hear her. She swallowed and affirmed his question with a soft *yes*.

Reaching out for a shoulder, Britton wrapped his arm around her, drawing her into his side. "Now, now…it's not even been a whole day. Tomorrow will be better."

"I hope so," she whispered, self-conscious of Makaias' gaze now that she was feeling so emotional.

"I know it will," Britton assured her, "but for now, I must beg your leave, for my head is spinning. I only wanted to wish you a pleasant evening before I go."

"Thank you for venturing down in the first place," she said, planting a kiss upon his cheek. "I'll come to you before I retire and see how you fare."

A parting blessing was on his lips, but he was interrupted by a firm hand to his shoulder. "This man needs no tending to, leastwise by a woman. Tis an insult! He will heal by sheer force of will—or so I would have believed last I laid eyes on him."

Though it was years since he'd last seen him, Makaias recognized the man immediately. He turned to Britton, knowing the man's voice would be both familiar and vexing to him, and wasn't in the least bit surprised when Britton's blindfold did nothing to hide his friend's expression of annoyance.

"Squire Harold, I presume," Britton said.

"*Sir* Harold, now," the man said, straightening his shoulders. "You've been gone a long time, my friend."

Makaias raised an eyebrow. Britton's *friend*. Surely, not. The man was obnoxiously self-absorbed and more like a bur one caught on his clothing and couldn't shake loose.

"Not long enough," Britton replied.

Sir Harold laughed. "What a jester you are. Same as always."

So far, the man had ignored Velena, but not for lack of wanting her attention. It was only for etiquette's sake he waited to be introduced. So, he stared at Britton's blindfold with an expectant expression for nigh on half a minute before remembering he wasn't looking at his eyes. Persistent, he glanced from Makaias to Velena and back to Makaias again. He cleared his throat.

Knowing what Sir Harold wanted but not wanting to give it to him, Makaias debated leaving the man in his awkwardness but decided against it. He opened his mouth to make the introductions—but not fast enough.

"Sir Harold, isn't it?" Velena asked, looking at the man with interest. "Is your father, Lord Barton?"

"He is, my lady. I commend your memory."

"Well, not too much, for that's all I remember, I'm afraid. But I thank you for attending our celebration, and I pray you've been enjoying yourself."

"I have, indeed. All that is left for me to do is dance…and have more to drink. Your father's wine is exquisite, and I must have my fill should it be a while till I attend my next wedding."

Makaias watched as Velena's smile dipped with the word *wedding*, as if she was truly remembering what the celebration was about in the first place. "I'm not wed yet, Sir Harold, so you may very well taste it again on that occasion."

It was the *yet* that caught the knight's attention and elevated his brows. "Tis the truth, my lady. Occasions such as these, only speak of the future and not of the *moment*. I, for one, have always believed men ought to live in the moment. Would you not agree?"

"No. She wouldn't," Britton cut in, crossing his arms in front of his chest.

Ignoring her brother's retort on her behalf, she linked her hands behind her. "I'm not sure that our Lord would express your thought in the same way, Sir, but I do adhere to what Christ said on the matter as recorded in St Matthew. '*So do not worry about tomorrow; for tomorrow will care for itself. Each day has enough trouble of its own.*' Perhaps we can agree on that."

Makaias noted the way Sir Harold let his eyes continuously slip down from her face, even while she looked on him with an even expression. Velena was trying to be kind, but Makaias knew she had no idea to what lengths one such as Sir Harold would go to twist her meaning—well intentioned though it may be.

"So, you worry not beyond the moment of the day. There's much to admire in that kind of thinking."

Britton yanked free of his blindfold and speared the knight with a look.

Velena gasped. "Britton, your eyes. They'll never heal if you—"

"You said you've yet to dance, *Harold*. May I suggest you do so now and kindly leave me to say good night to my sister."

Taking offense at Britton's omission of his status, Sir Harold narrowed his eyes and sulked off with barely a nod.

Startled by her brother's abruptness, she waited for the knight to move on before speaking. "Though I have no say in how you speak to *your* friend, he was *my* guest. And I'd have my guests treated with courtesy."

"He wasn't my friend, and he isn't your guest. He's Lord Barton's son—who's our uncle's guest—and who you barely remember."

"Nevertheless, it wasn't Christian behavior," she responded in an even tone.

Britton took a tolerant breath. "I think you need to submit to my judgment on the matter."

Not wanting to argue, Velena pressed her lips together and plucked the blindfold from his hand before moving behind him to tie it back into place.

"Velena…" he said, waiting.

A sly smile creeping onto her face, she looked past his head. "I'm thinking," she said, locking eyes with Makaias.

Britton sighed as he turned to face her. "If Stuart doesn't raise a hand to you a week into being wed than I'll owe you a shilling."

She smiled, but as Makaias witnessed when she'd first entered the hall, it failed to reach her eyes. "Then you owe me a shilling," she said, rising on her toes to kiss his cheek. "Off with you, now. I've more dancing to do."

What Britton dismissed as jesting, Makaias saw as truth. He turned away, scanning the room for Stuart. Had his cousin grown into the kind of man who resorted to abuse? Makaias had always equated such violence with weakness and began to question Stuart's character.

His face was solemn as he excused himself from Velena's presence and led Britton above stairs to his solar. Upon his return, Makaias scanned the room for his mother and brothers, but without meaning to, his eyes settled again on Velena. Easily done, for she stuck out like a rose amongst a sea of clover.

No longer dancing, she was speaking with Sir Harold. And, *again*, her expression held not the slightest hint of modesty but was entirely unguarded and intent on what the man was saying. *Foolish woman,* he couldn't help thinking as Stuart finally arrived at her side. A moment later, Velena was ushered from the room, leaving Sir Harold to stand alone, an overly confident smile pulling back his lips as his eyes trailed after.

Makaias rubbed his thumb over top his fingers, his hand itching to rid the man of the smug expression before a tap to his shoulder jerked him from his thoughts. Bringing his head around, Makaias was greeted by Sir Andret, offering both a smile, and a tankard of ale.

Makaias accepted the drink but turned his attention back to Velena. Quaffing a mouthful he kept Sir Harold fixed in his sites from above his tankard—his gaze silently penetrating the knight's motives as if taking aim at an unseemly boar.

When, finally, his quarry perceived he was being watched, Makaias merely lifted his drink in an acknowledging salute, a warning in his expression that caused the other knight to turn away in pursuit of better company.

Sir Andret chuckled at the exchange and then gestured that they should go outside.

Noting that his mother and Jaren were already waiting by the door, Makaias nodded and followed him from the great hall.

[23]**Garderobe:** A small chamber where the toilet is located.
[24]**Ablutions:** Reference to washing oneself.
[25]**Wastel:** Bread made of very fine flour, served to nobility.
[26]**Templar:** Head dress encasing the hair on both sides.
[27]**Fealty:** A formal acknowledgement of loyalty to a lord, country, or leader of some kind.
[28]**Bard:** A Poet.
[29]**Lute:** A stringed instrument with its lower half shaped like a halved egg.
[30]**Cittern:** A stringed instrument, similar to a lute, but with a flattened back.
[31]**Psaltery:** A triangular stringed instrument, plucked with one's fingers.

18

broken promises

"Where are we going?" Velena asked as Stuart led her from the great hall by the hand.

He looked back at her, the corners of his mouth lifting in anticipation. "Somewhere where I don't have to share you with other men."

Velena frowned as he pulled her into the library, keenly aware of how alone they were as the sounds of music and gaiety became muffled as he shut the door. "I was only talking to him," she insisted.

"I know," Stuart said, turning to face her, for once his eyes void of any jealousy, "but I want you to talk with me now."

Velena looked cross. "I'm not sure that requires this sort of solitude?"

Stuart gave her his most winning smile and circled around behind her, openly admiring his future wife. "It does for the kind of talking I want to do."

She whirled around to face him, but he only chuckled at her expression.

"And for that," he continued, "we needed to be out of view of your new would-be protector."

"Rowan?" Velena felt a small glimmer of concern. "I promise you I had nothing to do with that."

"I believe you," he assured her, then scoffed. "He can't stand not to be the center of attention. But nothing he can do can ruin this moment for me." Stuart took a moment to drink Velena in, allowing his eyes to caress her every visible feature before slipping his hands around her waist. He pulled her forward until he'd removed all space between them. "

Instinctively, Velena's arms came up, hands landing awkwardly at his shoulders, splayed in misgiving. But he was not put off.

Her voice wavered. "What are you doing?"

His grin broadened into a familiar smile, his eyes both youthful and seductive. "It's time," he responded simply.

Unable to look away, and knowing full-well what he meant, her eyes darted back and forth across his face. "T…time for what?"

He brought his lips close to her ear, the warmth of his breath penetrating through her head scarf. "I think you know," he whispered, sliding his cheek against her skin as he pulled his head back only so far that his nose nestled alongside her own. "You look beautiful tonight, Velena…more beautiful than I've ever seen you."

Velena could smell the alcohol on his breath but knew he wasn't drunk. He was fully alert and ready to claim the kiss she'd failed to deliver in the chapel. "Someone will notice we're gone," she said, offering no more than a pathetic amount of resistance when she ought to be insisting that he release her.

His arms circled hungrily about her waist, the tip of his nose now nudging her head back, preparing her lips for what he intended. "There's time."

By now, the blood was thrumming in her ears. She remembered her promise to Tristan, but it was only a brief remembrance as she felt her body respond in ways her heart had thus far refused. Conflicted by raw emotion, she began to recall what she'd told Daisy about wanting to love Stuart—or at least, wanting to want to.

"Are you willing?" Stuart questioned, breathing deeply against her chest.

Velena took an unsteady breath. "I don't know what to do," she confessed.

"Just say *yes*…" he whispered, his voice more breath than sound as his gaze caressed the smooth contours of her upturned face, "and I'll show you."

She was a hair's breadth from doing so when thoughts of Tristan appealed to her one last time. *Faithful are the wounds of a friend, but deceitful are the kisses of an enemy.* Those were the words written on the note he'd left for her. No personal sentiment—only words of wisdom from the book of Proverbs. And they spoke truth, for it couldn't be denied that Tristan had wounded her by leaving. But it was only a half-truth because no matter how much Tristan hated her cousin, she couldn't believe Stuart was her enemy.

Confused, she couldn't help but wonder if succumbing to Stuart might be the key to unlocking her feelings for him—or at least a small step in that direction. Because the truth of it was that Stuart was to be her husband whether she loved him or not. And in light of that, questioning the right or wrong of keeping her promise to Tristan seemed senseless.

"Say *yes*," Stuart's voice repeated, reminding her she had not but a moment to choose.

Why did she feel so helpless? Her insides twisted in indecision. *You promised*, she berated herself. "I can't."

"Then don't say *no*..." Leaving her no time to do so, Stuart caught her up with a firm hand to the back of her head, drawing her mouth up to meet his own. She stiffened but didn't struggle, thus he continued his course without wavering. The warmth of her lips ignited a fire in his belly, and he had to remember to go slowly, exulting in the fact that they were alone this time—no audience—no urgency.

After waiting for what seemed like an eternity—certainly long enough to have fulfilled any imprudent obligations—Velena pulled her face to the side in an attempt to escape what seemed to be ongoing. "Stuart."

"Velena..." He moaned, pulling away her scarf as he moved his attention to her neck and ear, thrilling at the shudder he felt course through her body.

Inhaling sharply, she shook her head in a frantic motion. "Please..." she said, her voice breathless, "no more."

Stuart pulled back, contentment radiating from his eyes despite her unwillingness to continue. His hands glided up past her arms and shoulders until he was cupping the back of her neck. He rubbed the pads of his thumbs along the lines of her jawbone, replaying the last few minutes in his mind with qualitative satisfaction.

He had to admit, however, that the experience would have been greatly enhanced had Velena made more of an effort to be a part of it. For outside of one or two very mild reactions, she hadn't actually kissed him back. But he was seasoned enough in his experience with women to know he could please one, so he excused this as nothing more than a lack of practice. And to that end, he was more than happy to do his part.

"Are you alright?" he asked, tucking one of her stray hairs back into place, allowing his fingers to linger at her temple. "Have I frightened you?"

Velena shook her head.

"What is it then? Was it not what you expected?" He grinned

playfully. "I wanted to make up for the first time."

To this, she raised her eyebrows, a nervous smile adding the first bit of animation back into her face. "You did that.

"And did you like it?" Stuart asked, smiling smoothly as he attempted to draw her close once more.

"Actually…" she put a hand between them, "it's too much," she said, looking apologetic.

At first confused, he soon thought he understood. "I admit I should have gone slower. Believe it or not, I tried. But Velena—being with you like this—it's exactly the kind of intimacy I've been yearning to share with you. This and more."

Velena bit her lip. "Then it's an intimacy best shared…after marriage."

Patiently, Stuart smiled down at her as though she were a child in need of instruction. "I promise not to ruin you…but as for this," he ran his thumb across her bottom lip, "there's no turning back now.

Cupping her face in his hands, Stuart delivered one of the most passionate kisses he could think to give. Yet, when he pulled away, she was visibly upset—and anything but impassioned.

"Are you done with me?" she inquired, an accusatory bite to her voice.

Uncertain how to proceed past his own wounded ego, Stuart's arms dropped away from her body. He opened his mouth to speak, but he hardly knew what to say. As good a lover as he claimed to be, nights spent in the company of harlots had falsely prepared him for the reality of a woman free from paid emotions.

Holding his gaze for several agonizing moments, she dropped them to the floor in regret. "I wish to rejoin the party," she said, simply. She moved to go around him, but he caught her by the arm.

"You're not a harlot for allowing me to kiss you."

"Then why do you treat me like one?"

"You know nothing of the world, else you'd know I did nothing of the sort."

Velena shrugged out of his grip. "I told you I wanted to wait."

"You could have said no at any time."

"Not saying *no* is not the same as saying *yes*."

"Don't play with my head, Velena. You were willing." Stuart closed his eyes in frustration. "I don't like saying this—but you're acting like a child."

Taking in but the smallest gulp of air, Velena gasped in indignation. "Then, clearly, I'm not ready," she exclaimed and hastened from the room.

19

in her defense

Crossing his arms against the chill of the evening, Makaias breathed deep of the night air wafting over his newly-shaven head. "This is Heaven," he said, ever grateful to be back in England.

"I can't ever remember it being so cold this time of year," Jaren muttered, rubbing his hands together.

"But better than France?" Sir Andret asked, doing the same.

Makaias smiled. "Better than France."

Together, Lady Margarite and her sons meandered a good twenty yards from the manor to one of several open fires which had been erected for guests who might need to get away from the stuffy interior of the great hall.

The gravel shifted position beneath Lady Margarite's best dancing shoes as she held out her hands to the heat, shuffling forward as close as she dared. The fire crackled and popped, filling her with the pleasant rhythms and sounds of the outdoors. "Well," she began, "Lady Velena certainly loves a good dance," she said with approval.

Andret chuckled. "She's not the only one."

Makaias opened his mouth in mock astonishment. "Do you mean to tell me you danced, Mother?"

She clucked at her son. "I did—and where were you, pray tell?"

"I had to take Britton above stairs. The commotion was making him dizzy."

"Poor boy," she said in sympathy. "How fares he overall?"

Makaias took a breath. "He's healing. Where he saw five of me, he now sees only two. But sitting idle wears on him, and he could do with some purpose to his day. In fact, if it weren't for his sister's constant attention, I think he'd go quite mad."

"She's attentive?"

"Very."

"A blessing then, but I'm not surprised. She was always such a loving child. I'm happy these past years of hardship haven't taken that from her."

Taking a wide stance, Jaren mumbled, "If anything, she's *too* charitable." He crossed his arms in front of him as shadowy flames danced across his face.

Makaias turned towards his brother. "What do you mean?"

"Encouraging Rowan, for instance. He declares courtly love for her, and all she does is encourage him when he should have been thrown out on his ear."

Out of habit, Makaias rubbed his chin, forgetting his beard was no longer there. "It was a shock, I'll admit. Does Rowan actually carry feelings for her?"

Jaren scoffed. "Only the carnal kind."

"All in good fun." Andret interjected.

"There's nothing *good* about Rowan's version of fun," Jaren answered him. "And you weren't there to hear what he had to say about her the time we went running in the forest."

Makaias looked surprised. "Running?"

"Yes, if you can believe it. Something Tristan talked her into, I think. I don't remember the details of it, but he brought men's clothes for her to change into, and when she went behind some trees to do so, Rowan spoke most disrespectfully—talking about wanting to take her for a roll in the hay and what not."

When Sir Andret snickered, Makaias had to fight to hold back a grin.

"I doubt he meant anything by it," Sir Andret said. "If so, he wouldn't have said it in front of Tristan."

Jaren looked frustrated. "All I'm saying is she's in the habit of keeping poor company. And Tristan was no exception. You know as well as I that had he stayed, it would've been a tryst in the making—no question."

Makaias raised an eyebrow even as their mother looked as though she might take her grown son over her knee. Looking around, she shushed him. "We're not so isolated as not to be overheard," she scolded. "Be careful you do not slander her without proof."

"I speak from my own observations."

"Which are limited, at best," Sir Andret said, shaking his head back and forth as though Jaren didn't have a clue in the world what he was talking about.

Makaias crossed his arms, making himself appear much the same as Jaren. A deep groove formed between his eyes as he glanced from one brother to the next, thankful Britton wasn't there to witness such talk of his sister. In fact, he wouldn't have tolerated a word of it. Makaias, now more mistrusting of women than he would have liked to admit, remained curious to hear what his brothers had to say of Velena's true character.

"You disagree with your brother?" Lady Margarite asked Sir Andret.

"I do. He thinks he's the expert, but his mere months' worth of observation is nothing to the three years when I was with Tristan and Lady Velena at Wineford. The Lady Velena and Tristan had an unusual friendship to be sure—but it *was* innocent."

Jaren shook his head. "Velena should count herself fortunate to have a man who would put up with that sort of *innocence* in a wife."

Sir Andret snorted. "He doesn't know the meaning of the word *innocence*. You waste your breath speaking ill of her when Stuart probably knows the name of every fallen woman from here to Exeter."

"Alright, that's enough," Lady Margarite reprimanded. "It's not Christian to carry on as we are. Let us be done with it."

Sir Andret returned his eyes to the fire. "Sorry Mother."

Unable to let it go, Jaren shifted his weight from one leg to the next. "Why do you always think so ill of Stuart?"

"Why do you always defend him?" Sir Andret questioned, his voice peaking for the first time.

"He's been a loyal friend."

"He's been your only friend," Sir Andret pointed out, "but he's still wanton, Jaren. Just be honest about it, else you appear the fool for defending him."

Jaren tried to speak, but Sir Andret pressed on. "If you don't care—fine—but if you do, stop turning a blind eye to it and exhort him to better behavior—at least for Lady Velena's sake."

"Admittedly, he's a sinner. I'm not denying it, but there comes a time in a man's life when he hopes to stop being judged by his every fault. Stuart strives to better himself. Look deeper and you'll see he's a good man—same as his father."

Mother and brothers all turned to Jaren with mouths agape as though he'd just taken leave of his senses.

"Magnus…a good man?" Sir Andret snorted as he snuffed out a wayward ember with his shoe. "Who convinced you he was one of those?"

"You don't think I know my own mind?" Jaren's voice was sharp.

"Jaren, please…" His mother's voice was gentle as she reached out to touch his arm. "Let this not be a source of dissension between you. I know you love your cousin well…but don't let it cloud your judgment of right and wrong if there's real reason to doubt his character. Remember that one rotted apple can ruin the whole barrel. So, too, an immoral man's rotted judgments can disease those who take company with him."

"We're like brothers," he exclaimed, giving no regard for the ones he had standing by. "I'm well aware he has faults, but I'll not shun him for them."

Letting her arm drop, Lady Margarite stared into the fire, sparks ascending into the inky blackness overhead. "Then lift him up in prayer. For prayer is a most powerful thing."

Silent for a moment, Jaren turned away from the fire. "I'm going back inside."

Rolling his eyes, Sir Andret spit into the flames, making a small hiss.

Unmoving, Makaias' eyes trailed after his youngest brother. "Well that certainly took a turn for the worst."

Sir Andret shrugged. "One too many opinions is all."

Makaias chuckled. "Last I remember, you tried not to have too many of those."

He agreed with a smirk. "And this is why."

"You were always a man of few words, my son. Too bad you didn't have a mother of few questions," Lady Margarite added, laughing at herself until her boys joined in. She feigned irritation, "You're not supposed to agree with me."

Makaias took the few steps needed to pull her into his side, relishing the feeling of having her near again—despite her reprimanding slap to his chest. He laughed. "You know we love you, Mother. And your many…many, many…many questions were ever the means to drawing our attention to our own hearts. Never were they a burden."

"Sometimes they were," Sir Andret teased, smiling affectionately at them both.

"Well, I have a question of my own," Makaias countered, "and I don't think I'm the only one. Did you notice the faces of Sir Richard's guests tonight as Lady Velena entered the room?"

Sir Andret nodded. "I did."

"Anyone with ears to hear should have known Rowan was setting them right with that little speech of his," Lady Margarite cut in. "The rest are nothing but a bunch of gossips."

Makaias appeared thoughtful. "I wouldn't put myself in the second category, but her leaving Stuart at the church to say goodbye to Tristan…are you sure Jaren's concerns hold no merit?"

Sir Andret sighed, growing weary of lengthy explanations. "Certainly, Tristan's presence has had its negative effects on her reputation. Can't say I haven't wanted to punch some sense into a few people a time or two, but you should have seen her before he came." He paused to fish around with his tongue for a bit of meat left stuck in his teeth. "I mean, you wouldn't know it to look at her now, but she was in a bad way after Lady Cecelia died. She spoke nary a word the whole journey to the castle. Sir Richard set me as watch over her and Daisy when we broke for camp, and I remember her having nightmares."

Unable to free the meat lodged behind his tooth, he dug at it with his finger for a moment and then flicked it into the fire before continuing. "And then after we arrived and got settled, boy that was it. She was planted and you couldn't get that woman to leave the inner bailey for anything. It was Tristan who changed all that. But Stuart wouldn't have anything to do with him, jealous from the beginning."

Makaias nodded. "Granted, but I can still see being jealous if the woman I wanted to marry was that close to another man."

Sir Andret shrugged. "If there was going to be anything between them, it would have happened before Stuart arrived."

"Do you really think you could have been any more trusting had it been you in Stuart's place?" Makaias inquired, skeptically.

Sir Andret gave him a sideways glance. "Either the woman you love is faithful or she's not. And if she's not, then let her go her own way and count yourself blessed to be rid of her. But if she is…there's nothing left to do but trust her."

Lady Margarite gave Makaias' hand a quick squeeze, knowing how much his heart must have wrestled with this very idea.

Sir Andret looked him full in the face. "You do well not to listen to Jaren, Makaias. I've seen Lady Velena grow up these last three years.

She may be free-spirited and headstrong—but she's true and she's faithful—a good Christian woman. And had Stuart put his trust in her as he should have, he'd have a fully devoted woman...and not just a body reconciled to warming his bed."

Makaias met his brother's gaze head on. "Strong words for someone who tries not to have an opinion."

"I might have gone without one, but for the day Stuart announced their engagement to Rowan, Jaren, and myself—the day you arrived, actually."

"What happened?" Lady Margarite asked, eyes rounded with interest.

"She burst into tears—right there on the spot. I've never seen anything like it. Just stood there and cried."

Acknowledging the account with a small grunt, Makaias remained thoughtful. "She made a comment earlier this evening that has me wondering if Stuart's been violent with her. Could this have something to do with it?"

Sir Andret scratched the back of his head. "I don't know," he said honestly, wondering now if this is what Tristan had referred to when he'd accused Jaren of *knowing* something—though what that something was hadn't been clear.

Lady Margarite laid a hand to her chest, "Let us leave off with this conversation here, for I now fear I already know more than is my right to know. Best to our knees in prayer and wait and see what the Lord will do." Bestowing a soft touch to the cheek of each son, she turned from the fire.

"Shall I see you home, Mother?" Sir Andret inquired.

"Shortly. I would first try my hand at unruffling your brother's feathers."

For a moment Sir Andret's face was unreadable. "You should never have sent him to Uncle Magnus for his training," he said flatly. His voice was of an even keel, but there was no mistaking the resentment in his words.

Firelight illuminated Makaias' face as he gave his brother a warning look not to suffer their mother any further disrespect. Still, he waited for her to answer.

Lady Margarite sighed. "How long could I have denied sending one of my sons to my own sister's household? Though it be a mistake," she rubbed her hands together in an attempt to gain back some of the warmth that had left them before shaking her head as if to rid herself of her own regrets, "I didn't want to offend her," she said, definitively.

"And now, how many people will Jaren offend?"

"Enough," Makaias said, softly, unwilling to allow another rift to form. "It cannot be changed, Andret."

Crestfallen, Lady Margarite managed a grateful look for her eldest before retreating into the manor.

"You think I should have held my tongue," Sir Andret said, as soon as the doors had shut.

"It's done," Makaias answered, assigning him no judgment. "You're not the only one to wonder why he was sent there." Growing too warm, he turned his back to the fire, arms still crossed.

"So," Sir Andret began, changing the subject. "Mother tells me you almost married some fish-monger's daughter in London."

Makaias exhaled through is nose. "Something like that," he answered, setting hands to his waist, his broad shoulders casting a formidable shadow as he looked out into a starless night.

"You loved her?"

"I trusted her."

"I'm sorry."

Makaias gave him half a smile. "Like you said, better to let her go her own way."

"And do you feel…blessed?" Sir Andret asked with a chuckle.

Casting a sidelong look at his brother, Makaias' smile grew with more humor than he felt. "I feel slighted, actually. It'd have been easier to swallow if she'd replaced me with someone better. As it was, he wasn't nearly so handsome as I am."

Andret chuckled. "A good many of us aren't."

"Well, don't feel badly about it," Makaias said, laying a hand to his shoulder.

Sir Andret's grin stretched the width of his face, "Oh, I wasn't speaking of myself."

Makaias laughed outright. "Get out of here."

He nodded. "I'll go apologize to Mother."

"You'd better."

With a final glance, Sir Andret retreated from the fire, stalking off into darkness until he reached the manor's double doors, where soft candlelight shown hazy through glassed-pained windows.

Hand barely on the handle, the door swung open before Andret could push, and Makaias watched as Velena nearly ran into him.

Looking flustered, she sidestepped as he gave her a respectful bow and disappeared inside, with the door shutting behind him.

Though Makaias was hardly hidden if one had a mind to see him, he could tell she hadn't as she looked around the bailey.

Stepping off to the side where her silhouette took on the nebulous glow of the window, her hands balled into fists, pressing into the pit of her stomach before traveling upwards, spreading wide at her neck. Pulling at her disheveled veil as if she were in want of air, she stripped it from her head, along with the pins that held it in place. Each one fell to the gravel with an inaudible ping at her feet as she paced, her chest rising and falling with every anxious breath.

Finding himself an accidental spectator for the second time, Makaias wondered at the point of her agitation. He'd no sooner decided to take a walk when the walkway flooded with light a second time, and Sir Harold stepped out through the doors.

Makaias narrowed his eyes as the errant knight found his target and approached, words drifting to his ears in the form of unintelligible mumblings. Determining to make himself known, Makaias moved to his left where he was sure to be well lit should Velena look his way again. For with Britton retired in his solar, Makaias had no qualms about taking on the role of elder brother should Velena need him. And with the posture Sir Harold was taking as he addressed her, he knew he'd better stay.

Velena balled up the veil around her fist and gazed out at the open flames semi-circling the front of the manor. For a moment, she thought to run over and cast it into the fire. In the next, she wanted to stuff the flimsy material into her mouth to stifle a scream she wished she had the courage to utter. It hadn't even been a full day, and she'd broken her promise to Tristan. Broken because she hoped that giving herself over to greater intimacy with Stuart would lead the way to loving him. But it hadn't. Not at all. Instead, it was lackluster and full of disappointments—the greatest being that she'd gone against her better judgement...and her word.

Velena shut her eyes to the ache in her throat, desiring nothing better than to give herself over to tears, when a glow behind her lids brought them back up. "Sir Harold," she exclaimed, startled at his presence.

Seeing her head scarf clutched at her waist, Sir Harold tucked his chin length auburn hair behind his ears and produced a roguish smile. "Lady Velena," he greeted, his voice smooth, if not a bit arrogant. "I see you've finally made your escape."

"Pardon?"

"From your fiancé. Very inconsiderate that he should pull you away from your guests—though one could hardly blame him. Who wouldn't want to be in the company of one as lovely as yourself?"

Velena blinked, uncomfortable with the compliment. "I had need of some fresh air."

"I had the same idea. Too many people indoors, don't you think?"

"I...I'm actually quite fond of being in the company of friends. And having been prematurely torn away—as you said—I should return to them. If you'll excuse me, I've been away too long already." She moved to sidestep him, but a quick step to his right blocked her way.

"I can believe that about you," he said, looking suddenly serious. "It was the banns that gave it away."

Velena's brow furrowed. "What do you mean?"

"I took careful note of you as they were read. Every word was a nail in your coffin. Your eyes said it all, and I thought to myself...now this is a woman who cannot be tied down to merely one companion."

"Your imaginings are quite colorful, Sir Harold, but imaginings are all they are. You saw no such thing in my eyes."

"Why should you deny it?" he inquired, smiling. "I'm the same way. As I see it, every moment is the potential for new experiences—every person, an experience worth pouring myself into." He crossed his arms and sighed. "I've often thought it too bad marriage has to be such a hindrance to our happiness. Our kind should never be caged."

"Our kind?" Velena repeated, feeling quite caged at that very moment.

A bold, but amused smile slid into place. "You needn't be coy, my lady. Your dissatisfaction with your intended is vividly clear." He produced a sympathetic smile. "And who could blame you?

Velena's mouth stood agape.

"Presumably, I thought you might find yourself desirous of another. And if you so choose, I can promise you'll find me a willing stand in. I'm quite discrete when it comes to these sorts of affairs."

Finding her voice, Velena nearly spat at him. "You, Sir, have made a gross error in judgment!"

"I find that hard to believe," he said, remaining sure of himself. "When you spoke earlier of seizing the moment, your meaning was quite clear."

"Can you not tell the difference between polite conversation and ill-mannered innuendo—the latter being a thing in which I do not partake?"

Sir Harold squinted his eyes at her until his confusion was replaced by a scowl. "I see." He swallowed. "So, your being out here...alone..." He took but a mere step forward, yet it was as if his very presence held her up against a wall.

Her insides recoiled, but she didn't back away. "Has nothing to do with you," she finished for him. It was then that Velena's peripheral vision caught a movement out beyond the shadows, bringing her eyes flitting towards the flowing ring. Flame and rising sparks outlined a man with broad shoulders and a readied stance. Having mistaken him twice in the light of day, the soft halo surrounding the newly-shaved head gave her certainty in the dark.

Makaias nodded in her direction and her breathing steadied. *Thank you, Lord.* She had nothing to fear from Sir Harold with her brother's friend looking on.

Alerted by the reaction in her eyes, Sir Harold followed her gaze out into the night. Humiliated though he was at being witnessed, he recovered quickly, shifting all his weight to one hip as if he cared not a bit that he'd just been rejected—or discovered. He smirked. "How foolish of me to believe I was the only one you might have had your eye on. You were meeting someone else...perhaps?" He leaned forward with a wink. "I think you are a great tease, my lady."

Velena's hand twitched with the desire to slap his face. "I was neither meeting him, nor anyone else. I was hospitable to you, but you've not repaid me in kind. I want you to leave."

"I think not."

"Leave, else I call that man to my aid."

"And say what? I doubt very much he could have heard us."

"He might have."

"No sword at my back tells me differently. You might not want to indulge in the *problems of today*," he said, befouling the words of Scripture with his insinuating tone, "but I might yet find someone who will. The night is not over—and there's much more wine to be had.

So," he said pursing his lips, "I think you'll have to reconsider your asking me to go."

"The only thing that needs any consideration at all, Sir Harold, is whether or not I'll be telling my father what sort of a man he's allowed into his home. Take your leave immediately lest I stand in the hall and give testimony to your words—rotten as they are. And see if Stuart doesn't run you through without a second thought—for a more jealous man you'll never find."

His eyelids sunk down into slits. "I think you're bluffing. You may try and shame me, but I'll not be the only one. There will still be those who'll doubt your part in it, saying you merely got caught...without your veil on." He shook his head. "And after what everyone witnessed at the church this morning—well..."

Speechless, Velena stood with her heart bleeding. Her eyes fell to the sheer material still in hand, fluttering in the night breeze like an apparition at her side. He could only be speaking of Tristan, which meant Rowan was right when he said they'd been drawing gossip. She wanted to believe he was wrong, but knew she'd acted shamefully, warranting the looks she'd seen in the eyes of her guests.

She looked up, now, into the face of the repugnant knight before her. He mocked the pain of their parting, but let it never be said that she was bound and helpless without Tristan by her side. Let it not be so, for she could see his face before her—goading her on—believing she had faith...and the ability to fend off whatever arrows should come her way.

So too, Velena found strength in Sir Makaias—even in his standing by at a distance. Had he felt her incapable, surely, he would have come to her aid by now.

Sir Harold looked smug. "Would you really dare risk your reputation any further...my lady?"

An unexpected lightness of mood lifted the corners of her mouth as she drew spare pins from her pocket and worked to replace the veil to her head dress. "I'll stand on a chair and say it in ballad form if you'd like."

"You bluff," he said again.

"Do I?" Her challenge was clear. Giving her head covering a slight shake to make sure it held in place, she sashayed past him without a second glance.

Opening the front doors, she found the foyer to be milling with people in want of fresh air and more room. Weaving past them, she made her way through the corridor and into the great hall where she veered neither to the left nor to the right in her quest to reach the dais. Reaching her place behind the table, she turned to find that the party had grown a good deal more raucous in her absence. The volume of music and conversation was so loud she doubted she'd be able to hear herself speak. So too, the temperature of the room was hotter and muggier than before, and she wished for a moment that she'd called upon Sir Makaias for help so that she could have remained outside and away from the noise and sour smells of sweat and spilt ale.

Too late for regrets, she craned her neck in an attempt to see around those dancers who'd filled in the gap between herself and the door, surveying the room to see if Sir Harold had followed.

He had and was presently standing by the door, arms crossed, mocking her with his very presence.

Scowling, she stepped up to her chair, daring him to stay.

Not only did he, but he began taunting her with puckered lips, blowing her a kiss and then laughing as she continued to glare.

Refusing to change her mind now, Velena took a deep breath. Then hoisting up the hem of her tunic with one hand, while steadying herself on the back of the chair with the other, she stood up above the crowd.

Instrument by instrument, the musicians in the minstrel's gallery ceased their playing until all began to notice, bringing the room to an awkward silence with every eye staring in her direction. It became so quiet, in fact, that a gasp or two was easily heard from those of the kitchen staff, who chose to peek out from behind the curtain wall.

Facing her audience, she lifted her chin and did her best to look as if all was perfectly in order—no small task. And worst of all, Sir Harold was still standing in the doorway, only he was no longer alone. Sir Makaias had come up behind him, locking eyes with her, questions swimming behind his even expression.

With naught to do but answer them, Velena cleared her throat. "If you would be so good as to lend me your attention, I..." Her voice trailed off as Sir Harold huffed out his indignation, colliding into Sir Makaias' shoulder as he finally vacated the room.

"Sir Harold," she called after him, her voice losing none of its sweetness. "Must you go?"

Immediately, the hall's guests turned their attention to the back of the room, but the knight was already gone from sight.

"Tis a shame to see anyone leave so soon," she said, looking down for the first time upon Stuart and her father who were staring up at her as though she'd completely taken leave of her senses—and perhaps she had.

"I trust you have something *important* to say?" Sir Richard queried, concealing any signs of displeasure for her sake.

Where was Rowan when she needed him?

"Rowan," she shouted out suddenly, causing all to startle. "I seek Rowan…" she said again, her voice a more even tone. She scanned the hall as did everyone else.

There, leaning against the fireplace wall with his arms and legs crossed, he stood grinning from ear to ear, knowing not what she had to say but enjoying every uncomfortable word of it. "I'm at your beck and call, my lady," he cried, standing straight before giving an embellished bow.

Smiling in relief, she dipped her head in return. "So you've said."

He looked convincingly wounded. "You doubt my devotion?"

Velena had a hard time not giggling with him staring at her like that—and from the look of it, so was he. "I seek only a show of it. It would please me if you'd join me here—"

He raised his eyebrows. "Here, over there? Or, here, on that chair?"

Hand on her hip, she dropped her opposite shoulder and pointed down. "Here…on the chair," she said, as if he were the daft one. "I'm giving you but an example of what I want, so you don't get it wrong. This is your first time following my directions, is it not?"

Laughter rolled along from one end of the room to the other, lightening the mood and distracting the guests from all impropriety.

"I appreciate your example," he said, strolling in her direction. "What would you have me do once I get there?"

"I would like…" She cleared her throat. "Um, a…a…"

"Shall I make something up, myself?"

"A sonnet," she blurted out.

"A sonnet," he repeated looking more amused by the moment.

"Certainly. All this talk of courtly love and devotion, and I've yet to hear a single original verse. Should not all declarations of love be proved thusly?"

"Here, here!" Makaias was the first to call out. Disapproving of her actions as he was, he thought he had an idea of what she was trying to do. In addition, he wasn't about to see Britton's sister embarrassed and hoped his enthusiasm would spur on that of others—and it did.

"Would you like to hear me declare my love for this lovely lady?" he exclaimed. Rowan held out his arms and spun around to unanimous calls of approval.

More cheers erupted, and even Daisy looked mildly amused.

Rounding the dais, Rowan offered up his hand as Velena stepped from her chair to the ground. "Rest assured," he whispered for her ears only, "I'll be paying you back for this little embarrassment."

Velena met his eyes, unflinching. "I believe you owe me for a great many embarrassments, already," she whispered back.

A thoughtful moment passed between them, every one of them full of mirth and challenge as a grin spread across his face. "So I do," he exclaimed with a goodly amount of glee.

In fact, he grinned with pride, recalling his great many antics. "So I do!" he said again, this time bounding atop the chair as comfortable as a bard in his element. Once on his perch, he looked down at Velena and laughed with the sound of sincere affection.

He stretched his arms out wide. "Then let us begin!"

20

un-sung serenade

Almost entirely lost in shadow, Daisy sat in the window seat of the outer sitting room of Velena's solar, in what was still the wee hours of the morning. Blanket pulled tightly about her shoulders and knees hugged snuggly against her chest, she placed her hand upon the latch of the window and pushed it open ever so slightly…and just breathed. Pungent and sweet was the aroma that wafted beneath her nose.

It was raining. Daisy leaned her head against the pane of glass that separated her from the outside world and listened as it pelted out a rhythm that no one could mistake for being anything other than one of God's most melancholy sounds. Sure and steady, it came down, soaking the earth and flooding dips in the ground that could contain no more.

More than a sennight had gone by since the banquet—since Tristan had left Landerhill, and since she'd stolen his letter. Daisy was regretful of her thievery, but now more than ever, she felt it was a necessary evil as she tried to move forward day by day, praying that God would forgive her. But time wore on like her mood, and what should have been the most pleasant days of late summer, were instead nothing if not unseasonably cold.

But in this moment, as dark turned to twilight, and twilight to a morning true and honest, Daisy had not the slightest inclination to ponder on such things as stolen letters or an early frost. She was far too consumed with guilt over her trip to the healer's home and how it had been seven full day since her last flux. She'd calculated them on her fingers at least a dozen times and always with the same devastating result.

It was best not to think too hard on her situation lest she come to an unsavory solution, so it was good when a sudden commotion at the window by her ear startled her away from her silent brooding.

Confused by the noise, she put her hand to the glass, just as a hail of small pebbles ricocheted off the other side, and a few making it past the small crack in the window to land at her feet where a spray of rain had sprinkled through.

Now light enough to see, she looked down just in time to see Rowan catapult another volley with his arm. Waiting for the assault to pass, she pushed the window open another few inches and leaned out.

Seemingly delighted at her appearance, he cupped his hands together over his mouth and shouted upwards. "Can you hear me alright?"

Daisy rolled her eyes, but her cheeks still dimpled.

"Are you decent?" he called again.

Despite the fact that he couldn't possibly have a good view of her, Daisy still peeked below her blanket to make sure the laces at the top of her shift were tied up properly. "I'm decent. It's pouring rain, though. What are you doing down there?"

He raised a hand to shield the water from his eyes. "I've come that I might call forth the fairest Lady Velena. My love demands that I sing to her."

"Do you even know how to sing?"

"We'll soon find out."

Shaking her head, she shewed him away with a wave of her hand. "Go away! She sleeps."

"Not likely," Velena said from behind her. "Not with racket such as this to be heard."

Daisy turned and waved her forward with her hand. "Come and see, my lady."

Across the cold wooden floor, Velena sprinted the short distance from rug to window seat, her shift billowing out behind her. Gone, it seemed, were the summer days of crawling into bed unclad. Pulling back from the window, Daisy withdrew the blanket from her own shoulders and draped it over Velena's, directing her to hold it tightly in front as she looked below. "Rowan?"

"Greetings fair Nenna."

"Rowan, you're getting wet," she called down.

"A very astute observation, my lady."

Velena grinned. "As much as I love seeing your face first thing in the morning, I must insist that you get in doors. You'll catch your death of cold."

"Rain or shine, my love is thine. I wish to sing to you."

"Stuart's here, isn't he?"

"Why should you think that?" Rowan asked, drawing up the corners of his mouth.

Velena laughed at him, compelled to reach out a hand to see what drops could be collected in her palm. "I don't mean to doubt the sincerity of your very *sincere* declarations of affection...but I have noticed that you only declare them when Stuart is in the vicinity. I can only then assume that your *lovely* behavior has more to do with him than with me."

"You accuse me of being false? How could you?"

An unexpected rap at the door had Velena holding out a finger for Rowan to wait. "Enter," she called, turning with Daisy to face the door.

Thomas Two-toes poked in his little mouse-eared face. "Lord Magnus has just arrived with the material for your wedding gown. Your father asks that you come down."

"My *uncle* brought the material?"

"That's what I was told, my lady."

"Is Squire Stuart here, as well...by any chance?"

"Yes, my lady. I laid eyes on him, myself."

Velena laughed outright and turned to point an accusing finger out the window. "You're such a liar," she said, shaking her head. "We've just now been informed of their arrival."

Rowan shrugged, grin fully in place. "Be that as it may, "I will sing to you."

"Sing to Daisy," Velena said, pulling herself back inside and swinging her legs down from the window seat to face the confused boy. "Thank you, Thomas. Tell my father that I make myself ready now. Also," she said as an afterthought, "have a man sent to Lady Rainydayas' home. I would have her and the Baroness LaDawn come and help me with the dress."

"As you w—"

"Send Rowan to do it," Daisy interrupted.

Velena laughed "Why not? Send Rowan."

"As you wish, my lady." Thomas Two-toes pulled his head back through the door and was gone.

Velena headed for the bedroom section of the solar. Peeking her head back out, she smiled at Daisy. "Indulge Rowan a moment more, then send him away. I need your help getting dressed.

From below, Rowan used both hands to brush his long, almost white, blond hair back away from his forehead, sending a small stream of water down his back. "Are you still there?" he called.

"Velena has to get ready," she answered.

"Then what say you, Daisy? Are you in the mood for a song?"

"Do you actually have one to sing?" she asked, leaning forward once again.

Rowan shook his head. "I was going to make one up."

"I'm afraid it'll have to wait. Lady Velena just sent Thomas down to fetch you."

"Fetch me where?"

"Lady Rainydayas and Baroness LaDawn are to help with my lady's wedding dress. You're to bring them here."

"In this rain?" He winked and then flashed one last smile before turning towards the stables, a light step to his stride despite the downpour.

Daisy watched him go—and for longer than she would have a sennight ago. Indeed, a sennight ago, she wouldn't have watched at all. But now…now, he was changed as promised.

The night of the banquet, Rowan slipped her a note telling her of his plans to declare courtly love for Velena. Though he owed her no explanation, still he'd left her with his reasons for doing so, assuring her she was not forgotten and that he'd still be available to her should she fear for her own well-being on any account.

Though initially perturbed as to why Rowan should feel the need to inform her of his personal doings, she soon realized he'd been attempting to do her a kindness. In fact, everything he'd done since then had been borne of the same motive. He'd ceased his flirtations—mostly—probably as well as he was able—and had instead taken up conversing with her for short bits of time as his training allowed.

At first, it was uncomfortable seeing him around so often—knowing that he knew what Stuart had done to her—but soon, such knowledge faded into the background as his manner proved over and over to be less than offensive.

Daisy's mouth curved into the smallest of smiles. She didn't know how he'd done it but seeing him down there below the window, all sopping wet and silly, had served the very peculiar purpose of reminding her that, once upon a time, she'd looked out upon an early morning…and been happy.

The thought of her current situation ought still to be raining down on her as the most dismal kind of despair, and yet somehow Rowan's presence in the midst of her initial sorrow proved to be a small mercy cast into the pit she'd thus been trapped in. He knew of her situation, and still he smiled at her. He knew…and saw nothing to be ashamed of.

Tristan's betrayal of her confidence had deeply wounded her, but as long as Rowan knew, might she trust him to be the advocate he proclaimed himself to be—to keep her secret and care for *her* interests and not just Velena's? A plan was forming.

She would stay with Velena for as long as she could keep her condition hidden. And when the time for that ended, she'd ask Rowan to take her to Tristan's home in Oxford. She'd take whatever work he'd deign to give her, have the child, and then—well, who knew what then?

Common sense reminded her that there was an easier way…but her conscience wouldn't allow it. Had not the Lord spared her from the Pestilence? This one act alone now gave her hope. Might the Almighty still have a place for her in this world? Would He, like the rain, wash her clean from the last of her despair and allow her the chance to make a new beginning?

Slipping her hand beneath the blanket on her lap, Daisy nestled it atop her womb…and prayed.

Standing in a puddle of his own making, Squire Rowan waited for Lady Rainydayas and Baroness LaDawn to descend the staircase. Hands behind his back, he rocked back and forth on his heels, counting the minutes and wondering if there might be some parchment about that he could pilfer while he waited.

"You, there," he said to a boy of about fifteen as he entered the foyer. "Might your mistress have some parchment lying about I could use. I'd like to write something down."

The boy nodded and rushed off to do as bid, leaving Rowan to compose a quick verse of prose in his head.

Chuckling to himself, he knew exactly what he wanted to write when the boy returned. Initially being a means of revenge against Stuart, penning love notes to Velena—albeit, more humorous than romantic—was proving to be more fun than he'd imagined. Although this one would be a trifle more serious than the others.

As there was no desk in the foyer, Rowan made his way to the small dining room off to the right of the stairs, and this is where Rainydays found him—head bent over his masterpiece, smiling like an idiot.

"So, here you are," she said, entering the room.

Rowan raised his head, a look of delight upon his face as he folded up two separate notes. "Was I difficult to find?"

"No." She approached him, stopping at his shoulder. "I had only to follow the trail of water."

"Sorry about that."

"No, you're not," she said, bending down to give him a kiss upon his cheek. "But I don't mind."

"Rainy—"

"Where have you been, Rowan?" Her voice became low—intimately so. "Every time I visit at Landerhill, you're nowhere around—and it's been days since you've come to see me. I've missed you."

Rowan rubbed the tops of his thighs. "I've been settling in I suppose. Makaias has us on quite the regiment. Exercise three times a day, along with weapons training and such. I'd be tempted to say that his methods are a bit excessive, except that I've seen him without his tunic on—and the results are quite impressive. I hear women are appreciative of that sort of thing, so needless to say, I've been doubling my efforts."

She laughed. "I certainly am. But only on the right person."

"Oh?" he questioned, rising from his seat. "You have your eye on someone, do you? What a fortunate fellow."

Rainydayas frowned. "You know very well I was speaking of you."

Pulling in his lips, Rowan sobered. "I know it."

"My admiration for you has never been a secret—and never something you used to mind. Has something happened to divert your attention?"

"I never gave you that kind of attention," he reminded her, scooting his chair back beneath the table.

"That could be debated…but still you sought me out."

"We're friends."

"How long shall we remain so?"

"For as long as you'll have me as one," he said, his voice sincere. "Your honest opinion—your blunt sincerity and understanding ear—holds a place of extreme value in my heart."

Holding her disappointment at bay, she smiled, both gracious and altogether too forgiving. "As long as I'm there somewhere."

"You are," he assured her, a grin full of charm and secrets breaking out across his face. "And I was hoping that you could give this to Nenna for me when you see her."

Rainydayas accepted the folded note.

"But not unless Stuart is present to see you do it," he added.

"More to do with your recent profession of love, I take it."

"More to do with placing a bur beneath Stuart's saddle."

"Do you think that's wise?"

"Probably not."

She sighed in resignation. "Alright. Consider it done. And what of the other one?"

"Other what?"

"The other note. There were two."

He waved his hand. "Something personal."

"Man or woman?"

Rowan pulled his lips to the side. "I could answer, but by your tone, I can tell that you already have a guess."

"I do."

"Let's have it then."

"Daisy."

Surprise registered on his face. "Impressive."

"Not that impressive. I've seen the way you look at her."

Rowan flexed his jaw. "How do I look at her?"

Rainydayas tilted her head and shrugged. "The way you look at every woman before you grow bored—and stop looking. Which is why I'm not worried."

"You make me sound fickle."

"Then I apologize. I meant for you to sound non-committal."

He raised his eyebrows at her forthrightness, unsure whether to feel insulted or annoyed at his own transparency.

"Have you had many occasions to speak with her?" Rainydayas continued.

"Yes," he answered honestly. "I make occasion to."

"I see."

"Careful," he said, pointing a finger. "You said you weren't jealous, but your eyes are almost as green as Velena's. Come now, there's no cause for that. Stuart treats her poorly, and I promised Tristan I'd look after her." He realized Tristan's last words didn't exactly include Daisy, but he felt it was implied.

"He cares for her?" Rainydayas inquired, with some skepticism.

Gwenhavare entered the room. "Who cares for who?"

Rowan turned to face the woman who'd come to be close to Velena over the last week. He bowed. "Baroness."

She waved him off with a laugh.

"I was just asking him if Tristan had feelings for Daisy," Rainydayas explained.

A curious expression passed over Gwenhavare face. "I meant to ask you about him. You said before that he went back to Oxford. Who were his parents?"

"Lady Isabelle and Sir Tobias Challener," Rainydayas answered, taking special note of the way Gwenhavare's face lit up at this bit of news.

"Fancy that," she said, working to control her smile, "I thought they might be. I'll have to tell Lady Velena."

Rowan looked confused. "How did you know him?"

"We're both from Oxford. I hadn't put it together at first, but after your riveting speech at the banquet..." Gwenhavare paused to give him an appreciative smile, amusement hidden within her eyes, "in which you said his name, I thought it had to be the same Tristan as I used to know."

"A fact sure to surprise her," Rowan said, exchanging a curious look with Rainydayas as he gestured for the women to proceed him from the room.

"I can't believe I didn't make the connection, myself," Rainydayas mused, expecting to revisit the subject with Gwenhavare at a later time. "But while we're still on the subject of Tristan, you didn't answer my question, Rowan."

"What question was that?"

"If he cares for Daisy."

"Oh, no." He shook his head. "Far be it for me to speak for another man—or provide fodder for gossiping women," he answered with a wink.

Gwenhavare looked shocked. "Women? Gossip? Never."

He laughed, then listened as the rain continued to pelt down upon the roof above them. "Shall we wait for the rain to stop?"

Rainydayas adjusted the cloak around her neck and pulled up the hood. "We'd be waiting all day if we waited for that."

"Then let us be off," he said, adjusting his own hood, still wet from his ride over. He plunged himself into the thick of it and then turned to help guide the woman past the deeper puddles.

As he held out his hand to Rainydayas, their eyes met, and he knew she was more worried about his infatuation with Daisy than she let on. Truth be told he wasn't entirely proud of himself for his deception, either. Rainydayas had always been an honest friend to him—and so he wished to be to her if only he knew what to say. His attraction to other women had always been merely that. Nothing serious and nothing worth confessing. There was no question that Daisy aroused similar feelings in him as others had—but was there more? He wasn't used to going beyond flirtation but for Daisy's sake, he'd done his best to stop. What was left for him to share, then, was something far more sincere...and vulnerable.

Rainydayas was also attractive, no question, but the thought of pursuing her for the sake of intimacy never lasted long in his mind despite her wish for it be otherwise. She was a kindred spirit but not a lover. He found no pleasure in tormenting her with his presence. She, however, continually assured him that he'd come to love her in time, and the *what if* of that had always drawn him back.

God forgive him for his selfish desire to keep Rainydayas close at hand when it was another filling his thoughts—and more and more so with each passing day. He knew he was nothing to Daisy, except a shield and a jester. And far be it for him to complain, for he'd always been those things—his size and wit his greatest strengths. But for once...he wished he was more.

21

busy bee

Now dressed and ready, Velena and Daisy stood at one of the long tables in the great hall, along with Sir Richard, Lord Magnus, and Stuart. Green velvet and rich satins of blue, cream, and gold were laid out before them in great folds, like ripples of water running down the table.

"Where did you get this?" Velena asked, stretching her hands out upon the yards of fabric. Daisy, too, fingered the soft velvet in admiration.

"In Avignon," Lord Magnus answered. "Finest we could find."

Velena watched as Stuart circled the table, coming to stand at her side. "I thought you went for indulgences," she said, wryly.

"That too," Stuart answered.

Velena looked across at her father whose top lip twitched beneath his mustache as her uncle went on in detail about the fine quality of the fabric, and the price he haggled over it. She lowered her voice. "Our marriage was hardly a surety at that point," she said, bending at the waist to have a closer look at the weave. "Awfully presumptuous of you, don't you think?"

"Not really." He eyed her the way she eyed the fabric. "It was only a matter of time—and I was willing to wait."

Velena turned her head to look at him. "Not patiently."

Boyish grin in place, "I never said *patiently.*"

She gave him a half-hearted smile.

"Do you approve?" he asked, handling a corner of it, himself.

She nodded her head. "I could hardly do otherwise. It is beautiful," she admitted.

He looked pleased.

"My lord," a voice addressed her father from behind them.

Velena turned.

"Yes, Thomas," Sir Richard answered.

"Lady Margarite has arrived."

Sir Richard's face broke out in a large grin. "Wonderful. Show her in."

A moment later, and Lady Margarite entered the room, accompanied by her eldest, Sir Makaias, who hung back as his mother advanced. She stopped just short of Sir Richard and her brother-in-law, Lord Magnus, to whom she delivered a small curtsy.

Waiting his turn, Stuart greeted his aunt with open arms. "God be with you, Auntie."

"And with you, Stuart," she said, returning his embrace. Then turning to Velena, she gushed. "And here is the bride. Are you ready for this old woman to teach you a thing or two about what she knows?"

"Are you to sew my dress?"

"If you find me acceptable."

Velena clutched her hands to her chest. "I do, indeed. What a godsend you are! I've sent for two others, thinking we'd have to muddle through on our own. I hope you're not offended."

"Not at all," Lady Margarite said, a smile on her face. "The more the merrier—and the quicker the work."

"Then we shan't get in your way," Sir Richard said. "Come, Lord Magnus, this is women's work. Let us find ourselves an occupation elsewhere."

He nodded. "Will you be joining us, Stuart—or do you plan on making a few stitches of your own?" he mocked.

Stuart raised an eyebrow. "If you're asking if I prefer the company of my aunt and fiancé to two graybeards such as yourselves, then the answer is *yes*. I'll meet up with you shortly."

Magnus grunted his disapproval before turning to leave, walking a straight line so that Makaias had to step aside for his uncle to exit the hall.

Velena gritted her teeth at her uncle's rudeness, thinking he ought to have at least offered a few parting words to his sister-in-law. She was, after all, there to help. Turning to Daisy, she received only a slight shrug of the shoulder in answer to her look of annoyance.

"So, you wish to help us cut, Nephew," Lady Margarite teased, unruffled by Lord Magnus' behavior. "Or you, my son? As I recall, you were quite handy with a needle when you had to be."

Makaias produced a crooked smile, leaving Stuart to answer. "No, indeed," he said. "I know very well that my talents lay elsewhere, but any extra moment spent in Velena's presence is a moment well spent."

Velena ducked her head appropriately at the compliment, though she felt no emotions equal to it. What remark she did raise her head to came from Daisy.

"Pretty words," she said, refusing to raise her eyes above the table. "Almost as pretty as Squire Rowan's of this morning."

Velena stood somewhat aghast. She hadn't heard Daisy intentionally speak up to Stuart since their return from Wineford Castle.

"Ah, yes," Stuart said, averting his own eyes and responding as if he'd received the remark from Velena, herself. "I did see him below a certain window upon our arrival."

Lady Margarite cocked her head to the side. "And what mischief is that nephew of mine up to this time?"

"He recites her poetry," Stuart answered dryly.

Velena tried to laugh away the seriousness of his tone. "Not this time. But he did threaten to sing to me."

"That would be a threat," Stuart said.

"Oh, but he *can* sing," Lady Margarite answered, beginning to maneuver the material on the table to a better position for cutting. "Quite well, actually."

Daisy's ears seemed to perk. "I wouldn't have thought so."

"A little-known fact, my dear, but a fact nontheless."

Velena tried to ignore the look of disapproval clouding Stuart's face as she wrinkled her nose as if Rowan's talents made no difference to her. "Well, then, what can I do to help?" she asked, directing her attention back to Lady Margarite.

"I'll need you to help me cut, so for that we'll need a good pair of shears. I've brought my own but if you have one or two pair more, we'll have this done in no time."

"I'll fetch them," Daisy said, taking her leave.

"Make sure they're good and sharp, my dear," Lady Margarite called after her, but she was already out of the room.

Makaias smiled. "I'll sharpen them," he said and quickly followed after.

"Now, it's time for you to go," Lady Margarite said to Stuart, shooing him away. "It's time to focus, and we'll not be able to do that with you mooning about."

"As you say, Auntie," he said with a quick peck to her cheek and a parting look in Velena's direction.

Velena knew that look—and it spoke volumes. He was wishing they were alone, but for Velena's part, she was glad they weren't.

When he lingered, Lady Margarite gave him a playful push and then pulled out a measuring tape from her pocket. "Now hold out your arms, dear Velena. I need to take your measurements."

Before long, Daisy was back with a single set of shears and an explanation that Sir Makaias was sharpening the other pair. Then with the measuring tape set aside, Lady Margarite went to work showing Velena how the material was to be cut. When all was laid out and ready, Makaias had still not returned.

A small knock on the wall caught their attention. "Look who I found," Stuart said, entering the room with Lady Rainydayas and Barroness LaDawn in tow.

At once, Velena rose from her place at the table to greet them. "Welcome! Welcome, I'm so glad you came," she said, embracing them both even as Thomas stood by waiting for them to shrug out of their wet capes.

"We wouldn't miss it," Rainydayas said, "though I warn you, neither of us have taken on a dress of this magnitude."

"It's true," Gwenhavare cut in, "and we apologize in advance should we do a poor job of it, but I think between the three of us, we should figure something out. Leastwise, you'll not be standing in church naked."

"Worry not," Velena said, turning to gesture towards Lady Margarite, who'd since risen from the bench. "We have an expert among us. "Lady Margarite, I believe you already know Lady Rainydayas."

Both women curtsied.

"But let me introduce to you Baroness LaDawn."

For a moment, Lady Margarite appeared somewhat awkward, but it didn't stop her from offering her greetings. "It's my pleasure to finally make your acquaintance, though it is I who should have been introduced to you. For that I apologize."

"There's no need," Gwenhavare said with a wave of her hand. "I would rather be seen as family than anyone's better."

Velena looked confused. "I don't understand."

Lady Margarite smiled warmly. "The Baroness is of a higher rank than I. In such cases, she of lower rank should be introduced to she of higher rank…and not the other way around."

"What did *I* do?"

"You introduced her to me as if I were her better."

Gwenhavare interrupted. "As I'm sure you are. If not in rank, then surely in wisdom. And I have no quarrel with sitting at the feet of my elders—no matter their station."

"Still," Stuart spoke up, from where he'd hung back by the door, "it's something she'll have to remember in the future." He looked at Velena. "You'll be the mistress of your own household in only a few short weeks."

"You're right," Velena said, looking at Lady Margarite, sheepishly. "I suppose I did mix it up. I'm sorry if I embarrassed you."

"Forgotten. Now let us begin with our stitching. Daisy, could you hand me that basket by your feet? It has my thread and needles in it." Once in hand, she began rummaging around for what she needed as the other women took their seats around the table. Once again, Stuart lingered, choosing to stand at Velena's shoulder, anxious to see the cutting begin.

"So," Rainydayas said as she seated herself on one of the benches. "Rowan tells me he was at your window this morning"

Stuart rolled his eyes. "Must he continually be the topic of conversation?"

Rainydays laughed. "I meant not to annoy you, but as I care for him a great deal, I should warn you that he is very often the topic of my conversation. So, yes, and back to what I was saying…" she turned to Velena, "he said he was at your window but that you didn't allow him the chance to sing. How very sad for you," she teased, "he's quite good."

"So I hear, though at the time, I had no idea of it."

Rainydayas quirked a smile. "Rowan doesn't attempt anything he doesn't believe himself to be very good at."

Gwenhavare giggled as though she thought this very amusing. "He certainly is cocky."

Daisy glanced up and then to Lady Margarite as she was handed her needle and thread.

"Offensively so," Stuart added.

"Well, I hope you'll take no offense in this," Rainydayas said, pulling Rowan's note from her pocket. She held it out across the table for Velena to take. "He asked me to give this to her."

Accepting it, Velena paused less than a moment before placing it directly into Stuart's awaiting hand with nary a glance in his direction.

Lady Margarite watched the exchange with veiled expression.

"No offense taken," Stuart said, unfolding the note, himself.

Rainydayas bit into her bottom lip. "Do you always make it a point to commandeer the correspondence of others?"

"Only if comes from other men," he answered. Opening it, he read aloud,

> *"Pretty as a flower,*
> *eyes green as the trees,*
> *a smile so fantastic,*
> *you beguile all the bees.*
> *One in particular has a fancy for you,*
> *but he's no gentleman bee*
> *but a deceiver through and through.*
> *He follows you thusly,*
> *neglecting his hive,*
> *taking you captive until I arrive.*
> *So, I'll slice off his stinger*
> *and pluck off his wings.*
> *You'll break free of his menace*
> *and escape all his stings.*
> *Remember who loves you,*
> *and won't let you fall.*
> *At the first din of trouble,*
> *let it be me that you call."*

To say Stuart appeared displeased was an understatement as the room was enveloped in an uncomfortably long silence. Even Lady Margarite looked apologetic over what she perceived as an unkind letter.

"How cryptic..." Gwenhavare finally said. "Squire Rowan certainly has an aversion to bees."

"Or to one in particular," Daisy added quietly, surprising Velena yet again with her bold remark. Unsure what had come over herself,

Daisy had the sudden urge to be away from Stuart's presence. "I think I remember having one extra set of sheers in our solar."

Ignoring her, Stuart addressed the women left at the table. "Tell me. Do you really find nothing wrong with this?"

Shaking her head, Lady Margarite answered before anyone else had the chance. "No need to stir up trouble, Nephew? I'm certain no one here would condone the action."

Velena frowned. "But Auntie, surely you know Rowan but jests."

"Yes, my dear, I know his ways, and his heart...but the Scripture says, '*If it be possible, live at peace with all men,*' and if what he's doing is causing division—unintended or otherwise—then he's in the wrong."

The room was quiet as if the weight of her statement rested on Velena to remedy.

"What would you have me do?" she asked.

"God's answers are far better than mine," Lady Margarite concluded, "so in my humble opinion—if it were me—I would start with prayer."

Unable to argue, Velena sat in silence, pretending not to notice the glances her friends were casting to one another.

Suddenly, there was the sound of footsteps as Makaias returned, breaking the silence for which Velena was glad.

"Your shears, Mother. I apologize for my tardiness, but Sir Richard had need of me. As it is, I must return to the training yard."

Lady Margarite gestured towards Velena. "It's her, who will be needing them."

He looked down at the material, now pinned and ready to cut. "Forgive me Velena," he said, placing them into her hand with a grin, "I had no intention of delaying your project."

"Thank you, Makaias," she answered, easily. "You were more than generous to take on the task in the first place."

Stuart stiffened at the familiarity with which Makaias and Velena used each other's given names. Even Lady Margarite raised an eyebrow, as her son bowed his head and exited the room.

"You shouldn't address him without his title," Stuart corrected.

Velena looked taken aback. "What?"

"You should refer to him as *Sir* Makaias.

It was all Velena could do not to roll her eyes. "Yes, of course."

"I believe Lady Velena has received enough correction for one sitting, Nephew. Let us leave her in peace for the time being, shall we…" Immediately changing subjects, she began directing the women as to where they should begin making their cuts.

"Lady Margarite," Gwenhavare said, making sure her sheers were lined up just so, "I hope you don't mind my saying so, but you have a very handsome son."

"He had a handsome father," she replied wistfully.

Rainydayas smiled. "All the Mannering brothers are worth a second glance to be sure, but Sir Makaias, especially. And I don't think anyone would argue with me."

Feeling the heat of Stuart's gaze, Velena toyed with her necklace. Did he really think her so foolish to answer?

Stuart ran a hand through his hair. "Well, as much as I'd like to stay and talk about how handsome my cousins are, I must return to my father. There is still much to be done in preparation for the wedding. Velena, would you do me the honor of walking me out. I'll have a word with you before I go."

Taking a deep breath, Velena placed her sheers on the table and excused herself to follow him from the room, polite smile plastered into place.

22

leverage

"What's wrong?" Velena asked, once they were alone

"Nothing. I'd just like a moment with you before I go. Once you all start your sewing, we'll have scant time together, I'm sure."

"Oh," Velena replied, genuinely surprised he had no further corrections for her.

"Do you really like the material?"

"I do," she assured him. "They're quite extraordinary."

He smiled. "It was my idea to get the green velvet for the tunic."

"I thought as much."

"It's my favorite color on you."

"I remember," she said, recalling a day at Wineford when she'd worn it, especially to please him. "But blue *is* more usual for a wedding garment."

Stuart's brow knit together. "I've noticed. Why is that?"

"It's the color of innocence," she stated, as if he ought to know.

"You can use the blue satin for the surcoat, but I wanted the green near your face," he said softly, wistfully, as if he were already imaging the finished product. "It looks best with your eyes."

Velena's smile wobbled as Stuart's hand came up to stroke the apple of her cheek. "I'd better get back," she said, ducking her head. "They'll wonder what's keeping me."

He shrugged his shoulders. "Let them wonder."

"Stuart."

"Alright," he conceded, knowing she wanted to go but telling himself she was merely excited to get started on the dress. He bent down to kiss her cheek, but she pulled away."

"Someone will see."

Straightening to full height, he exhaled in frustration. "See what? That I kissed your cheek?" he questioned, his tone a reminder of what he thought of her prudish ideals. "I don't care who sees."

"I do," she insisted.

Stuart began massaging the back of his neck as if the muscles had suddenly knotted up.

Velena waited for him to speak, but he seemed to be thinking. "Stuart?"

"What?"

"May I join my friends now?"

"Might as well…" he paused, searching for the right words. "Only take care what guides your tongue. Your friends were vulgar to talk about Makaias the way they did, especially in mixed company. I don't want you influenced by them."

"Here it is…" Velena said, exasperation in her tone.

"Here what is?"

"I knew there was something bothering you."

"Of course it bothered me. And when did you and Makaias start calling each other by your given names?"

"Even you neglect his title in private company," Velena pointed out.

"Yes, but he's my cousin."

"After the wedding, he'll be my cousin too, and besides that, I don't do it in public."

"You did it in front of your friends. How do you think that made me feel?"

Velena crossed her arms. "Probably the same way it made me feel to have been corrected for it."

He scowled, waiting for a better answer.

"He invited me to do so," she submitted. "I see him so often…with Britton, of course…I suppose it was just easier to dispense with formalities."

"Then learn to do hard things, because I don't like other men being so familiar with you."

Velena took a deep breath. His voice was condescending, but at least he wasn't yelling at her. Serious Stuart was easier to placate than angry Stuart, so she nodded. "Alright."

He raised an eyebrow. "Just like that?"

"Just like that."

"I expected you to argue."

"I'm working on being submissive."

"Since when?"

"Since I decided Sir Makaias' title isn't worth the argument."

Stuart smirked. "Decided just now, I'd wager...but thank you," he said, taking her hands, his eyes caressing the smooth skin as he brushed his fingers over her knuckles, a question on his lips. "You don't think...I mean, you don't really think Makaias is *that* handsome, do you?"

Also, not worth an argument, she firmly told herself. "I've not taken note of him if that's what you mean."

"Is that your denial?"

Was he pouting? Velena pulled her hands free from his grip, emotional exhaustion clouding her features. "Don't do this," she implored. "I'll not start lying just to ease your discomfort. Yes, he's handsome, but so are you and many other men—and you're simply going to have to start trusting me around them."

Stuart grimaced. "Like Rowan?"

"Back to Rowan?"

"You encourage him."

"Try *discouraging* him. You know him as well as I do."

"I do know him, and he's gone too far. Guessing his motives at the banquet was easy enough, but why does he continue with this charade?"

"It's as you say. It's a game to him. He doesn't mean it."

"And if he does? Now that he's at Landerhill, he has every occasion to find you alone when I can't."

Velena scoffed. "I'd say you do a pretty good job of finding me alone," she said, gesturing at the empty hallway.

"You know what I mean."

"Then be angry with him," she hissed, trying to keep her voice low. "I've made no declarations in return. Stop holding me accountable for his actions. *His* actions," she reiterated.

"You have a part in it," he insisted.

"Then I'll pray as your aunt suggests."

"Just tell him to stop."

"He's your cousin, Stuart," Velena said, holding out her finger. "Why don't you tell him to stop? It all has to do with you anyway."

"It can't all be my fault."

"I'm in earnest," she said, praying that her words would finally have an impact on him. "Not one verse of poetry—nor one single scrap of paper declaring his affections—has been spoken or sent unless you're there to witness it. It's not me he's trying to impress himself upon. It's you. So, who but you can figure the reason for it?"

A chill ran up Stuart's spine as the inkling of an idea impressed itself upon him, but he brushed it aside as impossible.

"Velena softened her words. "Please, Cousin, I tire of the enmity between us. Don't you? Let us be on the same side," she pleaded. "Do you remember that Hocktide[32] when we were children, and Rowan and Jaren chased me through the crowds trying to drag me away?"

"Yes," he said, failing to understand its relevance."

"Who did I call for?"

"Me."

"Who came for me when I did?"

"Me."

"Who did I stay with despite Rowan begging me to run off with him to the cock fight?"

Stuart's shoulders finally relaxed, his expression all forgiving. "Me."

"Then why do you worry? Rowan will ever be Rowan—but the person I'm standing with is…"

"Me," Stuart whispered, his mind holding tight to the memories she'd conjured. "You're light to my darkness, Velena, and yet you'd insist you don't love me. Is it not what you've just described?"

Velena looked down. If only it could be as easy as a word. "Of a kind."

His lips pulled to the side. "And how, pray tell, am I supposed to interpret that?"

She raised her face to him. "I'll ever be faithful to you. Is that not a form of love?"

"You know I want more," he said, searching her eyes for some spark of greater affection. But there was no hiding her hesitancy, nor disguising the way she shrank back from his question—if not in body, then in spirit.

She spoke kindly but without apology. "Then you'll have to be patient."

Stuart put a hand to his chest. "You think me anything else? How long since we kissed at the banquet, and I've not asked you for another?"

Velena looked him square in the face. "Haven't you, though?"

Stuart brought his voice to a whisper. "I can't stop thinking about it, Velena. How I wish you'd reconsider and grant me another?" He brushed his hand against her sleeve, ready to pull her forward, given even the smallest measure of encouragement.

"I've already told you how I feel about it. You'll not change my mind."

Stuart's countenance fell, leaving him to look every bit the part of a wounded animal.

"I'm sorry," Velena said. "I'm sorry, but I won't yield. And it's not right you should ask it of me." She twisted her arms in front of her waist. "Your patience will have to extend to the wedding."

"I'll tell you what's not right," he said, hurt written into every word, "granting me a taste of Heaven only to withhold it again."

Velena scoffed. "That's not—"

"Because that's what you're doing," he insisted. "Feeling you in my arms was like a piece of Heaven. I've waited to kiss you my whole life. That first time…it was like taking my first real breath of air. But at the banquet…" he licked his lips, "that was feeling alive—really and truly *alive*. Every night I pray that you'll forfeit marital obligations for sincere desire…and kiss me because you want to.*"

Velena slunk back against the wall. "That's not fair. How am I supposed to respond to that?"

Stuart came forward, caging her in with both arms. He didn't touch her, but the force of his gaze held her in place. "You know how."

"Oh," a woman's voice exclaimed in surprise. "Excuse me."

Stuart turned his head even as Velena pushed him away. Gwenhavare stood just outside the doorway of the great hall, hands clasped at her waist, eyes averted.

Feigning embarrassment, Stuart rubbed the backs of his fingers across his chin. "I see I've kept her too long." he said.

"We *were* wondering where she'd gone off to," Gwenhavare said simply.

"My apologies, Baroness. Allow me to return her."

Too embarrassed for a proper farewell, Velena dipped her head without ceremony and followed Gwenhavare back into the room.

Stuart frowned as he watched her go. Deep down, he knew he'd have to stop pushing her if he was ever to gain any semblance of this woman's devotion, but still it baffled him how she could be so cold to his advances. Frustrated, he turned to leave, but it was then he saw Daisy standing by the stairs at the end of the hallway, staring like an animal caught in a trap.

Most likely she'd heard them talking and was now working up the courage to move past him. No matter. He had a thing he wished to say to her as well, so by the time she began walking, he'd met her halfway.

"So, I'm the *bee,* am I?" he questioned, cold smile in place. "It was a bold statement on your part, Daisy, but any talent you think you have for words should be none but what you can do to keep them quiet. So, I'll be asking you to keep your comments to yourself from now on. I'm sure you understand."

Expecting her to cower, his smile faded as Daisy squared her shoulders in a way he hadn't seen since the day she'd gotten drunk and confronted him at the castle.

"You can say what you like," she stated calmly, "but so can I."

"Oh, Really?" He raised an eyebrow. "And where, might I ask…is this sudden bout of courage coming from?"

Courage? If only.

Daisy's hands trembled at her sides, and when she didn't answer, he looked on her with nothing short of contempt—though she would have been be surprised to know how much of it was truly for himself. For the truth of his misdeeds was always reflected in her eyes, and the longer he stared, the greater his propensity towards self-loathing.

"What I wouldn't do to erase you from my mind," he finally said, moving to step around her as if her presence had grown suddenly intolerable.

"I'm with child." She blurted it without knowing why. And as expected, everything stopped—stopped almost entirely as she watched him forget to take his next breath. *What have I done?* her heart cried as Stuart approached within a hand's breadth of her face.

His voice was a deadly calm. "What did you just say?"

Daisy swallowed, unable to say it again, his presence continuing to frighten her no matter what she wanted him to believe to the contrary.

His eyes narrowed. "Answer me."

"I carry your—"

Speaking one moment, gasping the next, Daisy lost her voice as Stuart's hand shot forward, gripping her upper arm in a vice-like grip. "You lie!" he exclaimed, knowing even as he said it that it was the truth, and he hated her for it.

Daisy endured in silence until she thought her knees would buckle. Desperate, she lifted her free hand between them but couldn't bring herself to touch him. "You're hurting me," she whispered at length, just as a noise at the front doors drew his attention away.

Having little choice but to release her, Stuart did so just as a servant entered, followed closely by the healer, who'd returned to examine Britton and hopefully relieve him of his blindfold. Daisy seemed suddenly unable to answer any questions regarding Sir Britton's whereabouts, so it was Stuart who sent them in what he hoped was the right direction—though anywhere would have been good so long as they left. And the moment they did, Stuart's attention was once more glued to the woman before him.

"If this is some sort of trick, so help me, I'll…"

"Yes, it's a trick," Daisy confessed, "only you played it on me. It wasn't good enough that you should ruin my life. You had to plant another for men to scorn as well."

"I never planned to touch you at all," he hissed. "I never wanted this—" his voice cut out abruptly as he tried to gain control over his racing heartbeat. He took a breath and continued in a rush of words. "I never wanted any of this to happen. I shouldn't have been drinking. You shouldn't have been ready to give yourself to Bowan. None of this should have happened."

"Is that meant to be an apology?"

"Let it be what you want—a poor explanation if nothing else, but I want to be done with this.

Daisy shook her head. "How can we be?"

Stuart continued breathing heavy as the silence beat between them like a drum. "Indeed," he said, as new understanding dawned in his eyes. "So now you wish to blackmail me."

Only then, fully comprehending what she'd done, did Daisy realize her newly elevated position. "I wish for you to leave me alone."

Surprised by the simple request, Stuart scoffed. "When have I ever sought you out?"

"Promise you'll leave me alone," she pressed.

"Happily," he answered without hesitation.

"And Velena."

"And Velena what?"

"Stop forcing yourself on her."

At this his patience failed. "I've done nothing of the kind."

"You think I don't see? You force yourself on her, and she doesn't like it."

"You're wrong," Stuart said, leaning forward—eyes taunting. "There's a great difference between wooing and forcing. Or perhaps you don't know the differen—"

"I know the difference!" she all but shouted, fists balled at the sides of her skirts, eyes squeezed shut as if a sea of glass had just shattered above her.

Unnerved, Stuart took a step back. Looking around, he half expected Velena and her friends to come charging from the room in concern.

Returning her voice to a whisper, Daisy stared him in the eyes. "Keep your distance…else I tell her of the child."

Tempted to take her seriously, Stuart's shock soon melted to nothing. "No, you won't."

Daisy lifted her chin. "I say I will."

Stuart's jaw shifted to the left. "I'll no longer do you the dishonor of doubting your bravery…but with all due respect, who would believe the child is mine? No one. Not when all I have to do is deny it. So, as I see it…we're right back where we left off."

"Far from it," Daisy said, a single tear trailing down her cheek. "Ruined before, I am now undone. Whether I say it's yours or another's, how long do you think I can hide this? Is there no decent bone in your body—no inkling of a conscience that bids you pity me for what you did?"

Stuart looked away, his conscience, indeed, taking a beating despite his pride. "Even if I did…" he began softly, but cleared his throat, deciding not to finish. "I'll leave you alone, Daisy. Have no worry of that. And, so long as you promise to leave before your condition becomes…apparent, I'll save my wooing for after Velena and I are wed."

Daisy blinked in surprise. "Where am I to go?"

"Surely, you know of someplace," he insisted.

Daisy bit her lip, thinking it unwise to involve Tristan or his previously made offer. "I do. But I have no way to get there."

Taking deep breaths, Stuart appeared at his wits end. "Money is no object. I'll pay your way and then some, only leave by wedding's end."

Daisy looked disgusted. "I don't want your money."

"Doesn't change the fact that you need it," he stated calmly.

"Then God forgive me for taking my help from the Devil."

Stuart made a fist between them and sneered. "If I'm such a devil, then why did you tell me?"

Silent for a moment, Daisy stared at the floor, tears falling to create small circles of color on the otherwise dull stones at her feet. "You're the only one I *could* tell…"

Mouth pressed into a straight line, his eyes drifted from her face down to her abdomen where they lingered until the reality of what existed there threatened to turn his stomach. Gritting his teeth, he turned away. "I wish you hadn't."

Leaving her then, he stalked through the front doors, ignoring the rain. He stretched his neck from side to side, working to release his tension as he headed for the stables where he'd left off Jaren talking with Sir Andret. Not bothering to skirt around the puddles, he sloshed muddy water clear up the front of his hose.

Bile rose in his throat, and he had to swallow hard, reminding himself that Daisy had done her worst…and failed. Nothing would come of it as long as she kept her end of the bargain and he, his. Still, he hated that Daisy should hold any sort of power over him and had to wonder if she'd truly just give up the only leverage she had for obtaining a better living? She might leave, but would his troubles go with her? He feared not. Not as long as she carried his child.

His child…

---

[32]**Hocktide:** A continuation of the Easter festivities, celebrated on the first Monday and Tuesday after Easter.

23

unexpected ties

Velena and Gwenhavare re-entered the great hall to find Auntie and Rainydayas leisurely engaged in a section of sewing and chatting merrily.

Gwenhavare took her seat beside Rainydayas and Velena across from them. Gwenhavare was quick to insert herself into the conversation, purposefully diverting attention away from Velena, who remained quiet.

Aside from the embarrassment of being caught in such a compromising position, her encounter with Stuart angered her. She hated the subtle manipulations that caused her to coddle him rather than stand her ground. She should have just walked away.

Distracted by her thoughts, Velena poked her finger with her needle and flinched. A bead of blood formed, which she quickly brought to her mouth before it could drop onto the material, though she hardly knew why she cared. She held no excitement for the garment that would bring her ever closer to a lifetime with a man she had no desire to be intimate with.

"Are you alright," Rainydayas asked, watching Velena suck on her finger.

Velena took a deep breath. "It's just a prick."

"I wasn't talking about your finger."

"You've been awfully quiet," Auntie agreed.

Velena shook her head. "I'm fine."

"Come dear," Auntie said, "you needn't mind my presence if that's your concern. Sometimes it helps to talk out whatever is bothering you. Whatever we keep in the darkness, it is always loses its power when brought into the light.

Velena pulled her finger from her mouth and then pressed it against her surcoat for good measure. "It's more than just one thing."

"Does Stuart always take Rowan's notes from you?" Rainydayas interrupted, as if the question had been on the tip of her tongue the whole time.

Velena rubbed at her nose, knowing it'd do no good to lie. "Yes," Velena confessed. "But really, it's alright. If it matters so much to him to have Rowan's poetry, he can have it. It means nothing to me, and it's worlds easier than giving him cause for further jealousy."

Rainydayas' eyes flitted towards Daisy as she entered the room and nodded. "Without question, jealousy is one of life's more gruesome things to contend with."

"The thing that's so difficult is that I thought it was only Tristan who made him feel so. Though, I suppose, jealousy isn't exactly what it is with Rowan. But still, I thought that after Tristan left, Stuart would be who he was…before. I was so hoping. But now…it's like he left for nothing.

Gwenhavare rested her hand on the table across from her. "I'm so sorry."

Velena smiled, but it did little to counteract her true feelings. "Some days I really am alright—just not today. Three times chastised for things I ought to have already known, and…well, you saw."

"I'm no prude," Gwenhavare said, giving her a reassuring smile. "And it seems to me that he ought to be the one apologizing for that."

"Still, it's one more thing to add to my list of wrongs for today."

"Of what do you speak?" Auntie asked, looking concerned.

Velena nodded for Gwenhavare to tell her. Somehow, it was easier that way.

"He tried to kiss her in the hallway."

Auntie quirked a smile as she returned to her stitching. "Well, perhaps, you think me ignorant of such goings on, but I'm not a stranger to love nor to its many devices. I was married a long time and even before that; I remember my Edwin stealing a kiss or two. You needn't be ashamed, dear. It's not so uncommon for a man to want to kiss the woman he loves."

"Better to suffer one of Squire Rowan's *pretendings* than his kind of love," Daisy muttered, biting a stretch of thread free from its spool.

"If you knew Rowan better, there'd be nothing to suffer," Rainydayas said, an unmistakable edge to her voice.

Daisy made no further comment but looked her full in the face. It was obvious her presence annoyed Rainydayas, but after what she'd just endured with Stuart, it'd be nothing for Daisy to meet her jealousy head on.

"Here," Auntie said, handing Daisy a section of fabric. "Start your stitching here." And then all was quiet until she turned back towards Velena. "So, I take it, his affections are unwanted."

Velena looked distressed. "I wish it were otherwise. You've no idea how much," she said, dropping her stitching to her lap. "When we were still at Wineford, there was a woman in the village who held nothing but disdain for her husband; I could see it in her face. She was cold—hard. I don't want that to be me."

Auntie gave her hand a squeeze. "I'd wager anything that woman didn't love God."

Velena looked at her.

"And you do, my dear. Trust in Him to give you the grace you need to love Stuart. Makaias tells me your father has given you his Bible to read. So, do something for me. I want you to read St. Paul's first letter to the Corinthians. He has quite a bit to say on the subject of love, and I think you'll find it quite appropriate to your situation. Memorize it. Drink it in. It's God's holy Word which sustains us—especially in the desert places," she said with a comforting smile.

"Then I won't delay," Velena said, reaching beside her to squeeze Daisy's knee. It was now only Daisy who truly knew how much she coveted God's word.

"I think we should stay with you tonight," Rainydayas said abruptly. "You need cheering up, and I'm a bit curious about this Corinthians letter. We could sit by a cozy fire, drink our fill of wine, and read it together."

Velena's eyes grew round. "Does it really interest you?"

"Why wouldn't it?" Rainydayas asked.

"You don't attend church."

"Just because I don't like church doesn't mean I don't like God."

Gwenhavare giggled. "She stays away on account of her brothers."

"Admittedly," Rainydayas said, then snorted. "They're degenerate heathens, and as soon as the Lord realizes who occupies his church, I'm quite certain He'll bring the entire building down around their ears. Therefore, it's safer for me to stay at home."

"I hope you have a prayer closet, at least," Auntie said.

"Are you saying I should hide myself in my wardrobe?" Rainydayas asked, one corner of her mouth ascending.

Auntie laughed. "In a manner of speaking. In Saint Matthew, our

Lord says, '*But you, when you pray, go into your inner room, close your door and pray to your Father who is in secret, and your Father who sees what is done in secret will reward you.*' If you claim to love Him, it's vital you meet with Him—and each other. The church is more than just a place of worship. It's accountability to Scripture, no matter the infinitesimal amount delivered to its saints."

"I sense some bitterness," Rainydayas exclaimed, examining her last stitch.

"Holy indignation," Auntie assured her with a smile.

Velena shared in a much-needed laugh. "Will you stay the night with us, Auntie?" Velena asked.

"I appreciate the invitation, my dear, but I'm sure you'd much rather talk openly amongst yourselves."

"Not at all," Rainydayas chimed in. "Who else will keep us from indulging in too much wine and writing scores of depressing poetry?"

Velena's smile grew. "Yes, Auntie, please stay. I want to build a prayer closet and we'll need your help."

"You've touched this old woman's heart," she said, looking from one woman to another. "If you really don't mind, then."

Gwenhavare clapped her hands together. "It's unanimous."

"Then stay I shall," she said, as a wide grin stretched the expanse of her kindly face.

Dressed in only her shift, Velena backed out of her bed chamber and shut the door. Blanket in hand, she turned to her right and smiled at the ethereal glow emanating from behind the bed sheets they'd strung up, ceiling to floor, in the corner of her sitting room. Half the window was blocked by the makeshift wall with the window seat itself serving as an entrance. Behind the facade, she could hear her friends whispering and see their shadows crouched low, knees scooched in to give each other room.

Moving to join them, Velena climbed onto the window seat and behind the curtain, waiting for Gwenhavare to hold the candle aloft so she could step back down to the floor on the other side. Candle replaced above them, they giggled in their new surroundings.

"It's a shame she went to bed so early," Gwenhavare said, speaking of Auntie who'd just retired to Velena's bed.

Velena smiled, as she adjusted the blanket over their legs. "I wouldn't call this early."

"Did Daisy join her?"

"I think she was asleep the moment her head hit the pillow."

Gwenhavare looked concerned. "She looked rather pale; don't you think?"

"Her stomach's been bothering her. She told me she got some herbs for it though. Hopefully those will help."

Rainydayas tipped her chin sideways, clearly unsympathetic to her maid's infirmity.

Velena frowned. "I know you don't like her Rainy, but I do wish you'd make an effort."

Rainydayas' mouth pulled sideways. "I'd like her fine if Rowan didn't."

Velena nodded. "I understand, but she doesn't like him."

"Yet."

"You don't know that," Gwenhavare scolded.

Rainydayas' eyes were all that shifted in her direction.

"She's as close to a sister as I've ever had," Velena said. "Please choose to see the best in her. It's not her fault Rowan is such a pretentious flirt."

Rainydayas pinched her lips together.

"For my sake…" Velena tried again. "Please."

Gwenhavare bumped her with her shoulder. "Come on."

Rainydayas rolled her eyes. "Alright. But I suppose we'll have to put this contraption to use and pray about it," she said, flicking the hanging sheets with her finger. "And you'll probably need to read me that bit about love again. My Latin was never very good," she said, searching for the over-sized Bible now hidden beneath the blankets.

Velena reached for it, caressing the gold embossed cover as she flipped it open.

Gwenhavare smiled. "How fortunate you are to possess such an item. And very rare to have the whole thing."

"It's only the New Testament," Velena admitted, but it is wonderful."

"How did your father come by it?"

"It was a gift from the king."

Gwenhavare's eyes rounded. "Again…fortunate. I've heard the church frowns upon anyone having an unsanctioned Bible."

"Why should they?" Rainydayas asked.

"Well…it's not the Scriptures themselves they frown upon but the risk of unsanctioned interpretations," Gwenhavare explained further.

Rainydayas scrunched up her nose. "So, let them frown. It's not our job to make them happy."

"I wouldn't want to be the one to make them upset," Gwenhavare stated. "Here, it may not mean so much as our priest is quite timid, but I've heard of places where they deal harshly with those who've taken to strange beliefs."

"What sorts of beliefs?"

"Denying the sinless nature of Mary…or the authority of the priests to forgive sins—even going so far as to publicly denounce indulgences and those who purchase them."

Velena leaned forward, gripping the Bible closer to her chest. "What happens to them?"

"Again, that would depend on the authority wielded by the priest. In many cases, they simply turn the people against them, threatening not to absolve them from their sins and what not. In worst cases… the offender is silenced."

"Murdered?" Rainydayas looked surprised.

"Only rumors, mind you," Gwenhavare admitted. "But I'll tell you something interesting I heard for myself. About a year before the Pestilence, I was touring the studium generale in Oxford with my mother. I wandered off through one of the gardens and I overheard a group of students discussing the possibilities of translating the Holy Scriptures into the common language. Can you imagine what that would mean?"

"We could interpret for ourselves," Velena answered quietly.

Rainydayas gave Gwenhavare a sly smile. "Well, you've read it, Velena? What interpretation do you take? Do you think all those rabble-rousing *heretics* might actually have it right?"

Velena breathed heavy through her nose. "I do…actually."

Rainydayas gasped. "Gwenny, our friend is a rabble-rousing heretic. I like her even better, now."

Gwenhavare laughed, and even Velena joined in. "It doesn't bother you," she asked.

"No, of course not," Gwenhavare assured her.

Rainydayas nodded. "It's true. As you're the only one of the three of us who has any knowledge on the subject—and as the priests have done nothing save threaten our eternal souls with damnation should we question their absolute authority on the matter—it'd do no good to contradict you. So, I say we throw in our lot. What do you say, Nenna? Will you teach us?"

Velena's mouth dropped open. "You're both in agreement?"

Gwenhavare nodded. "Absolutely. Why not?"

"I'd hardly know where to begin." Velena blinked. "I…um…I could at least read to you whenever you'd like. We could then talk about it…and pray, though I can't promise I'll have the answers."

"As long as our mass is in here," Rainydayas said. "I've never felt so at peace in my life. What a clever idea Auntie had."

"Mmhm. It was. I think Tristan would approve as well."

"Oh," Rainydayas exclaimed, a twinkle in her eye, "speaking of Tristan—we've just found out Gwenhavare actually knows him."

Velena looked shocked. "You do?"

"I only just realized it," she said. "I'm sure you've said his name before, but when Rainydayas mentioned this morning that he was from Oxford, it finally clicked, and I put two and two together."

"She's a bit slow," Rainydayas said with a wink.

Velena slapped her leg as she further questioned Gwenhavare. "Did you know him well?"

"More his sisters."

"Then…did you know that…his family died?" Velena asked, not wanting to hurt her but realizing it was next to impossible for her not to have entertained the possibility, herself."

"I did hear of it. A tragedy to be sure."

Silent for a moment, Velena mouth curved upward. "I'm glad you know him."

"Really, Velena, hardly at all."

"But it connects me to him—knowing that you do. It seems too great a coincidence to go unacknowledged, and I now have one more thing to thank God for."

"It's true," Rainydayas said, reaching out to grip their hands, bringing them into a circle of the friendliest kind of intimacy. "No one but God could have matched up our little trio."

"Furthermore, there's your Daisy," Gwenhavare pointed out.

"Mm-hm," Rainydayas said with a most awkward looking tight-lipped smile.

Velena and Gwenhavare laughed quite heartily at her effort to be nice.

"Alright, alright. You see that I'm trying. But my point is, Velena, you're not alone—and we'll be here for you in any way we can. So, let not a silly thing like an ill-matched marriage, or even a bygone friendship, allow you to forget it. Promise?"

Velena gripped their hands tighter, her heart overcome with emotion. "I promise," she said, hoping at that very moment, that Tristan had found his brother—and was at peace.

24

a man plans his way

Tristan sat bolt upright in bed, his chest heaving in and out, his skin drenched in a cold sweat. He swept his hair back from where it clung to his temples and forehead. It was only a dream.

He'd only just arrived at his family's castle that very night, and he was still exhausted from the long nine-day trip it took him to get there. Disturbed by the images that had now awakened him, he flung himself back upon the mattress and rubbed his hands up and down his face, recalling what he could as the dream faded.

There was a church. A priest. Velena and Stuart...ready to take hands. And behind Stuart, a woman with blond hair laid out upon the floor as if wounded, only Velena couldn't see her. Tristan tried shouting Velena's name—to confess to the kind of man she was to marry, but his voice wouldn't carry. Nevertheless, his silent words reached her heart, and she turned to him with new eyes, seeing all. Escaping Stuart, she ran to him, and together, they burst from darkness into light, rushing from the church as fast as their legs would carry them.

They ran until they could run no more. Stopping, feet apart from one another, he stood panting, she, rested and calm. For a while they simply stared, delighting in each other's company until a voice turned her head. It was Sir Richard, calling her name from a distance.

Smiling at her father's voice, she looked back at Tristan and then did as he'd come to expect she would. She held out her hand, asking if he'd walk with her. He might not have hesitated to take it, except that the intended destination was the church from whence they'd come. She was going back. But how could she? Why would she?

It was suddenly revealed. Though done with Stuart, Sir Richard would still see her married. Tristan had only freed her for the unknown—and she would now pull him into it. Shadows of all shapes and sizes began rising up around them, all horrifying and strange, except for one who stood quiet at his side. Hauntingly familiar, it appeared to be a woman—someone he'd known but had allowed himself to forget.

Oblivious to the trouble surrounding them, Velena spoke again. "Walk with me."

"But what about her?" Tristan asked, almost as if Velena should know better than he. But his question caused instant upheaval as the woman vanished and every shadow made its descent upon Velena, carrying her instantly from his sight. Spinning around, he screamed her name, but she'd been lost to the unknown he feared for her.

Eight days later...

Though not yet autumn, the dank chill of the morning air assaulted Tristan's lungs so much that he found himself stopping short of his run to walk the last half mile back to his parent's castle. Three times, he paused, coughing into the crook of his arm—once, twice, and then for such a spell that he had to stop all together.

After catching his breath, he wiped his thumb across the corner of his mouth to clear away some of the unpleasantness. Grimacing, he wiped the small bit of phlegm across the hip of his tunic and plodded on through patches of grass and overgrown weeds, taking care to avoid the ruts and divots pockmarking the neglected earthen road leading up to the castle gate.

It was now dawn, and he could see the smoke from the kitchen chimney making its lazy escape across an ever-brightening sky, whispering promises of a warm room and good company. His brother would be awake—and most likely waiting for him. With renewed vigor, Tristan quickened his pace, skirting around a smattering of men and women who'd come to kiss the gates.

Once into the inner bailey, he veered right of the main entrance and continued on towards the detached kitchen. Before his parents died, he would have gone straight to the great hall to melt off the morning nip in front of the gaudiest fireplace to ever embarrass England. Before the Pestilence, he would have taken drinks with his mother and sisters, and those drinks would have been delivered by any number of servants employed by his family—a family long since gone. Almost.

Tristan smiled in sincere praise of the *almost;* for by the grace of God, his brother had survived the Pestilence. Indeed, not only had he found Philip alive, but finding him had been no difficulty. In fact, it had been as easy as coming home, for their mother's home is where Philip had returned after the death of his wife and two children.

As for Philip, he'd heard rumors that Tristan had left Oxforshire, yet this was all he could learn, for there was no one left alive who could tell him where he'd gone. But certain that Tristan would return for his inheritance if at all able, Philip decided to stay, devoting himself entirely to prayer and whatever charitable work as was helpful to the friary[33].

Philip did this in honor of Friars, Daniel and Oshua, who'd come to the bedside of his mother at the pleading of her cousin, Lady Agnes. And this he discovered, because the friars had become something of a miracle to the people—and his mother's castle a kind of shrine—bringing in men and women of all ranks to touch the walls and kiss the gates in hopes of healing and future protection from sickness. For though the friars should have died from exposure, they'd continued from house to house, ministering across the countryside and preaching salvation to the lost and dying, all the while, seemingly immune to the Pestilence around them.

Whether the friars were still alive, Philip didn't know, but it seemed of little consequence to the people, seeking whatever power they might have left behind, bound up within the walls of the castle—never mind that Lady Isabelle hadn't survived.

Despite the comings and goings, Philip's life at the castle remained quiet. Many of his father's decadent furnishings had been pilfered before his arrival, but since material possessions held little value to him, he'd replaced only what was needed for daily living and few, if any, for additional comfort. In addition to this, their mother's servants had long since run off, and these also Philip replaced sparingly, hiring only those needed to work the fields plus one widowed woman, who kept house for him every other day from noon until dusk, thus allowing her to work her own small plot of land every morning.

This told, it was not surprising there were none this morning to serve Tristan drinks in the great hall whilst thawing in the glow of a grand flame. Philip cooked his own meals, lit his own fires, and consequently, warmed his own drinks. But what was this to Tristan after so many years of death and want. Their fireplace had always been to his discomfiture and their kitchen was now just as good as any great hall due to its company. And from all outward appearances, it seemed his brother's new life suited him, minus his adherence to certain doctrines Tristan had come to reject. Indeed, in the days following their reunion, they'd struck up several discussions on the subject. Timid at first, they'd grown quite lively in their debates, but never anywhere that brought them to any permanent discord. Oh, but it was good to see him again.

One last cough into the crook of his arm and Tristan entered his now favorite sanctuary. As expected, Philip was there—seated peacefully in one of two chairs placed strategically before the bread oven for maximum warmth. The feel of the room was peaceful and cozy as his brother sipped from a generous tankard of hot ale from one hand while proffering a second for Tristan to take from his other.

"Exactly what I needed," Tristan said, the metal warming his fingers, and the liquid accomplishing twice as much as it slipped past tongue and throat to heat him from within. A contented sigh escaped his lips, and he sunk down into the open chair, taking in the man across from him.

There was no doubt they were brothers. While Philip was taller and thinner, his face a bit longer, they shared the same look—the same coloring and shape of the eyes. Even the length of their hair was the same. Though in this, the similarity ended, for Tristan's unkempt hair could only be considered something akin to haphazard while Philip's was tidy, brushed smooth about his ears.

Philip took another gulp and smiled. "You have a nasty cough, Tristan."

Tristan nodded. "This will help."

"You've been running too much, I think."

"I pray better when I run."

"I gathered that," Philip swirled the liquid in his tankard, "but you should have made an exception for the rain."

"It was clear this morning."

Philip stuck out his lower lip and scratched at his cheek, shaved clean just the day before. "Still…the chapel would suit on days it does."

Tristan chuckled. "Next time it rains, the chapel it is."

The scrape of his brother's metal tankard set down upon the bricks of the bread oven let Tristan know his brother wanted to talk in earnest. "Have your prayers brought you closer to a resolution?" Philip asked, having already been taken into Tristan's confidence concerning Velena.

A distant look clouded Tristan's features as Philip waited for him to speak. He stared into his own cup, now half drunk and finally gave a slight shake of the head. "Only that I have to stop her from marrying him."

"Which you might have already done," Philip reasoned. "This Sir Richard sounds like a good man. Do you really suppose he'd still give his daughter to such a miscreant after reading your letter?"

"I hope not. But if it didn't matter to him what Stuart did, then why would it matter whom he did it to? And I still had no proof of it. I shouldn't have left."

"You were asked to leave," Philip reminded him.

"If she marries him, it'll be my fault. I should have told her."

"And what would that have accomplished?"

Tristan opened his mouth, yet thought and word alluded him. He leaned over his knees and pulled at his hair until it was left to stand on end. Restless, he rose to his feet. "When she finds out that I knew, it'll…" he sighed. "It'll feel like a betrayal. At least, if I'd told her—though it come to naught—she'd know I'd been honest with her. As it is, she won't understand my motives for keeping quiet."

"Which are?"

Tristan threw up his hands. "Which *were*…to protect her from further pain should I fail to keep them apart."

Grasping a rag in his right hand, Philip reached for the handle of the ladle, warm from swimming in a pot of hot ale. He refilled their tankards and then leaned back into his chair as if they had all the time in the world. "For arguments sake, let's say Sir Richard has ignored your letter—and your concerns—and the marriage is still on. If you go back, what options do you have? To openly accuse this Stuart person is to bring the maid's reputation into question. And without proof you could be charged with making false accusations. That puts *you* behind bars—not him."

Tristan smirked. "Sounds like I'd do better to just crash the ceremony and haul her off."

"If you think she'd go with you."

Tristan rolled his eyes, a sardonic tilt to his lips. "No. She wouldn't." He crossed his arms, thinking. "I have money—and now thanks to you, a lot of it. Perhaps if I offered Sir Richard compensation for whatever losses he might accrue due to breaking the contract, he might—"

"Wholly inappropriate unless you're offering marriage in the bargain."

Tristan returned to his chair and cupped his tankard with both hands, rubbing his thumbs up and down the heated metal.

"It *is* an option, you know," his brother finally said.

Tristan raised a finger to the inside corner of his eye and took a moment to clear something away. "Not for us."

"Why not?" Philip pushed. "Have you really never considered it?"

"Only when she asks it of me," he said, taking his last swig of ale.

Philip looked confused. "She's asked you?"

Tristan chuckled. "In my dreams only," he explained.

"Tell me of them," Philip prompted.

"There's nothing much to tell."

Philip raised an eyebrow. "Except the part about her proposing marriage."

"Well..." Tristan shrugged. "That might have been a bit of an exaggeration. What she actually asks is...for me to walk with her."

"Where?"

Tristan shook his head. "There's never a *where*. It's just what she says. She holds out her hand and asks me to walk with her."

"That's it—no other words?"

"Sometimes, but more often than not I can't remember them."

Philip now raised both his eyebrows. "And yet you feel as though these dreams are...some sign of a marriage proposal?"

Tristan bit his lip. "I know, I know. It doesn't make sense. It's...it's just confusing because they're all the same. I mean different, but pretty much the same...generally speaking."

Philip rested his ankle over his knee. "So, what happens next?"

"What do you mean?"

"In answer to her question, what do you do? Do you take her hand? Do you not?"

Tristan's eyes drifted, his thoughts searching the unseen. "I have. But I suppose that was when we were back at the castle—before Stuart. After that, it seemed like there were always things getting in the way of my being able to. Other times, I just wouldn't..." His brow furrowed. "I can't quite explain the difference...except that I used to think that friendship was all she was asking for. Now...it's like she's expecting something more of me. And when I resist…I feel like I'm failing her, and I don't know what to do."

Philip pressed his lips together and nodded until Tristan gave a nervous laugh. "Care to interpret? Because I surely don't know what they mean."

Only one side of Philip's mouth lifted as he placed his tankard down next to him. "Since you asked…"

Tristan waited.

"I think they're just dreams," he stated flatly, though there was more than a glint of humor behind his eyes. "Dreams that say more about you than her. In fact, I don't think it's she who's asking something of you at all. I think you're asking it of yourself."

Now it was Tristan's turn to be silent.

"Come brother," Philip prompted, "surely you know."

Tristan shook his head. "I know what you mean, I just don't agree. I'm sure that in most cases there is some degree of anonymity between friends of the opposite sex, each left to wonder what the other one truly feels. But it's not that way with us. We've spoken of it freely. I don't have to ask myself if I want something more because the nature of our friendship has always been understood."

"Then why did you almost kiss her?"

"Wait…wait. Hold on—"

"Certainly not an act of friendship…" Philip continued, folding his hands across his chest, his demeanor just as relaxed as if he were a cat settling down to do his daily duty of not much in particular.

Tristan pushed himself higher in his seat. "It was an accident—"

Philip smiled as if he'd caught Tristan in a trap. "Which, I imagine, you were very much afraid of repeating should you have stayed."

"No. We dealt with it."

"You, yourself, told me one of the reasons you left was because you were too close to her."

"And to find you," Tristan insisted.

"And now you have. So, go back. This friendship you think you have with her is—"

"Is what?" Tristan's middle finger suddenly leapt into action, tapping out a flurried tempo on this thigh.

"Unmaintainable," Philip answered without apology. "You don't know how to free her, because you won't think outside the boundaries you've created for each other. In your dreams, what if taking—or not taking—her hand is your mind trying to make sense of your heart?

More than likely, I think you love this woman and don't know what to do with it."

Without thought, Tristan laughed, an action which soon had him coughing into his elbow as a spasm took hold of his chest. "It's not that kind of love," he finally said. "And marriage between us would never work."

"What do you know of marriage, Tristan? How many marriages do you know that begin with the kind of love that you think you're looking for? And what if this is it—and you miss it?"

"She's my friend."

"And that's a better start than most men are blessed with. Don't make the mistake of thinking that what you feel for her now is all that can ever be. Love can grow. And it does grow. Consider my Anna. Before she was taken from me, our love could have rivaled the sun...yet when we first met, twas no greater than starlight."

"And yet you gave up joining the monastery for her."

Philip chuckled. "Shows you what a little starlight can do. Even a twinkle is enough to throw a man clear off his path."

Tristan frowned. Velena wasn't a twinkle of starlight—and he wasn't sure he wanted to be thrown anywhere, least of all into a hasty marriage.

"You can keep praying, Tristan, but the answer might be as simple as following after your heart."

This Tristan couldn't accept. "God's word says the heart is deceitful above all else. I'd be a fool to do that."

"So, what then? You have but two options."

"Two?"

"Yes. Go back, willing to offer yourself and your fortune to Sir Richard in Stuart's place. Else stay."

Tristan looked surprised that his brother would suggest it. "Stay...and do what?"

"Stay and do nothing. Allow her to marry Stuart in peace. Allow it to play out as it ought. If friendship is all you truly feel, then accept that it's not your place to save her."

This was too much. Tristan stood to his feet, pacing. Unwilling to get into an argument over poor theology, he instead, examined what he knew of scripture. Two things immediately coming to mind. The first being that greater love was indeed a man laying down his life for his friend—not abandoning them in their hour of need. And though this was a clear reference to Christ, its application ought to be carried over into what should be Christ-like behavior.

The second thing was that though it was in a man to plan his own way, it was God who directed his steps. Stilling both body and soul, Tristan realized this was the answer to prayer he'd been waiting for. Resting in this, Tristan made a decision as he took in one long, ragged breath. He *would* go back.

He would plan his return, preparing to offer himself and his fortune if need be. But he'd not stop praying. Moreover, he'd pray harder than ever before—giving himself over to it every moment of every day—trusting that God would thwart his plans if he was wrong.

"So, which is it going to be?" Philip finally inquired, unaware that he'd interrupted the first of those prayers before they had a chance to begin.

"I'm going back," Tristan stated, knowing at the same time, he was still wholly unprepared for Sir Richard's potential acceptance or rejection of his proposal—much worse, Velena's.

Philip smiled. "I think you do right, Tristan. She sounds like a worthy woman."

Tristan turned to look at him. "That has never been in question."

"Then it's marriage, itself, you fear?"

"I suppose it is. Ever since Mother expressed her desire for me to have a wife of my own choosing, I've feared choosing the wrong person." A tight-lipped smile creased his face. "It's a gift I don't know what to do with. Who would have thought such freedom would cause fear…"

Philip held him with his gaze. "I understand you, but in this case, your fears are for naught. Rather than fearing whether Lady Velena is the wrong person, simply ask yourself who else could be more right—for surely you've known none."

None but Isulte, his heart reminded him…and so Tristan allowed himself one final remembrance. But far from feeling sorrow, thoughts of her made him smile, for it now held more attachment to Velena than it did to the woman he'd not seen for three years. Isulte was Velena's name for Gwenhavare—the only name she'd ever known for her, having given it so that Tristan should never give up hope in the story book ending she'd dreamed for him.

But a life with Velena's Isulte *was* a dream. It was work of fiction amidst a reality he would no longer overlook. Thinking on it now, he was glad not to have sought out Gwenhavare upon his returning to Oxford. Nor would he now.

Convinced that his brother was right...and that God would direct his every move, he determined to return to Totnes come morning—and never think of Gwenhavare again.

[33]**Friary:** Dwellings occupied by a community of friars.

Glossary

Definitions are in the order they appear in Familiar Souls.

[1]Jerkin: A close-fitted, sleeveless jacket for men, often made of leather.
[2]Surcoat: An outer garment for men or women, made of rich material.
[3]Quoits: A medieval game, similar to Horseshoes, involving a ring of iron or rope tossed at an upright peg.
[4]Destrier: A knight's warhorse.
[5]Cabbage-eater: An insult, as cabbage was a food with an unpleasant aroma, causing equally as unpleasant side-effects; the food of peasants.
[6]Solar: A bedroom or living space.
[7]Plait: Braided (pronounced "platted").
[8]Tourney: Short for tournament.
[9]Indulgence: A grant from church authorities that absolved men of sin and kept them out of purgatory.
[10]Buttery: A pantry used for the storage of wine and liquor.
[11]Banns: Public Announcement of an intended marriage, announced for three successive weeks (usually in church). Purpose: to provide an opportunity for any objections to the union.
[12]Villein: A feudal tenant.
[13]Stripedhoods: Used to reference a prostitute. In some places, wearing a striped hood was a symbol, denoting their occupation.
[14]Sennight: One week.
[15]Dais: A raised platform used for a speaker, seats of honor, or a throne.
[16]Demesne: Land attached to a manor and retained for the owner's own use.
[17]Studium generale: Old name for a medieval university.
[18]Tippets: A long, narrow strip of attached material hanging from a sleeve or hood.
[19]Caul: Close-fitting headdress.
[20]Thurifer: In Catholic ceremony, it's one who carries the censer.
[21]Tryst: A romantic meeting between lovers.

[22]Wimple: A head covering made of cloth, worn around the neck and chin.

[23]Garderobe: A small chamber where the toilet is located.

[24]Ablutions: Reference to washing oneself.

[25]Wastel: Bread made of very fine flour, served to nobility.

[26]Templar: Head dress encasing the hair on both sides.

[27]Fealty: A formal acknowledgement of loyalty to a lord, country, or leader of some kind.

[28]Bard: A Poet.

[29]Lute: A stringed instrument with its lower half shaped like a halved egg.

[30]Cittern: A stringed instrument, similar to a lute, but with a flattened back.

[31]Psaltery: A triangular stringed instrument, plucked with one's fingers.

[32]Hocktide: A continuation of the Easter festivities, celebrated on the first Monday and Tuesday after Easter.

[33]Friary: Dwellings occupied by a community of friars.

Acknowledgements

What a journey this has been…for me as well as for Tristan and Velena.

I intended for this to be book three of four, but it was so long, it's now book three of five. I intended for it to be titled *Take Me Furthermore*, but with the introduction of so many new faces, it's become *Familiar Souls*. I intended for a lot of things, but characters seem to have a mind of their own…making it so that both writer and reader must hold their breath in anticipation of what happens next.

Delightful as it is maddening, the process of getting *Familiar Souls* from my head to your hands couldn't have happened without a tribe of people helping me. A very special thank you to my beta readers, Brittany, Carolyn, Adrea (whose inquiry into my progress got me setting a deadline and writing again), and Sabrina (my amazing mother and sounding board for every scene I get stuck on). Your help in catching my every homophone error has been invaluable!

A big thank you to Kayla Fioravanti (Selah Press) for all of your formatting genius, Christine Dupree for your amazing cover designs, Alisa Taylor for squeezing in time to complete your beautifully designed verse page before your vacation, and Loral Pepoon for all of your content editing and thoughtful comments, which help to put that final bit of polish on my story.

I'm most grateful to my Lord, Jesus Christ, for His loving direction (and redirections) in my life. And I acknowledge Him for any talent given me and for any successes I have as a result of it, none of which are limited to my writing. The successes I've seen in my marriage, in my children's lives, in our homeschooling, and in those very special friendships that become the heartbeat of how we do life—all are gifts sent from above, and I could do no less than kneel at His feet in total humility and unending gratitude, admitting complete dependence on Him for all of it.

I pray the same successes for you, my readers, who support me with your time, encouragement, and reviews. Acknowledge God in everything you do and never forget to thank Him. God bless you…and happy reading!

connect with venessa

To connect with Venessa through comment or question, visit her at Facebook.com/Venessaknizley or on her website Venessaknizley.com, where you can receive updates on her next book.

As always, if you enjoyed this book, let her know by leaving a review on Amazon and Goodreads. She welcomes your feedback.

CPSIA information can be obtained
at www.ICGtesting.com
Printed in the USA
LVHW030904111119
636963LV00006B/2747/P